58 Farm End

Natasha Murray

Best Wishes
Natasha Murray
2022
♡

Prologue

"I cannot undo what is done or tell another. Today is my birthday, my actual, 'birth' day. The day I emerged from the darkness. I am reborn. Everything I have, I have worked for. I ask nothing of anyone, but I am expected to give. Give my heart, my soul, my very being. There is only so much I can give!

"Those bad days are behind me. I am the sky, the sea, and the earth. I will walk barefoot through the fields, feeling only the soil under my feet and the sun on my back. I will watch the skylarks soar above me and I will swim in deep dark pools. I will never be alone again as soon my angel will walk beside me."

"If you should offer yourself to me, then it would be a crying shame not to. Wouldn't it?"

Chapter One

Jules Bridgewater thought that it was rather an odd group assembled at Emma Truleigh's "Welcome to the Baby" dinner. She eyed the baby suspiciously as Emma placed her in her arms. Baby Darcey seemed harmless enough, and much to her relief was sound asleep.

Anxious thoughts flooded her mind. *I mustn't drop her. I must relax. I can do this. I will just pretend that I am holding a lamb or a box of eggs.* "Darcey is beautiful, Emma. Her hands are so tiny." The baby's arms moved and her eyes opened for a moment to reveal bright blue eyes. "Oh, she's waking up. I think you'd better take her back. She might cry when she realises that it is not you holding her."

"Jules, don't panic. Darcey loves everyone. I am glad you could make it to the meal. I didn't think that you'd be able to get away from the farm."

"It was touch and go. The farm keeps us busy, and I don't really like to leave Dad in the evenings. It is so good to get out and see friends. Dad hasn't been too good lately so my brother and I are practically running the farm between us."

"I invited your brother, but I didn't get a reply to my message. Perhaps he's changed his number."

"I'm sorry, Peter's doing all my chores this evening and I'm going to get up early and help bring the cows in for milking in return. Oh, Emma, I think you'd better have Darcey back, my arms are aching from holding her, and I am frightened I might drop her."

"Ok, Jules. You are funny."

It was a relief to give Darcey back to Emma. Jules breathed a sigh of relief and watched with a half-smile as the baby was given to another unsuspecting member of Emma's so-called friends. She had been surprised that Emma had invited her to the meal. Even though they were in the same class, they had never been that close. Jules thought back to her recent college days with a mixture of sadness and regret. Studying and completing course work had given her a buzz but studying for exams had been tedious. In a few days' time, on 9 August, the 'A' Level results would be given out. Sitting the exams had been challenging for her. She was particularly worried about passing history, having made a classic schoolboy error, by missing a question on the back of the exam paper. That error could have cost her getting a good grade or even passing the exam.

Emma, she remembered, had been one of the more confident members of Worthing Sixth Form College. The tutors had high hopes for Emma's future and must have been disappointed when she left to have a baby. Her boyfriend, Kevin, was a lot older than her and had three children already. Her Dad had said that Kevin should have been locked up and thought that Jules needed her head examined to want to go to such a stupid meal. This had made her even more determined to go, to prove to him that she had a life of her own. Spending every day with her Dad and brother on the farm was proving to be suffocating. Her Dad didn't realise how much his depression was affecting everyone around him. It had been five long years since her Mum had died, and yet, he was still grieving over her loss. The subject of him getting help could not be broached. Everything was fine with him, apparently.

Most of her old friends were going to university in September. They were not at the meal and those that were now present with her were a random collection of misfits. To the left of her sat Roger, who had always kept himself to himself and hardly spoke. Knowing that he was a gamer, Jules had tried to talk about computer games with him but he was not willing to or able to say more than yes or no. Her knowledge about gaming was limited but a conversation was what was needed to make the meal a little more enjoyable. Roger was not going to open up, and she wondered why he had come at all. *This is one weird evening.*

Emma's best friend, Marcia, sat across the table from Jules and was shredding a chicken fillet with her knife and fork as if she was looking for something. Jules looked down at her own meal with alarm, she had eaten most of her chicken wrapped in bacon and hadn't noticed anything untoward. Jules wondered why she had been placed at the end of the table with her and Roger. Marcia was quite outspoken, and she and Emma regularly fell out. She was looking sullen and must have had a row with her. Exasperated, Marcia threw down her knife and then tugged at the neck of her blouse as if it was constricting her. She had expanded since Jules had last seen her and she was probably in need of some larger clothes.

Jules sighed, her own appearance was probably shocking to all those around her. Her Dad had insisted on her wearing a modest dress which he had found in her Mum's wardrobe. Her Dad had kept everything that her Mum had left behind and was unable to give away her clothes. She was almost the same petite size as her Mum, and she didn't mind too much about wearing the odd item of clothing. Some of her clothes were retro and trendy, but today was not the day to have the vintage look. The dress had a large lace collar which she had managed to remove. A pair of old sandals had been up-cycled by adding beads to the ankle laces. Her only saving grace was her sun-bleached, curly, honey-coloured hair that had complied when she had put it up into a fashionable messy bun. Working and riding outside in the sunshine had some benefits.

Jules was starting to feel cross again with her Dad. At eighteen, she really didn't need him to interfere with her social life. His controlling attitude had forced her to come to this disaster of a meal, just to defy his authority. *We need to talk.*

She jumped, her mind re-joining the party. Ivy Brown sat at the top of the table next to Emma and was laughing hysterically at something her boyfriend, Jake, had just said. Jake Hearn was laughing too, he brushed back his dark hair and tried to drink from his glass, spluttering as he drank. Jules remembered Jake at secondary school and back then they had been friends for a while. When he hit fifteen, he had started to go off the rails and then didn't have anything to do with her. He hadn't even acknowledged that she was at the meal.

Ivy's large breasts shook in a most undignified way as she chuckled and Jules noticed that Roger's eyes were almost popping out of his head as he watched her. Ivy had a bit of a reputation and had always been popular with the boys. There was no getting away from it; Ivy was beautiful and knew it. Using her good looks and ample chest to her advantage, Ivy reeled the boys in. Jules had always avoided her if she could. Ivy could be a bit of a bully too and they really didn't get on.

Jake and Ivy were sat next to Emma and were obviously in her good books which was a puzzle to her as they really were not Emma's sort of people. Ivy was giggling uncontrollably and had clearly had too much to drink. As well as her chest, her wavy, dyed blonde hair bobbed up and down as she laughed. Jake laughed again, banging the table with his hand. Jules frowned, they really were the most insufferable pair. *What had been so funny?* They didn't share the joke with her or her oddball companions sitting at the end of the table. She found it even more astounding that Emma was laughing too.

Jules decided that it was time to go, she was done with this meal and had promised her Dad to get home before it was dark. The ten pounds her Dad had given her was just enough to cover a main meal and a drink. Through a window, she noticed that the sun was starting to set. She took her phone out of her bag and noticed that it was almost nine.

"I've got to go now, Emma. I've got to be up early tomorrow," she said as she got to her feet. "Thank you for inviting me. I'll pay for my meal on the way out."

"You don't have to pay, silly. We are paying for tonight. You are our guest. Please stay with us and have a dessert."

"That's kind of you, Emma. I've had a long day and need to get to bed. As I said, I've got to help with the milking in the morning. Thanks again for inviting me."

Something she had said must have set Jake and Ivy off laughing again. She frowned at them.

"You're welcome. Come over and see us soon. I'm in most days."

"Yes, that will be lovely. I will." *That won't be happening.*

Feeling relieved to escape the pub, Jules walked out into Findon's sleepy village streets. The cool evening air filled her lungs and a feeling of joy washed over her. It was good to be free. The birds were chirping to each other as they settled down to sleep in the bushes along School Lane. The smell of cut grass made her remember playing with her brother in the fields near the German barracks when they were small.

Before they moved to Farm End, her Dad had been in the army. For most of her life, the family had travelled across the world and had lived in various army houses. Jules didn't miss that life at all and much preferred living permanently in Sussex. She was happy to be out of the Gun Inn and thought that it would be pleasant to sit on a bench on the edge of the village, before walking up Long Furlong to Farm End. She wanted to make her few hours of freedom last as long as possible.

She was glad to get to the bench as one of the beads on her sandals had slipped down and was rubbing against her skin. She took the offending sandal off and fiddled with the bead until it returned to its rightful place. The view from the bench was wonderful, the pale blue sky was streaked with pinks and reds. Tomorrow was going to be a good day on the farm.

After her Dad had left the army, they had inherited the farm from her Dad's brother, Mark. It had been a steep learning curve for them all, adapting to and running a dairy farm. Her Mum had got sick within weeks of arriving at Farm End and her Dad blamed this change of lifestyle to be the cause of her Mum's death. He had said that the farm was cursed and should have been called Cancer Farm. He wanted rid of it.

The farm was for sale but he had got too depressed to really bother about pushing to sell it and seemed to be running the farm in a chaotic fashion.

Her brother, Peter, who was two years older than her, loved being a farmer and he was turning out to be a good businessman too. The farm was just about holding its own and it was all down to her and Peter's hard work. She knew that things were going to be tough in the future as there was not enough income from the milk they produced.

Peter never spoke about their Mum or about their Dad's depression. Occasionally, he reminded her of an old man as he was always so serious and grumpy. What annoyed her most was that sometimes he acted like he was her Dad. This infuriated her. She missed her Mum, a lot; her Dad too - he was not the same person anymore. She found solace in the fields and farmyard, tending the animals and of course, there was her horse Connor and an old pony, Barney, to look after.

Really, if her grades were ok, then she should be going to university in September. This was only a pipe-dream. It was not practical for her to go as the farm needed cheap labour to continue. Although it was tough some days, there were aspects of working on the farm that were most enjoyable. There was something very wholesome about running a farm, but she had a dream, and that was to open a tea room. On the farm, there were a couple of derelict out-buildings that could be renovated and turned into a tea room, and this new idea filled her with hope.

With no wage coming in, money for her was an issue. Any profit the farm made went into the business account that only her brother and Dad had access to. Household expenses came out of this account but anything extra like socialising or buying clothes, she had to ask Peter his permission before she purchased anything. It was tiresome asking for money, so most of the time Jules went without. The ten pounds for the meal was beginning to feel like ill-gotten gains and not hers to spend. As well as socially, she wanted to be financially independent too.

A money-raising scheme was forming in her head. *Perhaps I could fit in my chores on the farm and get a part-time job in the village or at a livery yard.* Any wage she received would be put by to renovate the outbuildings and to open the tea room. She would talk to her Dad about her plan in the morning. Jules replaced her sandal and thought about how he might react to her news. *A negative response, no doubt.* Her courage was starting to slip away. There had to be another way to raise some money without upsetting him.

She got up and started her walk back to Farm End. It was nearly nine-thirty, and although the streets were quiet in Findon, it was usually busy on the A24. Sometimes, it was tricky to get across the roundabout to the Long Furlong.

Jules shivered a little, the sun had gone down now, and the evening air was cooling her hot skin. The night before, her bedroom had been too hot to sleep in. *I hope it will be cool in my room tonight.*

As she waited to cross the A24, she smiled to herself as a money-making scheme came into her head. Her tiny room was piled high with old toys and games that she really didn't need anymore. Throughout the house, there were plenty of things that could be sold. Any profit made could go towards renovating the barns and starting up her new business. Tomorrow was going to be a good day.

Chapter Two

Jules shivered, the evening dew was settling on her bare arms, the sun had long since slipped behind the hills. Soon it would be dark. Picking up the pace, she walked along the lane, relieved to have escaped Long Furlong's busy road. Farm End and the neighbouring farm, Crow Farm, were silhouetted in the half-light up ahead. Jules sighed as she imagined her Dad stood in the courtyard, tapping his watch, chastising her for being late. She hoped that this would not be the case. It was nearly dark, and it was highly likely that there was going to be a humiliating scene on the doorstep. It was not necessary and she could feel herself getting cross.

Jules had nearly made it home when she heard people giggling hysterically. Her heart sank. Ivy and Jake were nearby. Their voices seemed to be coming from one of Farm End's fields. Jake worked and lived at Crow Farm next to theirs, and he and Ivy were taking a shortcut home across their farm. She ran along the lane to try and locate them. Not wanting to talk to them, her plan was to wait out of sight until they had gone by. They were in the field where her horse and her old Shetland pony were kept. The two of them were obviously up to something. As Jules got closer, she was horrified to discover that they were both riding Barney. She gasped and blinked, hoping that this apparition would dissolve. Poor Barney was too old to ride, and he would struggle to carry one rider, let alone two. "GET OFF HIM! PLEASE! HE IS TOO OLD," she yelled.

"MAKE HIM GO FASTER," Ivy shouted, oblivious to her pleas.

Jake kicked Barney on. The old pony walked a little faster but he was unable to trot with so much weight on his back.

"GET OFF HIM, HE IS TOO OLD!" cried Jules, tears of anger and sadness pricking her eyes. She found a stick on the ground and started to run to the gate, with the plan to knock them both off of Barney's back. She started to climb up the gate and exhaled with surprise. Someone was standing next to her. He was wearing dark clothing and the hood of his jacket was up. *Where did you come from?*

"It's ok, I've got this."

Panic-stricken, Jules froze and watched as the stranger with broad shoulders, leapt over the gate and ran towards Barney.

"GET DOWN, BEFORE YOU HURT HIM, YOU MORONS!"

"Are you going to make us?"

"Yes, I'm going to make you, Jake, and you will wish I hadn't! Christ, you are such an eejit!"

The man stepped forward and looked like he was about to drag them off her pony's back, forcibly. Jake and Ivy stopped laughing and then decided that they had better do as they were told. There was something menacing about his tone. Still drunk, Ivy fell off Barney, face down into grass and Jake, despite his drunken state, dismounted properly and she could see that he had ridden before. Jules was fuming, *Jake should know not to ride a pony too small for him.* She was now shaking with anger.

12

Jake helped Ivy get to her feet, and then holding her up they made their way to the fence and climbed through. She wanted to yell obscenities but was too angry to speak. She watched them stagger down the lane towards Crow Farm. *Good riddance.* Her dark knight was still in the field. He was checking Barney's legs and back to make sure he was ok. *He obviously knows a thing or two about horses. Who is he?* He started to walk towards her, and she wanted to thank him for his kindness. He climbed through the fence this time, rather than leaping over the gate and smiled at her.

"Thank you for helping me. Those two are such jerks and Barney is so old; he's nearly twenty-eight. I'm sorry, I don't think I've seen you around here before. Are you from Crow Farm?"

"Yes, I am your neighbour. Most people call me Seth. I'm Seth Hearn. Jake and I are brothers, although you would never know it."

"Thank you, Seth. I don't know what I would have done without you." She had detected a soft Irish accent when he spoke but wasn't sure. He pulled down his hood, and she couldn't help but stare at his face, and even though it was nearly night, his dark hair, brown eyes and good looks were mesmerizing. Jules was surprised that she hadn't seen him around before and hoped he hadn't noticed her looking at him so hard.

"I think that you would have done alright," he replied looking at the stick that was still in her hand.
Embarrassed, she dropped the stick and laughed.

"I… I don't know what I would have done with it. Is Seth your real name then?" *Why am I asking you this?* She hadn't heard that name before and wondered if it was short for something.

"It is what I prefer to be called, but my Mam uses my formal name sometimes. I'm not going to repeat it," he smiled mischievously. "She uses it when I am in trouble. What are you doing out so late? I usually see your light go out at nine."

"Oh, do you? I um… I had to suffer a horrible meal at the Gun Inn. Jake and Ivy were at the table too. It was all a bit weird. I didn't really know anyone very well there."

"I would have gone with you."

Jules was surprised by his response and realised that he was hitting on her. Boys had asked her out before, but they had not been as confident as he was being. It was flattering, though. She wasn't sure why he was interested in her. "Oh, you would? Well, it was awful, you wouldn't have liked it. You had to hold a baby and make polite conversation."

"I can make polite conversation. If you are interested, my family is holding a shindig tomorrow night. Come along and I promise you won't have to hold any babies."

"I will have to see. I'm not sure what I am doing tomorrow. I…"

"I hope you can make it, Julia Bridgewater – we'll have fun."

Feeling a little stunned, she watched as Seth walked away. He looked over his shoulder and smiled at her and then continued walking home. She held her gaze for a while, trying to remember if she had seen him before. It suddenly dawned on her that he knew her name, her whole name. *Did I tell him my name? No!*

Since arriving at Farm End, they had kept themselves to themselves and hadn't had any contact with the neighbouring farm. From the top field, Jules had seen in the distance teams of men planting and harvesting crops or tending sheep. She hadn't really thought about who owned the farm or who lived there. All she knew was that her dead uncle disliked his neighbours, and they him.

She looked at the time on her phone and sighed, it was nearly ten and it really was dark now. Her Dad would be cross and she fully expected him to be pacing up and down the kitchen awaiting her return. Holding her temper would be key in this situation. She would stay calm and try and act like an adult even if he started crying again. Her Dad really was not himself these days.

She reached the courtyard and was surprised to see her brother stood there with his arms folded.

"Jules, it's dark. We've been worried sick."

"Peter, what the Hell? It's only just got dark. There was a problem with Barney, and Seth Hearn sorted it out for me."

"I thought so, what the fuck was you doing with Seth Hearn?"

"What do you mean exactly? Look, some drunk people were riding Barney and Seth saw them off."

"I saw him walk past our farm a moment ago. You do know that he is one of those tinkers that live on the farm up the road? Don't you have anything to do with them, Jules! They're nothing but trouble."

"Seth helped me, Peter. You shouldn't call them tinkers."

"Didn't you hear what I said to you? Dad won't be able to handle it if you get involved with him."

"Stop being such an arse, Peter. I'm not a child anymore!"

***

Jules groaned when her alarm went off. *It really can't be 4am!* With her eyes still closed, she patted the side table to try and find her phone. Finally, she found it and drew it near to her face and opened her eyes, trying her best to focus on the close alarm button on the screen. It had been a really hot night, and because of the heat, sleep had been sporadic. Slowly she sat up, pulled back the covers and placed her feet on the cool floor. Only now was it safe to turn off the alarm.

The smell of coffee brewing drifted into her room; her Dad was already up. He was fine in the mornings but by the afternoon he would disappear into his study, leaving her and Peter to milk the cows. Her brother would probably lie in for a bit, enjoying a rare morning off. She was still cross with him and really didn't want to speak to him for a while. He was becoming such a pain. It was almost as if he had become a parent to both her and her Dad.

Still on autopilot, Jules washed, dressed and made her way downstairs to the farmhouse kitchen. A chat show on the radio was broadcasting in the background, and they were talking about how to survive the current heatwave.

Their border collies, George and Pip, came over to her with their tails wagging. She ruffled each of their heads to greet them and then looked over at her Dad. He was sipping his hot coffee. He looked tired, and she guessed that he must have had a bad night too. His eyelids were red and swollen and his clothes looked like they had been slept in.

"Are you alright, Dad?"

"I'm fine. I just need this coffee and then we will be good to go. Do you want one?"

"I'll just have water. I'm gasping. It's too hot in this house, Dad."

The kitchen was unbearably hot and so she opened the kitchen door to let the cool morning air in. The dogs ran out into the courtyard to greet the rising sun. Jules picked up a glass from the draining board and ran the tap until the water became cold. After filling her glass up, she sat down at the table with her Dad. He eyed her questionably. *I know he is going to lecture me any moment now.* She was ready for him.

"About last night..." he began.

"There is nothing to talk about. No doubt Peter filled you in last night. I can look after myself, Dad. You don't have to worry about what time I get in or who I talk to. You need to tell your son to mind his own business."

"Oh, I see. Then there is nothing more to say then. Apart from..."

"No, nothing, Dad!"

The walk to the fields to collect the cows was a quiet one and Jules knew that her Dad would have his say when he deemed it to be the right moment. She was determined to stand her ground. She watched her Dad open the gate to the field where their Friesian cows were waiting in an orderly line. Hermione, the matriarch of the herd, led the others to the milking shed. It was as her Dad closed the gate that he gave her a concerned look and then looked sad.

"It's just that I don't want anything to happen to you, Julia."

"What do you mean by that?"

"I don't want you getting hurt."

"I really don't think a meal out with friends is going to harm me."

"No, I don't mean that."

"Then what do you mean?" *I know exactly where this conversation is going.* She was starting to get cross.

"I don't want you getting involved with the Hearns lot. They are bad news. My brother warned me to keep away from them, and I swear they were the ones that drove him to his death."

"Dad! You really can't blame them for that. Uncle Mark was an alcoholic and his wife ran away. It was the drink that killed him."

"You say that, but that lot gave him so much grief over the boundary line that it would have driven anyone to drink."

"Seth was really kind to me last night. He stopped Jake and Ivy from hurting Barney. The Hearns can't all be bad. This evening I am going over to Crow Farm for a shindig, a party. Seth invited me."

"A what? No, Julia! Have you lost your mind?"

"I'll be fine. I won't drink much, and I won't stay out too late."

"You're not going. End of!"

Jules wiped down each cow's udder and stripped them so that the cow was ready to release the milk. Her cheeks were burning with fury. Her Dad was treating her like a seven-year-old and she was tired of having to justify her actions. *I am going to this party, whether you want me to or not.* Her encounter with Seth had been brief. There was something intriguing about him. Out of the blue, he had said that he would have gone to the pub with her. He also knew what time she went to bed. *Why was he in the lane last night? Had he been waiting for me to come home, too?* Her heart rate increased just thinking about him. Jules wasn't sure if she was troubled by him or just bewitched. She would go to the party without her Dad's permission and find out. *What could her Dad do? Lock her up?* Her resolve to go out was failing. Her Dad's disappointed face filled her thoughts. She didn't want to make him even more depressed than he already was. *Perhaps I shouldn't go.*

After Jules had groomed the horses, her attention turned to gathering what she could to sell on eBay. When passing the dresser in the kitchen, her Mum's pink rosebud china collection caught her eye. The dusty cups and saucers were lined up neatly along the shelves. There were more sets in the cupboards below. *I wonder if Dad would let me use them in the tea room?* Nobody in their household drank tea from the delicate cups - they were just gathering dust. She thought about her Mum and smiled, knowing that she would have wanted her to use them. Her Mum didn't like anything to go to waste. At lunchtime, she would tell her Dad about her scheme. Just after lunch when he had eaten was always a good time to talk to him about things.

It took her a surprising three hours to photograph and log all her old games, toys and unwanted Christmas presents onto eBay. By the time she had finished listing everything, someone had already bid on Cluedo and had raised the bid from ninety-nine pence to one pound and ninety-nine pence. Her old bank account only had pence in it and although it was unlikely that she would make a big profit, it would be good to have some money coming in - it was a start anyway.

It had been so long since her bank account had been used that she had forgotten where her bank card was. It wasn't in her purse. Jules had checked in all the usual places, including the kitchen drawers but couldn't find it. She would have just one more look and then report the card as being lost if it didn't turn up. Her guitar was sat in the corner of the room and sometimes she hid her card in the front pocket of its case. *Not in there either. I haven't played my guitar or sung for ages. I must.*

As she walked into the kitchen, Dance Monkey was playing on the radio – *I like this song.* She almost forgot why she had gone in there in the first place. *Oh yes, dinner.* Supplies in the fridge were getting low. There was a chicken tucked at the back of the fridge that needed using up. She would cook it now and serve it later with salad and new potatoes. Her Dad and Peter would probably moan, but it was too warm in the kitchen to slave over a hot cooker later on.

The cooking was left to her as it turned out that she was the only one that didn't burn anything. They were in the fields gathering crops to make into silage for the winter months. It was a really hot day to be working outside, and they would return home tired and hungry. Peter would have to do the milking too, and she hoped that her Dad would see that his son needed to rest and help her with the milking instead of retreating to his study. She knew this would not be the case.

Jules looked out of the open kitchen door, the leaves on the trees were moving gently in a cool breeze. A gust got under the blind that was hanging on the kitchen door and it swayed, banging against the glass. Wanting to feel some cool air on her hot body, she walked out into the garden. Shutting her eyes, she breathed in deeply, appreciating the gentle gusts of wind. The breeze subsided and refreshed, she opened her eyes, ready to return to the kitchen to do battle with the chicken. Alarmed, Jules gasped and stepped back. Seth stood in front of her, only inches away.

Chapter Three

"What are you doing here?" She tried not to sound frightened. "Were you going to kiss me?" He smiled and his brown eyes sparkled mischievously.

"I might have. Who could resist? It's my lunch break, and I stopped by to say that I will pick you up at nine. You are still coming over tonight, aren't you?"

"I don't know. Maybe. Yes, I will. I'd like to. Ok, nine then - that's late. Don't you have to get up early in the morning?" She looked at his blue overalls and could see by the sweat on his face that he had been working hard in the fields.

"It's the weekend so the Hearns will party until late and some still go and work the land in the morning - hangover or not. I don't work on a Sunday."

"Is the party for a birthday? Should I bring a gift?"

"No, don't worry about that. It's a family gathering to celebrate the eejit Jake and Ivy's engagement. Really, it is a great excuse for everyone to get fluthered and to dance a jig."

"You are joking? This is Sussex, not Ireland. I can't do a jig. What should I wear?"

"Don't panic. Wear that cute thing you had on yesterday and you really don't have to dance if you don't want to. I'll take care of you."

"This is embarrassing to say, but my Dad and brother have gone all weird about me talking to you. I don't know why.

I am going to have to slip out of the house without them knowing. Do you have a phone?"

"Yes, I do. I thought that might be the case. They don't think much of the Hearns, do they?"

Jules picked up her phone from the kitchen table, selected the keypad to make a call and handed the phone to Seth. "Type in your number and then I'll call you so you have my number. Meet me by the horses' field where I was last night. I'll message you if I am going to be late."

"I'll be there. Wear your hair down tonight, it looks stunning that way. My Mam has a thing about curls and if she asks if you eat your crusts, then just say yes." Seth winked and smiled.

She leaned against the doorway and watched Seth as he walked back to Crow Farm. When he was about to go out of sight, he smiled and waved. He was clearly infatuated. *How could he be? He barely knows me.* She wasn't sure how she felt about him. He had a charming way about him, and she couldn't deny that he was curiously attractive. No boys had been of interest to her at school, only Jake perhaps at one time but not now – *no way!* Having such an annoying brother had probably put her off men for life. However, there was something about Seth that she liked. Liked a lot.

Jules didn't get a chance to speak to her Dad about the tea room idea. The evening passed by slowly and she was tempted to call Seth and cancel as her nerves were really shot. It was nearly eight and her Dad and brother were eating the cold chicken salad. They were worn out, covered in dust and they did not complain about the meal she had prepared for them. This told her that they were really tired – too tired to moan. Her Dad had managed to get through a whole day's work without disappearing. That had to be a good sign that he was coping with things better. Keeping her fingers crossed, she hoped that after they had eaten, then they would go and have a shower, go to bed and give her a chance to slip out. Her heart was already thumping in her chest with anxiety about sneaking out.

After dinner, Jules excused herself from the table and went to her room to read Chanctonbury. The words on the pages were not sinking in as her mind was elsewhere. Her brother had showered and gone to his room. As soon as her Dad had finished in the bathroom, she changed into her dress and put her dressing gown on to hide it. Her newly washed hair was behaving itself and hadn't frizzed in the humidity; it was getting really long. The new conditioner she had used was doing its job; it was worth spending the extra money. She was feeling really hot in her dressing gown but dared not take it off. It was ten to nine. Her heart was pounding hard. *Am I wrong to go to the party without telling them?* Her life was getting complicated.

Still wearing her dressing gown and with her sandals hidden within it, she crept barefoot down the stairs and into the kitchen. The dogs were asleep in their baskets and were too tired to bother with her. The outside light was on so getting across the courtyard would be fine as long as her Dad or Peter didn't look out of their bedroom windows. There were no streetlights in the lane, but it was a clear night and the moon was almost full. *I should be able to find my way to the horses' field without a torch.* Her dressing gown pocket got caught on a chair, and she silently cursed as the legs scraped against the flagstone floor. Jules held her breath and waited for a moment. *Is there someone moving upstairs?* She exhaled; the house was silent again.

She opened the kitchen door and slipped out into the night, closing the door gently behind her. It was good to be free again. Keeping close to the house, she put on her sandals and then in the shadows made her way across the courtyard and headed towards the horses' field where she and Seth had last met.

Jules waited patiently by the gate and felt in her dressing gown pockets for her phone and then realised that she had left it on her bedside table. There wasn't time to go back and get it. *How annoying! What if Seth is messaging me to say he is going to be late or to cancel?* She looked up and down the lane for him and then noticed that Barney and her horse Connor were walking over to her hoping for a treat. *Did they ever sleep?* Tomorrow, she would take Connor out for a ride, if the weather was cooler. The horses had belonged to her uncle, and they had inherited them from him when they took the farm over. Connor's large nose breathed warm air into her neck expectantly and she patted him gently.

"I'm sorry, I've nothing to give you tonight."

"That's a shame. I always like a treat."

"Oh my God, Seth! You've got to stop creeping up on me like that!"

"I like it when you're angry, you colour up."

"I do not. You idiot!" She said, smiling, knowing full well that her face was now pink from shock.

"I don't remember you wearing this yesterday."

"It's ok, I am dressed. It's just a cover in case I was caught going downstairs."

"It's a pity."

"What's a pity?"

"That you are dressed."

"Seth!"

"Are you ready for a night to remember?"

"I'll be honest, I'm feeling nervous. I'm going to leave my dressing gown in the bushes here and put it on later when we come back. I shouldn't stay out too late. Is that ok, Seth?"

"I'll have you home by midnight. Let's go and have some fun."

Jules turned away from Seth to undo her dressing gown, not wanting to give him the wrong impression. She rolled up the gown and stuffed it into a bush in the hedgerow. *It should be safe there for now and will be easy to find later.*

"There we go, I'm ready. I'm a bit uneasy, Seth. I think this is the first party I've been to in a while." It was in fact over five years since she had been to one. She didn't want to give him the idea that she was a complete loser, socially. *Which, I am.*

"Really, don't be nervous, you look beautiful."

He took her hand, and silently they walked up the lane to Crow Farm. Jules could feel her hand tingling, there was obviously some chemistry going on between them. She knew so little about Seth and the fact that he was wearing his black hoodie with the hood up made it all the more difficult to study him properly.

"Aren't you hot wearing a hoodie?"

"A little. I was feeling cold earlier. I'll take it off when we get inside."

As they approached the farm, she could hear Irish music playing and her nerves kicked in even more. *What am I letting myself in for?*

"How many people will be at the party?"

"I don't know exactly. I've got fifteen brothers and sisters. Their families will be at the party and there are the farmworkers too. Mam invited them and some of Jake and Ivy's friends. Ivy's Mum and Dad don't approve of the engagement so none of them will be there. Around sixty people, I guess."

"Goodness, you have one huge family. Do you all get along? I've just got my Dad and my brother Peter and they can be pretty challenging to live with."

"Well enough. We all look after each other. That is our way."

"Were you once gypsies? Oh no! That's so rude. I mean travellers. Sorry."

"No offence taken. In the past we were but not in my lifetime. Mam was born in a traditional caravan drawn by a cob, a bit like the one you were petting earlier."

"Oh, that was Connor. He's mine and Barney is his field buddy."

"I've seen you riding him along the bridle paths. You've got a good seat."

"You know about horses, don't you? You seem to know an awful lot about me, but I know nothing about you. You haven't been at Crow Farm for long, have you?"

"No, not long, just a few weeks. Long enough to lose my heart to a pretty girl, though," he said, squeezing her hand.

"Oh my! I see."

Jules, still holding Seth's hand, stood on the doorstep of Crow Farm and took a deep breath ready to enter into a new world. *Will they accept me?* Seth pushed open the door and they stepped into a dimly lit hallway. Photos of family in dark wooden frames adorned the walls. They passed a side table where she noticed a handmade lace runner laid out on it. Her

Mum would have loved it. They made their way to a brightly lit room at the end of the hall. As they got closer, the volume of the music increased and she knew that it would be hard to hear him. Seth stopped for a moment, he let go of her hand and took off his hoodie to reveal a slightly creased white short-sleeved shirt beneath.

"I don't need this anymore."

She tried not to look too hard at his muscular arms and chest, but couldn't help herself. It was obvious that he either visited the gym regularly or worked the land.

"Let's get a beer from the kitchen first." Seth led her through to a farm kitchen, not unlike her own. There were plates of party food spread across the kitchen table and two women were standing by a range waiting for a kettle to boil. Jules smiled at them. They looked at her and Seth, frowned and then carried on with their conversation. She was beginning to think that it was a bad idea to come to the party. They had to know who she was and there was evidently still bad blood between the Bridgewaters and the Hearns. Jules hadn't really expected such a cool reception. Seth picked up two cans of lager and passed one to her.

"No glasses, I'm afraid. Is that ok? Or did you want a soft drink?"

"No, lager is fine."

"Come with me, we'll walk through the party and go and sit in the garden and talk," Seth shouted.

Taking her hand again, Seth led her into the lounge and through the dining room. The furniture had been cleared to the side and a band of four played on a fiddle, accordion, whistle and drum. The Hearns and farmworkers danced wildly to the music. The dancers hurled each other around in time to the beat.

This vision was quite something to see and the music uplifting. Music always cheered her up.

Jules, now clinging to Seth lest she be swept away, wove her way through the dancers towards the garden. As they passed everyone, she looked out for Jake and Ivy. It was going to be difficult to speak to them again. It was unlikely that they would be very welcoming as they obviously both disliked her. Maybe it was a bad idea coming to their engagement party.

The French doors were open, and Seth led her out into a garden filled with fairy lights. It was good to be outside again. There were a few people in the garden but not many as most were dancing. At the back of the garden, there was an archway leading to another part of the grounds. The Hearn's garden was huge but nearly every bush had been lit up with fairy lights. *It must have taken hours to put them up.*

Jules spotted Jake and Ivy making out beneath the arch. She felt a little disgusted watching them. Seth looked over at them and shook his head and smiled. He found a couple of chairs and placed them so they could sit with their backs to the amorous couple. She sat down and opened her can which fizzed over her dress. Seth laughed and opened his can away from himself, and then taking a sip sat down next to her. She looked down at her wet skirt and felt embarrassed. "It will dry quickly, it is a warm night. Did you notice Jake and Ivy getting a bit carried away over there? They're not shy, are they?"

"They're always at it. Take no notice. They won't go all the way. Not until they are married."

"Well, that's a relief. Do you believe in getting married first then?"

"Mam and Dad like it that way."

"Did you see the way those two women looked at us in the kitchen? I don't think they liked the idea of you bringing a Bridgewater here."

"No, they are grand. Maureen and Doreen are my grumpy older sisters. They are going through a hard time at the moment. Their husbands are being unfaithful, and they are probably comparing notes. You can't really blame the husbands, though," he said, smiling. "Do you want to dance?"

"Let's drink this first and then maybe. I might need a bit of Dutch courage. So tell me about yourself, Seth Hearn."

"Oh, there's not much to tell, I grew up on this farm and then when I was twenty, I wanted to travel. I have been all over the world backpacking. That was a bit of a shock for everyone as you are really just expected to help run the farm and not have any dreams, let alone carry them out. I guess you could call me the black sheep of the family."

"Tell me about it! My Dad and brother think that I should be happy just working on the farm and not do anything else. I'm going to open a farm tea room soon and lead my own life."

"Good for you. You do know that you are the first girl I've brought home? When Mam and Dad have a band break, I'll introduce you to them."

"So have you had other relationships?"

"A few. I met a girl in Thailand once and thought that she was the one. I wanted to see more of the world with her, but she didn't want to leave her family. So we parted."

"It couldn't have been love then or you would have stayed."

"No, not love. It's different with you."

"I bet you say that to all the girls. You hardly know me."

"Don't be hard on me. I feel like I have known you all my life."

"How old are you, Seth?"

"Twenty-nine, not that much older than you."

"I didn't think that you were that old. My Dad would think that ten years difference is a lot."

"You're here with me. That says a great deal."

"You do know that I might not be here for much longer? My Dad wants to sell the…"

"Seth, what the Hell are you doing here with Jules?"

She looked up, Jake and Ivy stood before them. Ivy was wearing a short red sundress and her breasts were spilling out of it. Jake was looking angry, and Ivy, who was really drunk again, was having trouble standing. She couldn't help noticing that Ivy was holding a bra in one of her hands and wasn't really focusing on them properly.

"Don't fret, Jake. We're not staying long. Just one drink and a dance and we will be gone."

"You shouldn't be here. I didn't invite you. You shouldn't be with her."

"I'll do as I please. We're family. Now bugger off."

Jules was becoming concerned. There was something going on between Seth and Jake. Seth, seeing her worried face, stood up. "We need to talk, Jake." He grabbed hold of Jake's arm and marched him over to the edge of the garden. She watched in dismay as Jake shoved him in the chest. Seth was shouting at him and pointed his finger at him angrily. She gasped as she watched them argue. "What the Hell is going on, Ivy?"

Ivy staggered towards her and grabbed hold of the chair that Seth had been sitting on. Trying not to fall down, Ivy threw

30

herself on to the chair. "That's better. What did you say? Oh, Jake and Seth. Soon we'll be sis...scissors. Don't worry about those two, they're always arguing. It will be over... over when they hit each other. Are you enjoying the party? I'm not."

"I've only just got here," Jules managed to say as she kept a close eye on Seth and Jake. "Why are they arguing?"

"I'm not sure... I think it is because Seth was in priso... prison."

"What for? He didn't tell me that."

"He killed someone. I feel so... so tired. So..."

Ivy's head fell back behind her and with her mouth wide open, passed out. Her bra dropped from her open hand onto the lawn. Troubled and confused, Jules was amazed that Ivy was able to stay seated on the chair in her condition. At least she was breathing. *What had Ivy just said? Something about Seth being in prison. Did she say murder?* Her head was whirling now with questions. They would have to wait. At any minute Seth and Jake would soon be hitting each other. This was crazy, she had to stop them fighting and marched over to the two men. She didn't feel afraid and just wanted them to stop being so stupid. "For Christ's sake get over it! Seth, please? I don't know what's going on but if it's about me being here then you don't have to worry. I'll go."

Seth glared at her, his eyes dark and dangerous for a moment. Jake shook his head at her. "Go home, Jules. You don't know what you're getting yourself into. He's not worth it. He's a loser and mixes with losers. The Bridgewaters are not welcome here."

Jules, putting her hands on her hips, turned to face him. She was furious. "How dare you speak to me like that? I didn't want to come to your stupid party anyway. You keep away from

31

me, or I'll do something I regret, you bastard! You too, Seth Hearn!"

"JULIA! Julia, get yourself home this instant." Her Dad appeared from nowhere and was climbing through the fence into the garden from the adjoining field. "YOU LOT KEEP AWAY FROM HER!"

"DAD! Really? This has to be the worst night ever! I'm leaving now anyway. Don't worry!" Not looking back, she climbed through the fence into the Hearn's field, not sure where it would take her. She strode past the Hearn's farmhouse hoping that the field would lead her back to the lane. Her Dad followed behind; she couldn't speak to him at the moment. Her blood was boiling, and she needed to calm down. Finally, they came to the corner of the field, unable to continue. It was really dark. Her Dad caught her up.

He turned on the torch of a phone so they could see each other. *That's my phone.* Her fists were still clenched and realising this, she released them and took a deep breath. Her breathing was more even now, as she started to calm down. Her Dad looked strangely subdued. "Your alarm went off just before nine and kept going. It was annoying me, so I knocked on your door to ask you to turn it off. When you didn't reply I thought you were sleeping so I crept in to turn it off... I was proud of you back there. You really told the Hearns where to go."

"See, I can look after myself. You shouldn't have come here, Dad!" She was starting to get angry again.

"I told you not to come here. You need to listen, Julia. Our family has to stick together if we are going to survive. You know that the farm is for sale. We are not staying, and I really can't take any more headaches. Do you hear me, Julia?"

Jules looked at her Dad's worn and tired face and felt guilty. It was best not to argue with him and just go home to sleep. Tomorrow was a new day and she would help him get through the days to come the best she could.

"I hear you. Just get me out of this field and home. I'm not going through the house again."

"Come on then," he said pointing to a gate further along the hedge.

They walked along the edge of the field; the grass was making her feet wet. As her Dad opened the gate, she looked back at the garden and was almost sure she could see Seth's silhouette. He stood by the fence and was watching her go. A strange feeling of sadness swept over her. It was difficult to leave him all alone.

That night, Jules tossed and turned in a half-sleep, her mind replaying out the night's events. She awoke tired, sweating and her throat was sore. *Do I have a fever? No, I don't, it's just incredibly hot today.*

It was light and her Dad and brother were out milking the cows. Wanting to make herself a cup of tea, she looked around for her dressing gown and then remembered that it was still in a bush outside. It's *probably full of creepy crawlies.* Putting on a long grey cardigan over her bed shirt, she headed down to the kitchen for much-needed refreshment. Today was going to be a busy one, washing, ironing, tending the horses and milking. She also needed to find some packing material and tape to pack up her parcels. On checking her eBay account on her phone, Jules smiled as there was a bidding war going on. Many of the items that had been listed were going to be sold for much more than she had expected. The balance on her eBay account was nearly at two hundred pounds, and the auction still had a couple of days to run. She sighed. If her Dad did get a buyer for the farm then there would be no point in setting up a tea room on site. It would make sense to save up for an existing business somewhere in Sussex. She would also have to rent a few acres of land for the horses and find a place to live. That seemed to be a better plan.

As Jules filled the kettle, a police car sped past their house heading towards Crow Farm. This was not the first time she had seen one going their way. Perhaps the Hearns were bad news after all. They were passionate people, dancing, loving life, but there was also a dark, violent side to them too. Seth was a bit of an enigma, he had said that he was the black sheep of the family. She wondered if he ever planned to tell her that he had murdered someone. *Was Ivy serious or were these just drunken words? Ivy isn't the brightest person - looks aren't everything.*

"Right, Jules! I must do my best to forget about Seth Hearn and get on with my life." She doubted whether she would ever see him again. Her Dad had seen to that.

Chapter Four

Breakfast had been a disappointing affair. The fridge was nearly empty and all Jules could find to eat was the heel of the bread. It had got caught in the toaster and had set the smoke alarm off. After scraping away the burnt edges, she drizzled the last of the honey over it and then took this, along with her tea, into her Dad's untidy study. There was a pile of brown envelopes on the side which had been unopened – *more bills!* She fired up her Dad's ancient computer and logged onto the Sainsbury's website so that she could order some much-needed food. It took her a while to complete her order as she was lacking motivation. Cooking was her least favourite thing to do, and her Dad and brother only really liked meat, vegetables and potatoes. Curry and spicy food which she liked were not appreciated and eaten under duress.

Her order came to one hundred and five pounds and she felt pleased with herself, as this would provide meals for them for at least three weeks. The next hurdle would be pressing the order button and paying for their shopping. Hopefully, there was enough in the bank account to cover it. No doubt, Peter would quiz her later and run through the order, questioning her purchases. He needed to get a life. He spent too much time on the farm and never went anywhere else. When he wasn't working, he was locked in his room watching movies on his laptop. He didn't appear to have any friends. At the moment, things between her and Peter were not that great. Jules had once asked her Mum why he hated her, and apparently, it was all down to sibling rivalry. Her Mum wanted more than anything for them to get along as one day each other is all they would have. She didn't really understand what her Mum was talking about and guessed it was something to do with them accusing each other of being the favourite child. Jules smiled to herself. *I am Dad's little kitten.* Not that it mattered anymore, lately, he was being cold towards both of them.

Jules put some laundry into the washing machine, squirted a small amount of washing up liquid over the dirty clothes as they had run out of washing powder. She turned it on and hoped that she wouldn't see soapsuds spilling out of the machine. She finished her tea and left her cup on the side, ready to wash it. Washing up could wait until later and the floor would need mopping too. The horses needed to be checked and groomed next.

The morning was much cooler than it had been and it looked like it might rain soon. It would be a perfect day to take her lazy Connor out for a hack. It would give her a chance to think. She was doing her best to forget Seth, but he kept popping into her head. *Should I give him a second chance?* First, he needed to tell her why he had been in prison. *Wouldn't he have been given a life sentence if he had committed murder?* She had so many questions.

As Jules walked out of the courtyard and onto the lane, she saw Jake approaching. It was too late to hide; he had seen her. Her timing couldn't have been worse. Jake looked troubled and she hoped that he wouldn't be mean to her again. Jules decided to continue on her way and not acknowledge him, and quickening her pace she strode on, determined to extend the gap between them. Jake caught her up, and gritting her teeth together she waited for him to shout more abuse at her. Her worries were unfounded.

"Jules, wait! I'm sorry about yesterday. I was drunk and angry. Things got a bit out of hand, and something happened last night."

She took a deep breath and turned to face him. "Is that why I saw a police car going up to your farm this morning?"

"Oh them. No...they were looking for Seth. I got very drunk last night and now I can't find Ivy. Have you seen her? I don't think she slept in her bed last night. Nobody saw her go to bed. I saw you talking to her. Did Ivy say anything to you? Like where she was going, perhaps?"

Jake was looking desperately at her. "No, Jake, she didn't say anything to me. Ivy was really drunk and passed out as we were talking. I don't think she would have gone far. Didn't you see her after I had left?"

Jake shook his head. "I was still angry and had another drink. I don't remember anything after that."

Jules sighed. I'm sorry, Jake. Ivy will turn up I'm sure. Have you checked your outhouses? She's probably just sleeping it off somewhere."

Jake shook his head and gave her a downhearted look. "I'll check again." He turned around and started to walk back to Crow Farm.

Connor and Barney sleepily cropped the grass and then lifted their heads with surprise when they saw her. The field was quite dry and there was not much grazing left. When she returned from her hack, she would have to open up another section of the field for them. The summer grass had been good this year and both Connor and Barney had round bellies. She didn't want them to go lame and would have to find a way to restrict the amount of grass they were eating.

The stable block consisted of three stables and was located on the far side of the field. Two of the stables were left open so that Connor and Barney could wander in and out as they pleased. They often would shelter together in one of the stables if it was too hot or there was a storm brewing. They didn't like being shut-in, which she had to do occasionally if the weather was really bad. The third stable was where she kept the horses' blankets, tack and hay for the days when they were unable to graze. They followed her across the field to the stable block, now aware that there was a possibility that they would be going out for a walk. Sometimes she took Barney out on a lead rein alongside her and Connor. She decided not to bring Barney today as she wanted to go further than the old pony was able to walk. Jules felt bad, he would be disappointed. Her mind turned to Seth again and she wondered what the police wanted with him.

Jules opened the spare stable door and stepped inside to collect Connor's saddle and bridle. The bridle was quite high up on a peg. Her uncle had been a lot taller than her. Connor waited patiently for her to fit his bridle on his large head and lowered it so she could reach. She tied the reins to a ring attached to the front wall and then went back into the tack room to collect his saddle. She braced herself, ready to pick it up, but then stopped. Something odd had caught her eye. Sticking out from between the bales of hay stacked high along the side of the tack room wall was her dressing gown belt. Startled, she knelt down to free it and the belt came away without difficulty. It was covered in hay, so she brushed it off. *How did it get here?* She hung it up on the bridle peg and she ran across the field to retrieve her dressing gown from the bush. She climbed through the fence and made her way to the first bush along the field edge and peered deep into the foliage. *It's gone! Perhaps a tramp somewhere is walking along the lanes of Sussex wearing a multi-coloured silk dressing gown without a belt.* This still didn't explain why the belt had turned up in the tack room.

As Jules climbed through the fence back into the field, she noticed Connor and Barney were standing outside the tack room. This was not a normal thing to see. Usually, when she left the tack room door open they would both be inside feasting on fresh hay. Something was not right, and the hairs on the back of her neck were standing up. As she approached the stables, she collected a pitchfork from the dung heap, ready to protect herself. Jules didn't know why she was being so dramatic, it was just a feeling she had. *Somebody is in the tack room!* "Is anyone there? Come out, or I'll call the police. This is private land."

"Don't panic. It's only me." Peter appeared in the doorway holding the belt in his hand.

"Peter, you gave me the fright of my life. I thought you were out with Dad. What are you doing here?"

He looked flustered and then gazed down at the belt he was holding. "I found her here last night? I thought it was you. She was wearing your dressing gown."

"Who did you find here?"

"Ivy Brown was lying on some hay bales - just here. She was pissed and couldn't get up. She kept passing out. I... didn't know what to do with her. I thought it would be ok to let her stay in here and sleep it off."

"You do know that she has gone missing? You need to tell Jake. He has been out looking for her. Why did you think that it was me? How did you see all this going on from the house?"

"After Dad brought you back from the Hearns, I couldn't sleep. I went out for a walk and saw you and somebody else walking towards the stables. I thought you'd got out again and were being stupid."

"Thanks a lot! I'm not a senseless, grounded kid. What happened to the person that was with Ivy?"

"When the light of the tack room went on, he must have heard me coming and disappeared into the shadows. Ivy was helpless. Anything could have happened to her, so I shut the door and I was going to let her out in the morning. I didn't lock it, in case there was a fire. She might have just gone home."

"You need to tell Jake what happened."

"Seriously? He's a loser. I despise him. I hope she never turns up and that he lives a miserable life."

"You are so cold sometimes, Peter. You need to lighten up."

***

Jules and Connor stumbled down a chalky bridleway, high up above the Long Furlong road. From where they were, she could see the sea sparkling on the horizon. This had to be one of her most favourite routes and Connor seemed to be happy to be out for a walk and was his usual calm self. Even the flies didn't seem to bother him. She patted his neck happily, and he snorted as if replying. Up ahead was a peculiar wooden table and bench that looked almost like a high style. She decided to have lunch here. The view from there was amazing. In her backpack, she carried an out of date pork pie, a black banana and a bottle of water - *not the most exciting lunch.*

After a few more minutes of riding, she could see the benches and realized that somebody was sitting there. As she got closer, she saw a man get up and she was pleased as he was about to leave and she would be able to have her lunch alone. Jules dismounted and pulled Connor's reins over his head to lead him. The sun was getting high, and it was difficult to see ahead. A cloud passed in front of the sun. She could see Seth walking towards her. Her heart lurched inside her chest, and she felt awkward. *Is he here by chance or has he been waiting for me?*

Seth was smiling at her, and she was doing her best not to look pleased but it was hard not to give him a half-smile. He was wearing the same clothes that he had worn to the party, and his dark hair looked dishevelled. He needed a shave too.

"Have you forgiven me for not wrestling you away from your Dad last night? I didn't want to make the situation worse. You have quite a temper on you."

"I could say the same about you, Seth Hearn. I have a lot of questions to ask, and I need some straight answers," she said, sitting down on the bench. "I like the view from here and I often come up here with Connor. I guess you knew that already." Connor started to graze on the grass verge next to them.

Seth was looking a little apprehensive and sat next to her. For a moment they said nothing and just sat there looking at each other.

"So, what do you want to ask me?" He asked, taking up her hand. She could feel the warmth from his hand and felt disconcerted, but she couldn't take her hand away from his.

"I don't know where to start." Her first concern was Ivy. Ivy had been wearing her dressing gown and only herself and Seth knew where she had hidden it.

"Ivy has gone missing. Last night, Peter saw someone helping her into our tack room. She was wearing my dressing gown. Only you knew where I hid it. It was you, wasn't it? Why were you out with her last night?"

"Yes, it was me. She was wasted."

"What happened, Seth?"

"So it was your brother I saw following us. I thought it was Jake, so I ran off and left them to it. After you left the party, I just wanted to make sure that you got home ok and that your Dad wasn't giving you a hard time. He shouldn't be treating you like that. Like a child."

"Seth, he's not well."

"Anyway, I got to your house and waited until your light in your bedroom went out. It was then that Ivy appeared. I think she was looking for Jake and mistook me for him. She probably saw me go across our field when I followed you home. I don't know if you noticed, but the Hearns all look very similar - it's our Spanish blood. Ivy was in a bad way and her legs kept giving out. I told her to go home, but she went the wrong way. I'm surprised you didn't hear her; she was singing some horrible song. I kept telling her to come back with me, but she wouldn't listen. When I caught up with her again, she was shaking and kept saying she was cold. We were standing right by your horses' field. I found your dressing gown in the bush and put it on her. It just about went around her, but she was grateful. It was then that Ivy saw your horses and she fell through the fence on her way to see them. I saw your stables and was looking for a warm place for her to rest and sober up. Your tack room was

42

unlocked. You do know you should lock it? You could easily get robbed."

"I usually lock it but most of the time I forget," she replied, pulling Connor's head towards her. He was about to pull her off the bench. "I saw Jake this morning, and he apologised for what he said. That surprised me. He was really worried. He hasn't seen Ivy since you two had a fight."

"I wouldn't call it a fight, exactly."

"If I hadn't stopped you, then you would have been thumping each other. Why were the police looking for you this morning? What have you done, Seth?"

Seth let go of her hand. "That's a loaded question. It was nothing. What makes you think I've done anything?"

Jules could see Seth's discomfort. She didn't want to make him angry. It was almost as if a red mist was descending upon him. She changed the subject. "It's ok, you don't have to tell me. Are you hungry? I'll share my lunch with you, but I must warn you, it may kill you." She took off her backpack and produced a plastic box containing the old pork pie and black banana. She opened the lid and showed Seth the contents of the box.

"No, it's ok, I'll pass. Are you sure you should? I wouldn't like to lose you so soon." Seth was smiling again and she began to relax. She needed to give him time to tell her about his life. Connor's nose suddenly appeared in her lunchbox and he snorted, disgusted by its contents.

"You have an intelligent horse, Julia."

"Seth, you have to call me Jules. I can't bear being called Julia. Sadly nearly everyone, including my Dad, calls me by my birth name. My brother and friends call me Jules."

"So you consider me to be your friend. Anything more?"

"Well, that's a loaded question!" she replied playfully.

After Jules had eaten her lunch, which tasted a lot better than it looked, they walked along the bridleway holding hands. She led Connor, and he stumbled along behind them. She hoped that by holding his hand he would realise that they were something more than friends. Jules squeezed his hand gently, to let him know that she was there for him. He smiled at her and stopped.

"Do I get a kiss then?"

"It's probably not a good time." They had reached the road and in the distance, the fields of Farm End spread before them. "I can see my Dad in the fields over there. We don't want him to get his shotgun out, do we?"

Silently they continued on their way and took the track that skirted the edge of her farm. She knew that when they were in a secluded spot, Seth would try to kiss her. She wasn't ready to be that intimate and needed time to process things. The elephant in the room was her lack of experience with dating. She had read romance novels but was still a little unsure how to respond to Seth's advances. She didn't want Seth to be disappointed, and she also didn't want to disobey her Dad - *a maddening situation to be in!* Her mind had become a whirlwind of torment, and she really needed some more time.

"Seth, I'm going to have to give Connor a quick canter or a trot at least. He is getting fat and lazy and needs the exercise. We can meet up tomorrow if you are free. Dad and Peter are taking some of the cows to the abattoir tomorrow. I have to take some parcels into the village if you want to help?"

He shook his head. "I've got a meeting tomorrow, but I will stop by on my way back and bring you a proper lunch. Later, I have to help with the harvest. I've got your number." He sighed and looked uncertain. "I have to get permission to text you or see you for that matter."

"Oh! You don't have mean parents too, do you?"

"No, I should have told you this before. I'm on parole, and I have to let them know my movements. I'm not allowed to even text someone or see someone without telling them. It's infuriating. Jules, I didn't want to tell you. I didn't want you to go off me. I'm not a bad person and haven't done anything terrible. I know I have a temper and sometimes I do things I regret. I would never hurt you, Jules. You do believe that, don't you? I forgot to go to report to my parole officer the other day, and that is why the police came 'round to check I hadn't run off. Luckily, they only warned me."

"It's ok, Seth. I know you have been in prison. Ivy told me. It's really ok." She found herself hugging him. He looked so distressed. "We'll get through this."

Seth rested his chin on her head for a moment and then releasing her he stepped back. He was smiling, and she breathed a sigh of relief. She didn't like to see him sad.

"Do you want me to give you a leg up? Although your horse does not look like it can canter let alone trot."

"On a good day, he has been known to break records!" she said lightly, placing the reins over Connor's head. Seth stood by the horse's side and joining his hands together, crouched a little so that she could put her left foot in his hands. Holding onto the saddle, she sprung up and simultaneously Seth stood up giving her a boost so she could get her leg over Connor's broad back and drop into the saddle.

Seth patted Connor's neck. "I have a Cob like this in Ireland, called Moss. When I get some money together, then I'm going to get him sent over here and we can go hacking together."

"I knew you were a horse person, I could tell."

"You have a good seat. Let me see what your horse can do."

Jules drew up her reins and walked Connor on. She knew that she was going to have her work cut out to even make him trot. As Connor's ears began to flick as he became aware of the pending change of pace, her phone pinged as a message came through. She stopped Connor and took her phone out of her pocket. The message was from Sebastian Hearn, and she read.

'I LOVE YOU! ☺'

Chapter Five

The next morning, Jules came down to the kitchen and saw that the shopping had been delivered. The bags had been lined up neatly by the back door. She wondered how long it had been sitting there. Her brother and Dad were enjoying some bacon sandwiches for their breakfast and were listening to the radio as usual. Her Dad didn't like a quiet house. They had done the milking, and she could see the truck outside in the courtyard. It was ready to take some of the older and dry cows for slaughter. It would bring some money in and there was no point in rearing cows that didn't produce enough milk. You had to be hard-nosed to be a dairy farmer. Jules tried not to think about what happened to cows at the abattoir.

"Food, Jules! You're the best!"

It wasn't often that she got a compliment from Peter. She started to put the chilled and frozen shopping away and then looked anxiously over at her Dad who seemed to be in deep thought as he ate.

"Are you alright, Dad?"

"I'm ok."

No, you're not, are you?

"I will feel a whole lot better when I see some money going into the bank. We should get a few pounds for the cows we're going to take today. I'm sorry, Julia; I have to take Hermione this time, she's getting too old to have another calf and has been dry for a while now," he added sadly. "I'm going to get in touch with the agents later. I really can't believe that there haven't been any sales enquiries about the farm this month. I can't carry on like this for much longer."

"Perhaps things will improve when August is over and everyone is back from their holidays."

"Do people still go on holiday?" their Dad asked.

"I believe they do," Peter said, looking at their Dad with a concerned face.

"What are you up to today, Jules?"

Jules sometimes felt guilty that her brother did more than she did on the farm. Running the house was hard work too, but this was a thankless task. "I've got loads to do around the house. I've got the horses' field to pooh pick and the milking too. There's never a dull moment in my life!"

Jules started to run the hot tap and then filled the washing-up bowl with water and soap ready to wash the dishes. There was a substantial pile of plates and cutlery building up next to the sink and she planned to have everything looking spick and span in the kitchen before Seth arrived. Jules didn't want Seth to think that they were slobs. She was also feeling a bit weird about inviting him in behind everyone's backs.

"I'm going to try and cook something exotic for dinner later. What time will you both be back?"

"We should be back by four," Peter said, throwing his plate into the bowl. "You know I don't like anything too spicy?"

"It's ok, I'm not going to set your mouth on fire again. I've worked out what the difference is between a teaspoon and a tablespoon. I haven't decided what I'm cooking yet. Are you going to take the dogs out with you?"

"No, not today. The cab will get too hot and I'm not sure how long we will have to wait at the abattoir," said her Dad, looking for the lorry's keys. "Peter, we'd better get the cows loaded on the lorry."

"Don't worry, Dad, George and Pip can hang 'round with me today and help me pooh pick. I'll take them for a walk too."

"Thanks, kitten."

The truth was, that she wasn't going to cook anything exotic and just wanted to make sure they were both out of the way when Seth turned up. Jules smiled to herself, remembering Seth's first text to her. *So, Sebastian is your real name.* She preferred to call him Seth. *Could he really be in love with me?* Jules wondered if he realised that Sebastian Hearn showed on her screen when he sent a text.

The morning passed quickly and after Jules had made the kitchen shine, she hunted through cupboards and drawers for materials suitable for packing parcels. She watched with excitement as the furious bidding war continued on each of her items for sale. At eleven twenty-three, the last item sold and after doing a few sums, deducting the usual selling fees, she worked out that she would have nearly four hundred pounds in her bank account. This was a step closer to her being financially independent.

Jules brought down to the kitchen all her sold goods and started to pack them up, ready to take down to the post office later. It was a good thing that her Dad was not around to see what she had sold as some of the items her Mum had given to her. There was a chance that he might be annoyed that she wanted to get rid of them. He could be funny like that.

August was always a hard month for them all. Jules checked the date. It was 7 August 2018. In three days' time, it would be her Dad's birthday, and he would be fifty-eight. If her Mum had been alive, it would have been her birthday too and she would have been fifty-eight also. They had always laughed about being the same age and having the same birthday. Jules dreaded 10 August, it was a depressing day and made them all miserable. Her Dad did not want to celebrate his birthday and usually went to bed early. Each year since her Mum had died, she had heard him sobbing in his room. This birthday would not be any different and perhaps even worse as her Dad's fifty-eighth birthday was significant – she couldn't remember why.

Jules stacked all her parcels into carrier bags and left them in the corner of the kitchen. *Am I going to make it to the post office without pulling my arms out of their sockets?* An idea came to her, she would put the bags of parcels in the wheelbarrow and wheel them down to Findon, hide the barrow at the edge of the village and then carry them in the bags the rest of the way. It was going to be hard work.

Jules looked up at the clock and saw that it was approaching midday. Seth would be here soon. It really was a hot day, but she felt cool in her sundress and flip flops. She looked down at herself and realized that she had forgotten to put a bra on; it really was too hot to wear one. *I'd better put one on.* She ran upstairs and then inspected herself in the mirror. Her cheeks were looking flushed, and her hair was on the verge of frizzing. Jules sprayed some anti-frizz serum over her curls and quickly brushed her hair through.

When Jules ran back downstairs, Seth was standing in the kitchen, holding a French stick and a bag of shopping. She barely recognised him. The stubble had gone, his dark hair was brushed through and he wore a neatly ironed shirt and shorts. Jules couldn't help but stare. "You scrub up well. Did your meeting go ok?"

"Thank you, I think that was a compliment. I can now legally see and text you. They overlooked my unauthorised message to you as I came clean and they have forgiven my no-show. I talked them 'round. I'm good at that, at least." Seth was smiling, she knew he was going to be cheeky. "I've brought some edible fare to share with you. It is all the right colour and is in date. Is it ok if we go and eat it in the shade outside? It's weird being in this kitchen again."

"So you've been in here before? I didn't think the two families got along."

"Once they did, many years ago. My Mam used to be good friends with your aunt. She sometimes brought some of us kids over to see her. I've had cookies and milk sat at that table."

"I never met Aunt Ann. She left my uncle when I was young."

"Did you know that she had a baby and left him on our doorstep with a note, asking Mam to look after Jake?"

"Your brother Jake?"

"Yes, that nut job."

"Oh my! Is that why you don't like him? Because he is a Bridgewater?"

"No, I don't have any grudges against the Bridgewaters. I've always thought of Jake as family. We all do. Mam was sad that Ann didn't say goodbye and just looked after Jake along with her own. Jake was fine when he was young and then turned into a nightmare as a teenager."

"Didn't my uncle object?"

"No, he once said to my Mam that he was not father material and wouldn't have a clue how to look after a baby. He didn't give her any money to raise him and Mam never asked."

"How strange. Goodness! That means Jake and I are related. I think that makes me his cousin?"

"Does he know all this?"

"He does."

"That explains why he hates the Bridgewaters so much. I guess he feels let down."

"Maybe. It all looks exactly the same in here. Don't you have your own furniture?"

"We have some but not a lot. When the army moves you around all the time into different accommodations, you learn to travel light."

"So your Dad was in the army, then?"

"Yes, he was. We were stationed mostly in Germany. I can speak and sing in German which might come in handy one day. You never know."

"Now there's a surprise. Are you ready for lunch? I want to know everything about you. Do you have a couple of plates and a knife or two? I hope you like cheese and pickle? I would have bought some wine too, but I don't want to get you drunk on our third date."

"That sounds great. Third date, you say?" Jules found a couple of old plates and some knives. Then she remembered Ivy. "Any news on Ivy?"

Seth shook his head. "I expect she saw what a heap of shite Jake was and has gone running home." Seth looked down at the pile of parcels in the corner. "Now I know why you wanted my help with these parcels. You could get a courier company to collect. It would be much less of a headache that way. That's what I would do."

"That headache has earned me four hundred pounds. I will take them down to the village later. I had thought of getting them collected but I just chose the drop off option as it was a bit cheaper that way. I have to save money where I can."

"Are things that bad?"

"The bills are piling up, and we just have to get a buyer for the farm. You don't know anyone that wants a dairy farm that makes hardly any profit, do you?"

"Perhaps your Dad could grow soya bean plants instead."

"Peter suggested something like that to him but he's really not interested in farming. I think that he took the farm on so he could find a place for us to stay for a while. I don't think he really knows what he is doing at the moment. He is so depressed."

"I'm sorry. You are bound to have some good luck soon. You've met me! That's a start. Talking of farms, I've got to take my turn driving the combine harvester at two. Let's go for a walk first. I want to show you a secret pool on your land that I used to visit when I was little. I bet you haven't seen it before. My Dad calls it a silent pool."

"No, I haven't. I'm not going in, though. I don't want to drown. I'm not that good at swimming and my hair does odd things when it dries. I might frighten you. Is it ok if the dogs come too? I can tell that they are restless and need a walk. They prefer to be out in the fields with Dad rather than stuck in here."

"No problem. The pool is not too far from here. It's a really deep pond. Are the dogs likely to jump in? They might have difficulty getting out. The banks are really steep."

"Not a chance, these two stinky boys are water phobic."

Along with the plates and knives, Jules collected a blanket to sit on and realising that it belonged to one of the dogs, left it where it was as it was covered in dog hair and too disgusting to bring. Jules picked up her phone and keys and they stepped out into the sunshine. The dogs, with tails wagging, ran on ahead and were excited to be out in the fresh air. The temperature had to be near boiling point. Jules couldn't remember a hotter August. This was great news for those harvesting grain crops and cutting hay, but it was too hot to walk in.

Because of everything they were holding, Jules was unable to hold Seth's hand, and so she walked beside him wondering where he was taking her. He led her towards his farm and then helped her over a style. They walked together, down the side of a field, towards a small wooded area. In all the five years she had been at End Farm, she wasn't able to say whose field belonged to who. It then occurred to her that this must be the boundary that had caused so many problems in the past.

"Is this our field or yours, Seth?"

Seth smiled. "I'll give you ten out of ten for observation. I am pretty sure that this field belongs to you. My Dad would say different and swears that a hundred years ago my grandfather bought this field from your grandfather for ten pounds. There are no papers to prove this and my Granny is too cuckoo to remember. If you can't prove it, then the original deeds stand."

"Did I see your Granny at the party, Seth?"

"No, she went back to Ireland years ago and lives with an aunt."

"Do you ever see them?"

"When I was travelling, I stayed in Ireland for a year. It was a bit of a journey to get from Cork to Dingle so I couldn't see them that often."

"Did you buy Moss in Cork then?"

"I lived with a friend in a village near Cork and she shows Cobs all over Ireland. I bought Moss at a horse fair and kept him at her stables. At one time, I thought that I would stay in Ireland, but I also wanted to see more of the world and my family. I miss that horse. You get attached to them. Have you ever been to Ireland?"

"No, but I'd like to go one day and kiss the Blarney Stone."

"Well, that's just five miles from Cork. I will take you there. Now you know why I am charming and never stop talking."

You are right, Seth Hearn, you really do know how to charm the girls.

The wooded copse was filled with young trees that needed coppicing. Birdsong echoed in the woodland as they approached the silent pool; Jules noticed that it was covered in flowering lilies. It was a magical place. The dogs ran around the pond and realising that they might get wet, went off to explore the wooded area.

"Oh my God!" Jules dropped the plates and knives she was holding and they clattered together, smashing as they hit the floor. He was staring at the pool too and had a look of horror on his face. "Seth, is that my dressing gown in the middle of the pond? It is, isn't it? Oh my God! Is that a body? Seth, is that Ivy? I think she's dead, Seth."

"Christ! I think you are right."

"Is she dead? We should get her out and try and revive her. We should call the police."

"It's too late, Jules. Believe me, she's dead! Look at her pale face. Fuck!"

Chapter Six

Jules could feel tears welling up, she was determined not to cry and got her phone out of her back pocket. "We have to call the police, Seth. I really hope this is just a tragic accident and not something worse. Her poor family. Poor Jake." Jules looked up at Seth for reassurance as she started to type in 999. He looked pale.

"Wait, Jules. Don't call them just yet."

She stopped dialling. "Why?"

"I can't be here when they arrive. The police can't know anything about me seeing her in the lane the other night or that I walked down to the pond with you. Have you told anyone?"

"No, of course not. You are joking? Are you crazy? What am I supposed to say? That I came down here for a walk with the dogs?"

"That will do. I can't have this one pinned on me. If they know I was involved, then they will send me back to prison for sure. I am really not going back there again. Never!"

Jules was beginning to lose her patience. "How do you know that Ivy didn't fall into the pond by accident? If you told the police about last night, then it will help piece together what happened to her."

"Jules, listen to me. It doesn't work like that. Once you have been labelled a villain, you will always be treated like one. You will never have respect and will always be the first they come looking for when something bad happens. Guilty or not. So don't text me about this or mention my name at all. Will you do that for me?"

"Isn't honesty the best policy? What on earth did you do, Seth? You're starting to freak me out."

"Christ! Give me a break. I am going to go back home for work. I'll give you a call soon. I need to clear my head. You have to trust me on this one."

Seth picked up the knives and broken plates, put them into his carrier bag and left. Jules watched him go. Tears started to roll down her cheeks. *Come back*! He had deserted her, leaving her with the horrendous task of sorting out this terrible mess. Jules felt sick with worry and didn't like the idea of lying to the police. *Am I committing a crime myself, by lying?* Taking a deep breath, she dialled the last nine and trembled. It seemed to take forever to be connected.

"Hello, Emergency Service operator. Which service do you require?"

"Um… Police, please."

"I'll connect you."

Jules waited, she was still crying and hoped that whoever she spoke to would understand her.

"Thank you, go ahead, caller. You are through to the police. What is the address or location of your emergency?"

"I'm by a pond in some woods, near End Farm in Findon. The farm is off Long Furlong. The postcode. Oh, I can't remember, it's gone from my head."

"That's ok. Can I take your name, please?

"Jules… No, I mean, Julia Bridgewater."

"Ok Jules, what is the nature of your emergency."

Jules sighed. "I've found a body, in a pond, on our farm. I think that it is Ivy Brown. She has been missing for a couple of days, and she is floating face up in the middle of a deep pool."

"Are you sure that the patient isn't breathing?"

"No, she's dead. I think that she has been there a while."

"I have managed to locate End Farm. Please, do not touch the body. Can you please wait at the farmhouse for the police car to arrive? I have marked your call as urgent."

"Ok, thank you."

Jules walked slowly back to the farmhouse. The dogs, sensing her distress, followed at her heels, looking up at her now and again. In the next field, Jules could see farm workers gathering runner beans. One of the workers stood still and was watching her. *Oh no*! She realised that she and possibly Seth might have been spotted walking down to the woods. She forced herself to be rational and then repeated in her head, several times, that all she was doing was walking the dogs.

When Jules got home, she put leads on George and Pip, picked up their water bowl and sat on a bench in the shade at the back of the courtyard to wait for the police to turn up. The dogs lapped at the water. After twenty minutes, two police cars arrived. She stood up, told the dogs not to bark, and walked towards the nearest car. Jules was relieved to see a female officer get out of the car.

"Julia Bridgewater? You've reported that you have found a body?"

She nodded and could feel the tears starting up again. *I can do this.*

"Can you show us where you found the body?"

"Yes, I was walking the dogs and was looking for somewhere cool to walk. I heard about a pond on our land and thought that it would be a good place to go." Jules was surprised how easily her story was coming together. *I mustn't say 'we' when I tell them what happened, I mustn't. Remember, Jules. It was just me who found her.*

After tying the dogs' leads to the bench leg, she patted them and took all four police officers up the lane towards Crow Farm and then down through the fields to the pond. When they reached the edge of the wood, she was unable to go in. "The pond is just a few meters in. Ivy is floating face-up in the middle of it. You can't miss her. I'm sorry, I really can't go in there again."

The female officer smiled kindly. "Don't worry, it is better if you don't. We don't want to disturb a possible crime scene."

The police officer looked concerned. "So you said Ivy. How do you know it is her? Sometimes plastic floating in the water can look like a body."

"It was definitely a body. I am pretty sure it is Ivy. She went missing the other night. Nobody has seen her since her engagement party." It was then that Jules realised that she was covering for her brother too. "I just have a bad feeling that it is her." Tears rolled down her cheeks.

The police officer's radio crackled and Jules listened to the conversation as the officers in the wood confirmed that the body had been located.

"Look, let's go back to your house and I will make you a cup of tea. I think that you are in shock."

"Yes, please. I've never seen a body before." Jules looked up and then noticed a man in blue overalls running towards her. She realised that it was the field worker that had been staring at her earlier. It was Jake. Her heart sank, and she really couldn't face telling him what had happened.

"Oh no! That's Ivy's boyfriend, Jake. What do I say to him?"

"Walk with me and let me handle it."

Out of breath and with sweat dripping down his face, Jake reached them and by the wild look in his eyes, he instinctively knew that something terrible had occurred.

"Jules, what's happened? Why are the police here? It's Ivy, isn't it? Is she hurt? You need to get an ambulance!" Jake started to head towards the woods.

The police officer grabbed his arm. "Hold on, Jake, we are securing the area. You can't go into the woods. A body has been found, but we have not identified it yet."

Jake stood still and his red face looked stunned. "A body?" He looked at Jules and frowned. "Did you see it?"

Jules nodded and then looked away, frightened that her eyes would reveal her secrets.

"I need to take some more details from you both. I am almost sure that we haven't had a missing person filed but I need to check, Jake. Is that ok?"

"Yes, of course," he replied and then followed Jules and the police officer up to the farmhouse.

As they walked, she tried not to look at Jake but couldn't help noticing that he was glaring at her.

***

Feeling drained, Jules sat at the kitchen table with her head in her hands. Taking a deep breath, she looked out into the garden trying to concentrate on the roses growing there to calm herself down. The police officer had made both her and Jake a cup of tea which had been too hot to drink. Sipping the now cold sugary liquid, she remembered Jake crying into his tea. *He cried a lot and must really love Ivy.*

The police officer had taken both their full names and addresses and contact details and the little that Jake knew about Ivy. He didn't even know what the name of the road she lived in was, let alone what number. The police officer had told Jules that she might have to make a statement at the police station soon and to expect a call. It was two minutes to four, her Dad and brother would be back soon. Jules wondered if she should call her Dad to tell him what had happened but decided to wait. She was curious to see Peter's face when she told them the news.

Jules could hear the empty truck rattling as it pulled up in the courtyard. The dogs barked outside, and she felt guilty that she had forgotten about them. *At least they are in the shade with water.* Jules was feeling nervous and was not looking forward to retelling her version of the afternoon's events.

Her Dad came into the kitchen with the dogs, and he was holding the dogs' leads. Peter followed and looked hot. He picked up a glass and filled it with water from the tap.

"Why were the dogs in the courtyard? Have they been annoying you?"

"No, Dad, they were fine. I... Something awful has happened."

"Are you ok?"

"I've had a bit of a shock. I took the dogs out at lunchtime and walked through our fields. I was feeling really hot, and I saw a wooded area ahead and thought that it would be a cool place to walk through. At the centre of the copse is a pond. I found a body in the pond, Dad! I'm pretty sure that it is Ivy Brown's body."

Jules looked at Peter and watched him nearly choke on the water he was drinking. He coughed and got his breath back. "Are you sure, Jules?"

"Ivy was face up, her skin a deathly white and I recognised her red dress and my..." *lovely dressing gown. I'll miss it. For goodness sake, Jules! Ivy's dead and you're worrying about a stupid dressing gown!*

"You poor kitten." Her Dad's face had drained of colour. "We will have to call the police."

"It's ok, Dad. I called them. They have closed off the woods. I think it has become a crime scene." As she said this, she saw an ambulance drive past their house. "They must have got the body out of the water. I just saw an ambulance go by. A nice police lady made us some tea and took both mine and Jake Hearn's details."

Her Dad's face darkened. "What was he doing here?"

"Jake saw me taking the police down to the woods and ran over. You do know Ivy and Jake were engaged to be married? They haven't identified the body yet, so he's hoping that it is not her. I didn't tell him that I thought that it was Ivy. He was really upset, Dad!"

He shook his head. "This farm is cursed. If only..." Near to tears again, he sighed and went off to his study to be alone.

Peter looked really pale and was lost in his own thoughts and there was a haunted look in his eyes. She wasn't sure what to say to him. *What is going on in his head?*

"That pool is really deep and dangerous. The Hearns should have fenced it off a long time ago. Jules, I was the last one to see her alive. What if…"

Jules could see that he needed to talk. He didn't normally confide in her and if he needed to get something off his chest then it would be better to talk privately. Seeing her parcels in the corner gave her an idea. She got up and walked over to them. "Peter, I need to post some things. Would you give me a lift to the post office, please? We need to talk."

Under normal circumstances, he would have told her where to go. He had the use of the old Land Rover and had only once taken her to the village for a doctor's appointment. He nodded. "Ok. I'll get the keys."

Jules loaded her bags onto the back seats of the Land Rover and climbed into the passenger seat. The car smelt musty, it didn't get used much. She wound down the windows to get some air into the car. A robin was singing in the shrubbery nearby and she searched the branches looking for a red breast. As they drove away, the robin darted out of the bush and perched itself on the top of a fence rail to watch them go.

Peter seemed a bit more focused and she was pleased, as his driving skills were poor. As they pulled out onto the road, he stalled the car. Fortunately, there was nothing coming. "Damn, this clutch is so stiff."

"It's hot and you're probably a bit tired after your trip out with Dad."

"Yes, it's been a rough day. Did you…"

"What you are going to ask me is, if I mentioned that you saw Ivy on the night she went missing. You don't have to worry. That didn't come up. They are not sure if the body is Ivy's. If it is, then there will be questions asked."

"Well, that's a relief. I hope it's not her. Did you know that I went out with her for a while? It was a couple of years ago."

"Really? I don't remember. In fact, I don't remember you ever going out with anyone. I never see you leave the farm apart from going to the bank."

"That was when I was at college. My life hasn't been the same since Mum died. There is so much to do on the farm and I don't think Dad could handle me seeing someone."

"So I'm not the only one that is having trouble in that department. I can understand Dad being overprotective with a daughter but not with his son. Do you think there is something wrong with him? I think he's depressed. Don't you?"

"Yes, I guess so. Perhaps he will feel better when he gets rid of the farm; the millstone around his neck. The farm is draining the life out of him. When he left the army, he had no plan. The army used to send him around the world. Now he has nobody to direct him. What are we planning to do? Buy a house somewhere? Where are we moving to?"

"God knows!"

Peter pulled up outside the post office. "Do you want me to wait?"

"Yes, please. No, actually, it's ok, I wouldn't mind the walk back to clear my head. I'll be back in time for milking."

"If you are sure. Jules, if the police question you, then please don't say anything about me finding Ivy in the tack room the other night."

"Really? It could be important."

"Please, Jules."

"Ok, but… Fine!"

58 FARM END

Jules collected her parcels from the back seat and then watched him drive out of the village. She sighed and hoped that the body was not Ivy's. It would be very difficult not to tell the police everything if it was. *Was it Ivy's body lying lifeless in the lilies?*

Chapter Seven

As early evening slipped over the Sussex Downs, a cool breeze made Jules shiver a little. Holding her hands in the small of her back, she stood tall and stretched the muscles to stop them from aching. It was tiring forking up the horse dung from the field; it was not one of her most favourite jobs. Helping with the milking had also taken its toll. She wasn't as fit as she used to be. The sky caught her eye, there was a beautiful sunset forming in reds and oranges and she was pleased to be outside in the fresh air, away from all the madness.

After a pleasant but hot walk back home from the village and after checking for toxic weeds, she had opened up fresh pasture for Connor and Barney to graze on. As soon as the tape had been removed, they had galloped up from the bottom of the field, overjoyed to be let loose on fresh grass. If only Seth could have seen them, then he would have really been impressed by their athletic ability. She eyed Connor's belly doubtfully, there was no getting away from it; her horse was getting fat.

The wheelbarrow was full of manure, so she wheeled it down to the heap by the gate, tipped it up and started to fork the dung to the top of the steamy pile. As she took the wheelbarrow back up the pasture to finish off her task, it was then that she saw Seth walking across the field towards her. He wasn't smiling. *Is he cross with me? He shouldn't be here.* She looked towards the farmhouse and was relieved to see that the hedges between the field and house screened them from prying eyes. Seth was wearing overalls and looked tired and dusty from working in the fields. She longed to see him smile again and wasn't sure if she was ready to engage with him. Today had been really emotionally draining. *I'm not going to argue with him.*

"Jules, I'm sorry about earlier. I shouldn't have just left you like that. You do understand why I had to go, don't you?"

Jules just stared at him silently, not sure if he was really apologising.

"How did you get on with the police? Jake said he saw you. He's drunk again, by the way."

Jules looked at Seth's worried face but was still feeling hurt. "They took the body away but have not confirmed the identity yet. It's ok, I didn't mention you at all. Just like I didn't mention anything about Peter seeing her in the tack room. What is wrong with everyone? They are not stupid, the police. If it is Ivy, then there will be an investigation and Jake and I will have to make a statement at the police station. It's been a tough day, Seth. I don't like lying!"

"I really am sorry. I understand how you are feeling. I have had to lie for someone, to save them from going to jail. It is not easy. I want to tell you about it and then perhaps you will forgive me. Can we go for a walk? I don't want your Dad to see me here. I don't want to cause you any more trouble."

"I'm tired, Seth, I walked back from the village earlier and I've got to make dinner soon."

Seth was looking so hopeless that she couldn't bear to let him go home without allowing him to share his story with her. She doubted if it would help things. "We could sit behind the stable block. Nobody can see us there, and there's a nice view. That is where I watch the sun go down and where I sit when I need to think."

The sun was just above the horizon line. Seth followed Jules to her suggested spot and they both sat side by side on a small wall, and in silence stared out at the fields below. She didn't want to be the one to start the conversation. This was his chance to confide in her and prove that he really did care for her.

"So you know that I was in prison, don't you?"

She nodded but said nothing.

"I got a three-year sentence, for a crime I didn't commit."

"Just three years? Ivy told me that you murdered someone."

"Did she! Someone did die but it was accidental and it wasn't my fault." Seth was doing his best to remain calm but was having difficulty.

"So what happened then?"

"You must never repeat this. I've never told anyone about what really happened. Two years ago, I was at my sister Maureen's wedding and the party finished just after midnight. She had a big do in Worthing and there were loads of people there. I wasn't feeling great that night. I was coming down with a bad cold and had dosed myself up, so I didn't drink anything. Jake had just learnt to drive and had got himself a new car. Just an old Ford that I got cheap from one of my friends. It was around ten and I was starting to feel really rough as the flu set in. Proper flu, not just man flu. Jake offered to take me home. He had one or two drinks and he kept telling everyone that he couldn't drink much as he was driving."

"He drinks too much."

"I know, but I thought he was ok to drive." Seth sighed. "The ride home was a journey that I am never going to forget. He shot out of the car park like a bolt and was laughing and showing off. He was driving his car like a maniac. I think he was high on something. I was really shocked. We hit the pavement several times and I was yelling at him to stop. He was acting the maggot and was being such an eejit. He was laughing so much that he didn't see someone step out onto a crossing. He ploughed straight into an old man. Killed him outright! The car hit the pavement too and turned over. Jake lay in a crumpled heap, stunned into silence. We climbed out of the car, and I ran over to the old man but his eyes were wide open and lifeless. A car pulled up behind us and the driver got out to help. He tried to revive him, but it was no good.

Jake was in a terrible state, and he was crying and shaking. He had been in trouble with the police several times and kept saying he was going to prison. I told him to calm down and that I would think of something. I kept thinking about what Mam would say. She was at her wit's end with him and was so proud when he passed his driving test. She would be devastated if he went to prison. I didn't want that."

"So why did you go to prison?"

"I told the police that I was driving."

"But that is crazy! Didn't they see you on camera? What about fingerprints on the steering wheel? Were there any witnesses?"

Seth smiled at her. "You're a right Miss Marple, aren't you? I had driven the car home from my friend's house so my fingerprints would have been on the steering wheel. The police believed that I was driving. The cameras didn't capture who was at the steering wheel when it happened and even if they did, it would be hard to tell who was driving as Jake and I look so alike. I thought that I would get community service, but I got three years for dangerous driving and for not having insurance to drive the car. I am on a year's probation for good behaviour. As much as I liked Ford Prison, I really don't want to go back there. It is a lonely and dark place."

She looked at his face and felt sorry for him. His dark brown eyes looked so lost. The sun was slipping down behind the horizon. There were still questions she wanted to ask.

"So why were you arguing with Jake the other night? He should be grateful that you helped him."

"You are going to laugh when you hear this. He has no recollection of that night. It was probably the shock that did it. The car was totalled and now he wants me to replace it."

"No way! I would have punched him!"

Seth sighed, "A weight has been lifted from my shoulders. I am glad I told you but I didn't think that you would believe me."

"Why wouldn't I believe you, Seth?" She took his hand, and squeezed it and then kissed him gently on the lips.

He looked surprised and then smiled. "I could, of course, be making this all up so that you would feel sorry for me and kiss me."

"That would be a very wicked thing to do! I would know if you were lying to me. I feel like I've known you all my life," she said quietly. "Seth, you need to always be honest with me, if we are going to be together."

Seth smiled. "I meant it you know. I do love you. I can't help it. You are the one. Now about the kiss, I think that you can do better than that! Let me show you how it's done?"

Slowly he leant forward, placed his hand behind her neck and kissed her tenderly. She could smell him, a pleasant mix of citrus, earth and hay. Shockwaves surged through her body and for a moment she was lost in a dreamlike state. *So sensual, so….*

Grinning, Seth pulled away from her. "How was that?"

She opened her eyes and smiled, she hadn't remembered closing them. She looked directly into his brown eyes and could see how happy he was. She could feel a warmth emanating from his hand, and she knew that she would always be his.

"I love you, Seth Hearn."

Chapter Eight

Today was 10 August, the day that both Peter and Jules had been dreading. The tension in the air was almost tangible and to make matters worse, storm clouds were gathering overhead, acknowledging her Dad's and her late Mum's fifty-eighth birthday. Determined to make the day a special one, she had made him a card, like she did every year, leaning against the toast rack for him to find before milking.

When Jules came down to the kitchen for breakfast, she noticed that the envelope had not been opened. *Oh dear! Perhaps he was in a rush and hasn't had time to open it yet.* Her Dad and Peter were out doing the milking and would be back soon for breakfast. Her plan was to bake today and on her list was a birthday cake and some cupcakes. She liked to bake. She would try and pretend that this was just a normal birthday.

Jules poured herself some cereal out into a bowl and added some milk. As she sat eating, butterflies were circling around in her stomach. Something was bothering her. There were a couple of things that were troubling her and one worry was that yesterday the exam results had been released, and for some reason, she had forgotten to go and get them. In some ways, it was a good thing as her friends would probably be really happy and get the grades they were after. It would be really humiliating to get bad results and then have to pretend you are happy with them. After breakfast, she would have a look online and see if they could be accessed that way. *What if I've failed all of them? What then?*

Seth had a lot to do with her anxious state. The last few days had been magical, and she was surprised how much Seth occupied her thoughts. It was a busy time on both their farms and Seth spent most of the day out in the fields helping with the harvest. In the evenings after she had helped with the milking and had made dinner, she had gone up to the horses' field to check on them. It was not unusual for her to do this but the time she spent with them was longer than normal. Seth was always behind the stable block waiting for her. She felt a little guilty being deceitful but all anxiety dissipated when they met. They talked about absolutely everything and of course, kissed and held each other a lot too. *I will have to be strong and tell Dad about Seth, but not today.*

Jules had asked Peter why their Dad had been dreading this particular birthday so much. He had raised his eyes to Heaven and reminded her that their Dad had discovered an Ouija Board in his grandmother's house when he was young and he and his friends had asked the spirits various questions. She vaguely remembered him telling her this. The spirits had supposedly guided a pointer they were touching around the board, spelling out answers. Not knowing that you were not meant to ask when you are going to die, he had asked the spirits. The pointer had taken him to five and then eight – '58'. This memory had always played on his mind.

She shuddered and searched on Google to see if Ouija predictions came true and chose to believe the BBC's article about us making involuntary movements without realizing it. *It was a load of nonsense. Wasn't it?* Her phone pinged, making her jump. She found the Ouija thing a bit disturbing. The message was from Seth.

'Can I meet you at 1pm in Worthing and take you out for lunch after my meeting? Do you have the bus fare?'

She thought about the ten pounds she still had in her purse, leftover from the meal in Findon. That evening seemed to be an age away.

'Yes, that would be lovely. I am a rich woman now and am looking forward to another date with you. Where shall I meet you?'

'On the pier in the Pavilion Café. I think that it used to be called the Denton Lounge. It's attached to the theatre. I promise this date will not be as traumatic – no dead bodies!'

'I'll find it. Did you sleep ok?'

'I would have slept better if you had been next to me <3'

Jules looked at his message and grinned. It was strange but she hadn't thought that far ahead and was enjoying just meeting up with Seth every evening. Her body was starting to tingle at the thought of sleeping with him. He had French kissed her just for a second or two and that erotic sensation had sent electricity through her body. He had stopped and smiled when he heard her gasp. She would have to wait a while for that day as the Hearns were perhaps Catholics and didn't believe in sex before marriage.

'Behave! See you at 1pm. I've got to sort the horses out before it rains xxx'

'I always behave myself. One day soon! ;) xxx <3.'

As she left the kitchen, the rain began to pour down and thunder rumbled in the distance. She ran back inside and put on her waterproof coat and wellies. She looked at the sky and decided that the rain looked like it was set to pour for the morning at least.

The rain made everything smell heavenly and as she walked across to the horses' field, the dry ground eagerly sucked in the much-needed water. Connor and Barney were in the same stable with their rear ends facing her. They often hid together when a storm was brewing and it was unlikely that they would graze today. Jules decided to get them some hay and collected the hay nets. She reached into her pocket and pulled out the key to open the tack room. She really didn't like going in there. In her mind, this was a crime scene. Trying her best to touch as little as possible, she dragged out a bale of hay, ready to break open on the covered veranda.

The rain was really heavy now and water streamed along the gulley in front of the stable block. She tiptoed back into the tack room to get a knife to cut the string holding the bale of hay together. The knife had been left on the floor, under the bridle peg. She remembered hanging up the dressing gown belt on the peg and she also remembered Peter holding it. It wasn't there now. *Where has it gone? Peter must have taken it away with him. Was he removing some crucial evidence from the crime scene?* Its disappearance was probably a good thing and if poor Ivy had been murdered, then he would be in the clear. *I think.*

Jules enjoyed going on the bus to Worthing, this was always a pleasure and her chance to get away from her responsibilities on the farm. At Worthing, she loved sitting on the beach and looking out to sea or taking photos of the seascape, the pier, or unusual objects washed up on the shore. Many of these photos had been uploaded onto Instagram and she had quite a following. There was a good chance that she had passed her 'A' Level Photography. Her dream job would be to work as a photographer. *Maybe I should?* She toyed with the idea of buying herself a decent camera; her dream of being a tea shop owner had slipped away.

She got off the steamed-up bus and stepped out into the pouring rain. Although she was wearing her long mac, it was not that waterproof and was already leaking. She ran towards the Pavilion Theatre, climbed the steps up to the café entrance and found Seth waiting for her in what appeared to be a small information centre.

"I'm here," she announced. "I am drenched!"

Seth wasn't wearing a coat, he smiled, pulled back her hood and kissed her gently on the lips. "You look lovely in that mac. A sweet little dote. Let's go in and sit by the window so we can watch the sea. I've got something to show you."

She took off her dripping mac and was horrified to see that her t-shirt was wet. Fortunately, it was mostly her shoulders and sleeves that were damp. As they sat down, Seth took a newspaper out of his backpack and looked anxiously at her. She knew something was wrong.

"Did something bad happen at your meeting?"

"No, that went well. It's just a bit tiresome that I have to go to them so often. I don't want you to freak out," he said, passing the newspaper to her. "But Ivy and another have made the headlines."

She lay the Worthing Herald out on the table in front of her and saw the headlines.

'Two Bodies Found at a Pond in Findon'

"Oh my! Two?"
"Yes, two. Read on, Jules."

'Police have identified a woman who was found dead in a deep pond in Findon, on Monday 6 August as 19 years old Ivy Brown from Goring-on-Sea. The post mortem has revealed that she died from drowning. Her death is being treated as unexplained and the investigation is ongoing.'
Detective Inspector Simon Black said;

'It is likely that Ivy may have fallen into the pond accidentally and had been unable to climb out due to the pond's steep sides. The investigation is ongoing and until it has been completed, we cannot say for sure if this is what has happened. We are appealing to anyone who may have seen Ivy on the evening of Saturday 4 August, after her engagement party. Ivy's family have been informed.

Remains of a second female body have also been discovered by divers while searching the pond for evidence. The body has been identified from dental records as being Ann Bridgewater. The

pond and woods have been fenced off while the investigation of both deaths continues.'
– DETECTIVE INSPECTOR SIMON BLACK, SUSSEX POLICE

"Oh my, Seth! This is mad! Poor Ivy and now Ann? They both can't be accidents. What the Hell is going on?"

"I really don't know. Jules, I'm starving. Let me get us some tea and a sandwich. Or would you like something else?"

"No, thanks, a sandwich is fine. I'll have whatever you're having. I suddenly don't have much of an appetite."

"Ok, there's only one in the queue, I won't be long."

As Seth waited to be served, she watched the waves rolling onto Worthing beach. She was feeling a little numb inside and knew that in the next few days she would probably have to make a statement to the police. Her good mood had ebbed away, and all she could think about was Ivy's body, floating lifelessly amongst the lily pads.

Seth returned to the table and peered into the teapot to check the tea. "I think this needs a few more minutes. The sandwiches are cheese and pickle." He sat down, and Jules could see that he was looking worried again. "There's something I need to tell you. I promised that I would be honest with you."

She sighed. It was not going to be good news. "Tell me then."

"When I helped Ivy over to your tack room, she told me something. She told me that she was three months pregnant and was going to get rid of the baby."

"But you said that she and Jake wouldn't go that far."

"Ivy also said that it wasn't Jake's."

"Oh, that's not good. Wait until Jake finds out." She looked at him thoughtfully for a moment. "Why would Ivy tell you that?"

"She was drunk and needed to share this with someone. There is another reason she might have told me this and I should have told you."

She was starting to feel alarmed, and she could feel the heat rising up into her cheeks. "It's not yours, is it?" She immediately regretted saying this as Seth looked shocked.

"No! Why would you think that?"

"I'm sorry, I am just overthinking things."

"Before I went to prison, we went out for a couple of months. It was going nowhere, and we stopped seeing each other. I am sad that she is dead, but she means nothing to me, Jules."

She looked away from him and tears started to roll down her cheeks. This revelation had hit her hard and there was one thing that she already knew the answer to.

"Did you sleep with her?"

"Just the once. We were drunk and it meant nothing." Seth was starting to look pale as he studied her face. "It was a long time ago. Do you want to go for a walk?"

She nodded, it was embarrassing crying in public. She put on her wet mac and made her way out of the café. An old lady gave her a sympathetic look as she left, which made things even worse. Seth followed her out into the rain.

Silently, they walked along the seafront, and the rain hit them hard and laughed at her naivety. She wasn't sure why this information had upset her so much. Seth must have had relationships before her but they were, in her head, insignificant and in distant lands. The thought of Seth having sex with Ivy

Brown sickened her. She had believed that, because of his upbringing, he would still be a virgin. She chastised herself for being so stupid. Most people had several sexual relationships before finding the right one. *Why am I so mad with you, Seth Hearn? I shouldn't be acting so crazy. Get a grip, Jules!*

She stopped and looked back at Seth who was a few steps behind her. His shirt and trousers were soaked through and his dark wavy hair had been flattened by the torrent of rain.

"Haven't you got a coat?"

Seth shook his head and was clearly waiting for her to say something more. She didn't like to see him in such a sorry state. His shirt was almost translucent and dark green tattoos on his upper arms were showing through. She hadn't noticed them before. "There's a shelter further along. We need to get out of the rain. I can't have you dying of pneumonia on me."

By the time they got to the shelter, she had calmed down enough to smile at Seth and she saw his anxiety dissipate. "I don't think that I've seen anyone looking as wet as you do."

"It's a small price to pay, just to see you smile again. I'll dry off eventually. I've got my hoodie in my bag."

"I'm sorry about lunch. I think that they have probably cleared it away by now. I'm sorry that I lost it back there. I just had to get out and clear my head. I guess what I'm trying to say is…"

"It's ok, I should have told you before. You have a right to be mad," Seth replied as he unbuttoned his shirt. She couldn't help but watch him as he removed his shirt and revealed his muscular body and delicate tattoos on the tops of his arms. She thought that they were perhaps Celtic motifs. Seth noticed her watching him closely and smiled. She found herself blushing. "Do you go to the gym, then?"

"I used to, when I was in prison but just working on the farm keeps me in trim these days."

She stepped closer to examine his tattoos. "Did you get these done when you were inside?" She asked, running her fingers over the woven patterns. "They are so intricate."

"No, you wouldn't want to get a tattoo done in prison. I had them done when I stayed in Ireland. They are Celtic knots; Dara Knots to be precise. They symbolise the oak tree, which represents wisdom, strength and the Earth's power. I really will take you to Cork one day."

"I like tattoos but my Dad would go mad if he saw them."

"My Dad would too, so I keep them covered up when I am at home."

"What's your Dad like? I didn't get a chance to meet him at the party."

Jake put on his hoodie and then sat down on the bench and looked out to sea. She sat next to him and held his wet hand.

"He is a difficult man. He runs the Hearn household with a firm hand. He dotes on his daughters and he demands respect from all of his sons. He doesn't take fools lightly and always speaks his mind – good or bad. I am not sure how my Mam puts up with him. She says that he is just a lovable scoundrel."

"Oh my. I am not sure I want to meet him after all. He sounds scary."

"The thing is, he is a charmer and he will love you. He will love you, like he loves his daughters."

"This is sounding like a period drama. What does he think about you?"

"I'm not sure he really knows who I am. My brother Patrick is his favourite and will inherit the farm. The other sons he regards as employees, I guess."

"So will you keep working for him or do you want to do something else?"

Seth smiled, "I have a dream and this dream includes you."

"It does?"

"When my probation is over, in ten months' time, I would like to go back to Cork with you, and your horses of course. As well as breeding cobs, my friend has a riding school and is always looking for instructors or stable hands. She's in her eighties now and although May is as fit as a fiddle, she could do with an extra pair of hands. We could rent a cottage from her, work for her and ride our horses out. She also has an old barn that could be turned into a tea shop."

"Wow! That sounds idyllic. You've really thought this through. Are you serious?"

"Of course, and now I'm getting nervous and need to know what you think."

"Are you sure you want a mad teenager to accompany you, who is prone to having temper tantrums?"

"I will take a chance and will make an honest woman of you yet!"

"Then I accept your kind offer. Is that a proposal, by the way?"

"It could be," Seth said with a cheeky grin.

A phone started to ring, and it took a moment for her to realise that it was hers. She took it out of her pocket and checked who was calling her. "That's odd, it's Peter. He never calls me. I hope nothing is wrong."

Chapter Nine

The journey home back to Findon had been unbelievably slow. The bus was crowded with old age pensioners taking advantage of their free travel passes. They chatted to each other about the foul weather and about which shops they had visited in Worthing. Jules was feeling lightheaded and hoped that she wouldn't faint in the hot bus. Each stop was a torturous wait as people slowly alighted or joined them on their journey. She was anxious to get home as soon as she could. It was a comfort to have Seth next to her, keeping her calm and holding her hand; otherwise, she might have cried.

Peter had sounded worried on the phone. He had said that he couldn't find their Dad. During milking, he had been strangely happy and had even whistled happy birthday to himself. This exuberant behaviour was not normal for him. At midday, they had eaten lunch in the kitchen, and a police officer had arrived. He wanted to ask some questions about Ann Bridgewater and Ivy Brown. Peter had said that the news of a second body being found in the pond had come as a shock. He thought that the news about the double deaths had sent him over the edge. When the police officer had left the farmhouse, Peter said that their Dad had just stood up, walked out of the kitchen and into the rain, without saying a word. He hadn't gone after him as he thought that he needed some space. For an hour he had waited for him to return. They had planned to clear some ditches that were backing up with water. He was going out to look for him and would need her help to find him and see if she thought he needed to see someone.

As they got off the bus, the rain continued to pour down on them but she didn't seem to notice. When they got to the courtyard she realised that Seth was still with her and hadn't gone on to Crow Farm. Peter came running out of the house to meet her. His blond hair was plastered down his hot face. He looked upset and then glared at Seth.

"You don't have to do this, Seth," she whispered.

"No, I want to help."

"What's he doing here, Jules?"

"Peter! Stop being an arse. Seth is going to help us find Dad. Perhaps Dad drove to the village?"

"No, the car is still here. I've just come back from the field where we were going to work and I have checked the house again. I just can't find him."

"What about the pond?" suggested Seth.

"Why would he go there?" scoffed Peter.

"It was just an idea. Have you checked the gun cupboard?"

Peter's fist clenched and he looked like he was going to hit Seth. She gave Peter a warning look. He relaxed and he shook his head. "I've thought of that. He hasn't taken a gun with him. I'm going to check the milking shed, there was a fault on one of the milking units." A quick smile was replaced with a concerned look. "Yes, I bet that's where he'll be."

She was not so sure. "You have a look there, and we'll check the barns and outbuildings. Like you said, he might just need some alone time."

He tore off towards the milking shed on the other side of the farm, and she and Seth headed towards the outbuildings.

"I'm sorry about Peter. He shouldn't have talked to you like that."

"It's ok, he's upset. I've dealt with worse. Where should we look first?"

"Let's start here," she said, pointing to a barn that housed farm machinery.

They ran from outbuilding to outbuilding and checked every corner and space that could house a distressed person but found no one. The rain beat down on them mercilessly and made their search more difficult. The last place to check was the hay barn, which was a field away on a flat piece of land. The black barn was old and decayed and was a blot on the landscape. She shuddered, and knew instinctively that this is where she would find her Dad. She had an overwhelming feeling of doom. Tears and rain ran down her face.

Seth looked at her with concern.

"There's just the barn to check now," she sobbed.

"Don't cry. It will be ok. We'll find him."

Through the driving rain, and taking a shortcut across the field, they ran through the long grass towards the barn. One of the doors had been left slightly open. Seth pulled it back abruptly. They stood there for a moment, shocked by what they saw. Her Dad, with a noose around his neck, was hanging from a black cord attached to one of the barn's rafters.

"NO, PLEASE!" she screamed as she ran towards him. Horrified, she looked up at her Dad's red face and then saw his body twitch. "I think he is still alive!"

Seth looked desperately around him for something to cut the cord with and then called to her. "Take off your mac and climb up the hay bales to the rafter. I'll hold him up, and you untie the knot. Quick now," he said as he placed some hay bales under the dying man's feet. Seth leapt up onto them, and bear-hugging him, he lifted him higher so that he was no longer hanging.

Jules threw her mac on the floor and climbed the haystack as quickly as she could. The black cord attached to the rafter was a meter away and difficult to reach. She stretched out and picked at the knot, which was bulky and tightly tied. She needed something to loosen the top strand of the knot. She had her door keys in her jeans pocket and as she pulled them out, she nearly dropped them.

"Oh God! Please help me!" She held onto the keys, and using her front door key she managed to loosen the knot.

"How are you doing, Jules? I won't be able to hold him up for much longer."

"It's ok, I'm nearly there." The first part of the knot came apart and the remaining knots loosened easily. Finally, the nasty black cord fell to the floor, and she watched Seth and her Dad collapse into a heap. She scampered down the haystack to help.

Peter ran into the barn yelling at Seth. "What have you done to him?"

She was furious and flew at her brother, shoving him in the chest. "You arsehole! Seth has saved his life. Don't you see? Dad has tried to hang himself!"

"I didn't realise…"

"Jules, call an ambulance. He's stopped breathing," yelled Seth as he pushed hard on her Dad's chest and gave him mouth to mouth.

She ran to her mac and pulled out her phone and called 999. She was too shaken to talk and passed the phone to Peter to speak to the emergency services.

***

Jules and her brother followed the ambulance in the Land Rover as their Dad was blue lighted to Worthing hospital. He was breathing but needed assistance as his airway had been damaged.

The rain poured down, making driving conditions difficult. Seth had wanted to go with them and then much to her surprise, Peter had asked him if he could find someone to milk the cows. Regardless of what happened, the cows would need to be milked. Seth had agreed, and kissing her on the cheek, said that he would text her to see how things were going.

Jules' phone rang, and she looked at the screen but didn't recognise the number. The number had a local area code. She was feeling drained and too tired to talk and let the message go to answer phone. "If it's important, then I will ring them back." She played the message out loud.

'This is Worthing Police Station. This is a message for Julia Bridgewater. We would like you to come down to the police station at 2:00pm tomorrow to make a statement; regarding the Ivy Brown case. If you are unable to attend, then please contact us.'

She stopped the message and looked at her brother. "Shit!"

"Do you want me to come with you?"

She nodded. "Please, I…"

Peter's phone began to ring and he looked scared. Without looking at the number, they both knew that it was the police again. "They must have seen my messages on her phone."

"Ivy's phone? Why did you leave her messages?"

Chapter Ten

The hospital car park was really busy, and after driving around it a few times she saw an old red Vauxhall reversing out of a space. Peter waited patiently for the car to leave. She could see his anxiety building as he prepared himself to park. It took him several attempts to get the Land Rover into the small space and she dared not speak to him in case he cursed her for distracting him. He was in a foul mood, and she decided to delay asking him why he had been messaging Ivy. For the moment, she needed to concentrate on dealing with their Dad's attempted suicide. "Do we have to pay for car parking now or later?" she asked and then jumped down onto the tarmac.

"I think we pay when we leave. Where do you think they have taken him? Shall we ask at the A&E reception desk?"

They were directed to the resuscitation unit and were then asked to wait in a small room nearby. They were told by a nurse that their Dad needed urgent medical attention and that someone would be over to see them with an update soon.

Jules sat on a soft green chair in the waiting room but could not get comfortable. She stood up, went over to the door and looked out of the window. "I don't like being in this room. I wanted to stay with Dad. Do you think that he will be ok? He can't even breathe for himself."

Peter looked cross. "I don't understand why he would do a thing like this. Didn't he realise how much his suicide would hurt others? Didn't he think how we would feel?"

"He wasn't thinking right, Peter. He's been hiding his depression for a while and if you do that then you get really sick. If he recovers from this, then they will give him counselling. He so needs it!"

He put his head in his hands, and she could see that he was very upset. She wanted to comfort him some more but she didn't know what she could say. In many ways, her brother was quite similar to their Dad and kept any emotions he had locked away inside.

After an hour of waiting in the tiny hot room, a doctor wearing scrubs knocked on the door and asked if they were Michael Bridgewater's family. He asked what relation they were to him. They told him, and he sat down on one of the chairs and had a serious look on his face. She was starting to fear the worse.

"We have assessed your father, and you will be glad to know that he has not fractured his neck but the muscle tone has been compromised. He also has injuries to his airways and the arteries in his neck. We are going to have to do some repair work to his arteries and he will be going into theatre shortly. He is heavily sedated and will need to be kept on a ventilator for a while longer. If your father recovers from this partial hanging, then it is likely that he may have suffered some brain damage as the blood supply to his brain was cut off for a while - this is known as ischemia. We will only know what the extent of the damage is when he is conscious and well enough to breathe for himself."

"Do you think that he is going to make it?" she asked, almost in tears.

"I have to be honest with you, there is a twenty-percent chance that he may die from his injuries, despite our best efforts to save him. On a positive note, the good thing is, that you got him to the hospital quickly and that can only improve his chances.

"I know this is a hard time for you both and things must be difficult for you. It will be a few hours before you will be able to see your father so I would suggest that you go and get yourself something to eat and drink. You need to look after yourselves too."

***

She had no idea what the time was and not seeing a clock on the wall of the café, she checked the time on her phone. It was nearly half-past six and way past the dogs' dinner time. The café was busy and she watched other diners enjoying eating a main meal oblivious to all that was going on around them. *My life is in chaos.* She delicately picked at the dried edges of a sandwich Peter had bought her and sipped the hot sweet tea. The warm liquid slowly began to revive her. Her nerves were in tatters, and she knew she should try and drink and eat something to keep herself strong so she could be there for her Dad when he woke up. *If he woke up.* If anything, it was good to be out of the miserable waiting room.

"Peter, the dogs! We forgot to ask Seth to feed them. I don't think we locked the house, did we? Shall I ask him to feed them for us?"

"I don't really want him poking about in our house when I'm not there."

"Why do you hate him so much? I know he's a Hearn but he's not like them. He saved Dad's life today. You need to give him a break."

Peter sighed. "You're seeing him, aren't you? Believe me, he's bad news. Do you know that he used to go out with Ivy, and one day he just walked out of her life for no reason at all? He's a bad egg and will do the same to you. It took her a long time to get over him, and it was a good thing that I was there for her."

91

She looked thoughtfully at Peter for a moment and was glad that Seth had told her about Ivy, otherwise she would have been in shock. Avoiding his first question. *Who I see is my own affair!* "I know about Seth and Ivy. But that was years ago. When did you stop seeing Ivy? She has certainly been through her share of men!"

Her brother gave her a bewildered look and threw his sandwich down onto his plate. It was then that she realised that he hadn't stopped seeing her. "Oh my God, Peter! You haven't ended things. You've been seeing Ivy behind Jake's back. You do realise that if they decide that Ivy's drowning was not an accident then you will be a prime suspect." His face was ashen white, and he looked like he had seen a ghost. "Now I understand why you have to give a statement to the police. Peter, did you know that she was three months pregnant?"

He shook his head.

"Do you think it is yours?" she asked gently.

"I don't know. It could be. Do you think that they were able to tell if it is mine when they do the post mortem?"

"Oh Peter! Of course, they will. They will probably check your DNA with the baby's."

He looked sad. I knew there was something up. "She wasn't going to stay with Jake you know. She despised him."

"Did she?" she replied, trying not to remember Jake and Ivy passionately making out at the back of the garden.

"So why do you think I would be a suspect? You've got to believe me. I didn't kill her. I… I loved her."

"Ok, so what if the police think that you are a jealous ex-boyfriend and you lost the plot when you found out that she was going to get rid of your baby. Or what if you have been sending threatening messages to her, demanding that she leaves Jake for you." She saw a look of horror spread across his white face. "You said that you had been messaging her."

"Yes, but nothing malicious."

"The police will be going through her phone and will see who she has been contacting and read all her private messages. I've seen it in films. Tomorrow, you are going to have to tell the police everything. If you withhold anything you will be hunted down."

"I know, I will tell them everything. You watch way too many films! I just want them to find the person that pushed her in the pond and want to know why they did it. There is no way, in her drunken state, that she would have been able to get down to those woods on her own. I bet that man that ran off, came back later to finish her off."

Jules wondered if she should tell Peter about Seth helping Ivy into the tack room but decided against it; she wasn't sure how he would react.

"If it is any consolation, she said that she was looking forward to being sisters with me. She actually said scissors. Although she got engaged to Jake, I don't think she was happy about it. I actually believe that she came to our house looking for you. Did you know that Jake is our cousin? Seth told me that."

He looked like he was going to cry but then she realised that he was angry. Just saying Seth's name had triggered something off in his mind.

"I bet that bastard killed Ivy!" People in the café were starting to stare. "If it's Seth, then..."

"NO, PETER! I know it's not him. He is no murderer!" she said this trying to keep her voice down.

"Whoever pushed her in the pond knew her and it was somebody that she trusted."

As they walked back to the waiting room her phone pinged. It was Seth.

'How is your Dad? How are you doing?'

'Dad is in theatre having the arteries in his neck repaired. We are worried that he might not make it.'

'He is a strong and healthy man. He will make it. I want you to come back to ours when you come back. Mum insists. I don't want you to be by yourself tonight. Peter can stay here too, if he wants to.'

For some reason, she thought that he would spell 'Mum' as 'Mam,' the way he said it.

'That is very kind. We might not be back until 9ish. I will ask Peter.'

'Peter says he will be fine. He needs to look after the dogs.'

He had actually said "no way!"

'I will be happy to sleep on the sofa. It's been a tough day! I just need a hug.'

'I would prefer it if you stayed in my room. I will be the perfect gentleman.'

'Won't your Mum and Dad think that I am a loose woman if I stay with you?'

'No, Mum thinks I need to look after you, and Dad does what Mum tells him to. Dad will be back late tonight. He is playing poker with friends.'

'I know this is a lot to ask but could you let the dogs out for a wee and feed them. They just have biscuits. The bag of biscuits is in the

dresser in the kitchen. I think that the kitchen door is open. We forgot to lock it ;/ How did the milking go?'

'I milked your cows with Dad this evening, and a cow chased me. I didn't realise that you had such a fierce herd. Dad used to work on a dairy farm back in Ireland so knew what he was doing. I am not sure that I would make a good dairy farmer. I am better with things that grow. Does Peter want me to help him tomorrow? Dad has got to go to the market in the morning. Don't worry about the dogs, I'll sort them out. They don't bite do they?'

'They will probably lick you to death. Peter says yes thank you. He will see you at 5am by the milking shed.'

Peter hadn't said yes straight away and he was hoping that she would help him. He had then looked at her sad tired face and reluctantly agreed. She hoped that Peter would be kind to Seth, and there wouldn't be any trouble. In fact, she had warned Peter that he should try and get along with him for her sake.

'Mum wants to know if you would like anything to eat. She has made a shepherd's pie, 2 actually. She will save you some. A meat one and a vegetable one for the vegetarians (the veg one is my favourite) Let me know x'

'We have just had something in the café and I won't be able to sleep if I eat late. Thank her, though. Are you a vegetarian? I have only seen you eat cheese.'

'Yes, I am one of those odd people that cannot stomach anything that drips blood. I live for cheese!'

58 FARM END

'Oh my, you must have nearly died when you saw me eating that old pork pie in front of you! You should have said something!'

'I forgive you. You will, however, have to promise not to do it again. I am only joking by the way. I'm walking over to End Farm now. Text me when you are driving home and are on Long Furlong and let me know how your Dad is. I will meet you at yours in the courtyard. If I am not there, then I will be on your kitchen floor being eaten by hungry dogs ;) LY4E'

Chapter Eleven

All Jules could do was hold her Dad's hand and stare at his bandaged neck. He was covered in tubes and wires and his face had a white strap across it, holding a tube which fed into his mouth. The miserable sound of the ventilator breathing for him above various machines that were beeping and clicking was beginning to get to her. Every so often, a blood pressure cuff around his arm would inflate and deflate, making her jump, adjusting the figures on the monitor above his bed. Each time they both looked up to make sure that there was no decrease in blood pressure, not really understanding what all the numbers meant. *He's alive, thank God!*

Peter was sitting on the other side of the bed and was looking weary. He was starting to look at the time on his phone a lot and then kept looking across at her. She knew that he wanted to head home but she wanted to stay a little longer. She was worried that something might happen to their Dad if they left; it was his fifty-eighth birthday after all. A couple of intensive care nurses were carrying out checks and she started to feel that they were in their way. *We should go now, it's getting late and Seth is expecting me.*

"Shall we go home, Peter? Will it be ok to come back tomorrow morning?"

"Yes, I don't mind driving us. Dad's stable and I am sure they will ring us if anything changes."

"Of course we will call you, but I am pretty sure he will improve," a nurse volunteered. "You need to rest. We will look after him, I promise."

In tears, she kissed her Dad's hand and hoped that this wasn't going to be the last time she saw him. She also hoped that he realised that they were both there for him.

She messaged Seth to say they were leaving the hospital and that her Dad was stable. In the warm car on the way home, her eyelids started to close; she felt guilty for sleeping when Peter was awake and driving but she couldn't help herself.

"Jules, we're home and he's here! Jules, wake up?"

"I am awake," she said sleepily. "Who's here?"

"Seth."

She climbed out of the Land Rover, yawning into the back of her hand. As her eyes started to focus on the dark courtyard, Seth put his arms around her and gave her the hug that she needed so much. She could feel Peter's eyes boring into her back. *I don't care.* It was just so good to be engulfed in a warm hug from someone that really cared for her.

She pulled away. "Oh, I'm sorry, Seth. I didn't message you when we were on the Long Furlong. I fell asleep."

"That's ok, I guessed that you were only half an hour away so I came over to keep the dogs company while I waited for you."

"They didn't eat you then?"

"No, I survived? They like a hug too."

Peter was looking uncertain and made an attempt to smile. She could tell that he was going to make an effort to be pleasant to Seth.

"Thanks for doing the milking earlier. Are you sure you're ok for the morning?"

"I'm usually up at five anyway. I'll be there. I think I've got the hang of it. Dad showed me what to do. By the way, he fixed one of your milking units. You had two wires shorting each other out."

"Great. Thanks for that. I'm beat. I'll see you both tomorrow. We'll go over to the hospital at ten, Jules. On the way back we will have to drop in at the police station. I'll wait for you in the car."

"Sleep well, Pete, I know I will."

Peter locked the car and then made his way to the house. Jules, holding Seth's hand, walked towards Crow Farm. The evening was warm and dry and very different from earlier.

"I forgot to tell you. Peter and I have to make a statement at the police station tomorrow. I'm dreading it. I only hope that Peter tells them everything."

"Mam said that Jake has to make a statement too."

"Do you know when?"

"First thing, I think. Why?"

"Oh good, we are going in at two. Peter's dropped a bombshell. Did you know that he had been seeing Ivy behind Jake's back? He thinks that the baby could be his."

For a moment Jules saw a flash of anger flit across Seth's face and she wished she hadn't said anything.

"Peter? You would never have guessed. He doesn't seem that upset."

"I think that he is upset. He is just not that good at showing it."

"It doesn't surprise me really that Ivy strayed. Jake is a drunk and an eejit. I know you shouldn't speak ill of the dead but let's face it, Ivy was a bit of a slapper. Peter needs his head examined."

"I know. When Jake makes his statement tomorrow, do you think that the police will tell Jake that Ivy and Peter were in a relationship? They've probably checked the messages on her phone. There will be another fight if he finds out."

"No, not tomorrow. They will probably want to take mouth swabs from the both of them for DNA checks. Don't worry about giving them a statement; the police will just want to know when you last saw Ivy and if she said anything that might indicate that she was unhappy? Just tell them what you can."

"Can I mention that I was at the party with you?"
Seth was silent for a moment. "Of course you can." He squeezed her hand to reassure her.

Seth took her around the back of the house and in through the back door into the kitchen. The house was surprisingly quiet. No wild music throbbing in the background. She could just hear a clock ticking loudly in another room.

"Where is everybody? Actually, I'm glad that it is quiet. I don't think I would be very good company. I feel a bit spaced out."

"Everyone will be in bed; we all have early starts in the morning. The Hearns only stay up late on weekends. Apart from Dad, of course. I am sure you will see Mam before we go to bed. She would have heard us come in and will be down in a few minutes. She won't be able to help herself but I have warned her not to ask you too many questions. She can talk the hind legs off a donkey. Mam's a typical Irish mother. I'm sorry there is nothing I can do to stop her. I won't let her loose on you for long. I'll be there to protect you."

He was smiling again, and all talk about Peter, Ivy and Jake was forgotten.

"Do you want a sandwich or some tea? Two sugars?"

"Yes, tea with sugar that would be great. Shall I make it?"

"No, of course not, I know my way around the kitchen. Well, to make tea at least." Seth filled the kettle with water and turned it on.

Feeling sleepy, she sat down on a wooden chair at the table and fiddled with the edge of a lace runner. "Your Mum likes lace, doesn't she? There's a lot of lacy things in the hall too. My Mum would have liked them."

"Some of my sisters sew. It is a family tradition to make lace - part of our gypsy heritage," he was smiling mischievously at her.

"So how many of your family live in this house?"

"Now that is a question and it might take me a while to tell you in detail so I will keep it short. Some of us live in converted outbuildings with their husband or wife and children. Including Mam and Dad, there are eight of us living in the farmhouse. My youngest brother Mark lives in a caravan at the end of the garden. Mam delights in the fact her whole family, apart from my aunt and granny, live on the farm with her. The last headcount came in at around forty-six."

"So many! Where does Jake live?"

"In the pub mostly but when he is home, he stays with Mark in the caravan. They both like the drink too much." Seth found two mugs and dropped a tea bag into each with some sugar in both and poured water into them. As he opened the fridge to get some milk out, a large grey-haired woman appeared in the kitchen doorway holding a hot water bottle. She was wearing a long white nightdress, and her long grey hair was plaited into a braid on the left of her round face. Jules thought that she looked like a character from a fairy story. She smiled at Jules and tipped toed into the kitchen as if she was trying not to disturb them. Seth smiled at her, and raising his eyebrows, gave Jules an all-knowing look.

"Seth dear, you wouldn't fill up me hot water bottle? I'm feeling cold tonight."

"No problem, Mam," he said, taking the hot water bottle from her. "You do know it is going to be a hot night?"

"Is this your young lady you were telling me about? The one from Farm End?"

"Yes, this is Jules, Mam."

"Hello, Mrs Hearn."

"Oh no, really, it's Margaret. You know that you are the first girl Seth has brought here. Our Seth keeps his cards very close to his chest. You must have won his heart."

"Mam!"

"Oh dear, listen to me going on when you've had all these troubles. I'm sorry to hear about your father and your lovely aunty Ann. It makes my heart bleed to think of Jake's wee lass and my poor dear friend floating about in that old pool. Such a horrible week. How is your Dad doing? Seth told me what happened."

"He's... he's…" She could feel the tears welling up again.

"No, it's ok, don't say anything. I understand. Your father will mend, I just know it. Seth will look after you. He's a good boy these days. Are you sure you don't want anything to eat? I've got some ham in the fridge. Unless you don't eat meat, like Seth."

"No, I'm fine, thank you."

"You look worn out. Seth, get this child to bed before she falls down. A good night's sleep will serve you well. You'll see, things will seem so much better in the morning."

"We're going upstairs now with the tea, and I promise to bring the cups down in the morning."

"You do that, Sebastian Hearn. I'm tired of collecting empty cups from around the house. You sleep well, Jules. Did you know that you have hair just like Ann Bridgewater and your mother, come to that? You have curls just like she did. So pretty. They are both angels in Heaven now – so sad."

Seth picked up the cups and signalled behind his Mum's back to her with his head to get up. If she hadn't been so sad, then she would have laughed at this comical first meeting with Margaret Hearn.

"Thank you for letting me stay," she said, getting up from her chair.

"No trouble, sleep well and in the morning we can talk."

Jules followed Seth out into the hall and as they got to the foot of the stairs Seth whispered that his Mam liked her very much.

"She's very sweet and kind but not how I imagined her to be. I haven't seen her before. Does she ever leave the house?"

"Sometimes, but I guess she has a lot to do here. Mam may moan about looking after us all, but she loves it, really."

As they reached the top of the stairs, the front door opened and a man fell into the hall.

"Dad's home early! He will kick off but take no notice. Even if I was on my own, he would still have something to say."

A tall thin man with thick white hair cursed the doormat and carefully closed the front door as if he was trying not to wake anyone. He turned around, swaying a little, and then caught sight of her.

"BEJESUS!" he exclaimed, holding onto the wall to steady himself. "No! It can't be. It's Ann Bridgewater risen from the dead! For the love of God, why have you come back here, of all places!"

She was taken aback and didn't know what to say.

"Dad, be quiet. You'll raise the dead shouting like that! This is Jules; she's staying the night. Her Dad is in hospital."

"Christ boy, you can't sleep with Ann!"

"Jethro? Is that you? Come to the kitchen and leave those two alone. What a noise you are making!"

"What is it now, woman?"

In a stupefied state, he stumbled forward, forgetting that they were stood there.

"Come on, Jules, quick! This way. He'll have forgotten what he said by morning."

She followed Seth along a narrow corridor that seemed to go on forever. Seth's bedroom was at the very end of the house, and it was a relief to close the door and get away from Seth's eccentric parents.

Seth turned on a lamp to reveal a large white room that had a vaulted ceiling with exposed beams. This part of the house looked much newer than the rest of the farmhouse. She guessed that the Hearns had extended the old farmhouse at some point, encompassing a barn. Seth had a double bed under a window and the part of the room they were standing in had been made into a mini lounge.

"This room is amazing!" Seth put the tea down on a coffee table and smiled.

"You didn't expect this, did you? My sister and her husband wanted more space so they moved out into one of the cottages on the edge of the farm. I moved out of a box room into this. I'm still getting used to living in such a large space. It's even got its own ensuite. It beats sleeping in a cell," he added.

"It's lovely. Seth? Do I look like Ann Bridgewater?"

"A little. Your hair is similar but that's it. I'm going down to talk to Dad. He shouldn't have said that to you; drunk or not."

"It's ok, I'm not upset. Seth, I'm exhausted. I need to sleep. I've just realised that I haven't brought anything with me. I don't want to get in your nice white bed wearing grimy clothes."

"I'll find you something. There's a new toothbrush in a packet in the cabinet. Would one of my t-shirts do to wear?" Seth walked over to a white chest of drawers, he opened a drawer and started to look through it for something suitable. "You can have a shower if you want. There's towels in the cupboard in the ensuite."

Seth pulled out a crumpled navy t-shirt and attempted to flatten it out for her. "It's clean. I did my washing the other day. It's not ironed, though." He handed the shirt to her.

"This will do just fine. Are you sure it's ok for me to shower, I won't be a minute? I just want to wash the day away."

"Go ahead. If you need anything, just yell."

She picked up her cup and drank some tea. Seth sat down and it was then that she noticed how tired he was looking.

"You did a wonderful thing in the barn today. I will never forget what you did for Dad."

"Anyone would have done the same."

"No, they wouldn't. Ok, I'm going to take this tea into the shower and then we must sleep. You have an early start tomorrow."

Jules showered and felt refreshed as the grime from the day swirled away down the plughole. She towel-dried her hair the best she could and brushed her teeth. The t-shirt was nice and long and came down past her underwear. It felt good to be wearing Seth's clothes. When she came back into the room, she found him asleep on the sofa. She studied him for a moment and realised how in love she was with him and was glad that they had found each other. Feeling really tired, Jules looked over at the bed. Not wanting to get into it without him, she walked over to him and kissed him gently on the lips. He opened his eyes and smiled.

"Did I drop off? You smell lovely, like mint and lemons."

"I used your shower gel and toothpaste. I've left the wet towel on the side of the bath. You're as tired as I am. Let's go to bed."

"How can I refuse an offer like that?"

Seth stood up and pulled her to him. He pushed her wet hair over her shoulder and gently nibbled and kissed her behind her earlobe, working his way down her neck. Surprised, she exhaled. She quivered with pleasure as goose bumps covered her body.

Seth stopped kissing her and smiled. She could see the desire in his eyes.

"Ok, enough!" He sighed and led her towards the bed. "I've promised to be good, but you are making it very hard for me. You are beautiful, you know? What side do you want?"

"I don't mind. Right, I guess."

She slipped into bed and then sighed with relief as her head hit the cool pillows.

"This is a dream of a bed."

"Not bad, is it?" Seth turned off the lamp and then started to undress in the half-light.

She could feel herself getting drowsy but held her gaze on Seth as he stripped down to his boxers. She heard him go into the bathroom and knew that it would be difficult to keep her eyes open for much longer.

As Seth got into bed, he drew up next to her and gently pulled her into his arms so that they were spooning and kissed her gently on the cheek. It was wonderful to feel his body against hers. He whispered in her ear that he would come back for her after milking and to sleep. She could stay awake no longer and drifted off into a troubled slumber, dreaming of black knotted cord, ventilators and silent pools.

Chapter Twelve

The night had passed slowly and Jules had been woken up several times by disturbing dreams. Each time Seth had woken and held her a little tighter. He had whispered to her that she was ok and could sleep.

The morning light began to illuminate the room and as she began to wake up, she realised that Seth was no longer holding her. *He's gone to help Peter and will be back soon.* She turned over, and lying on her back, opened her eyes and looked up at the high ceiling. Despite her weird dreams, she was feeling a lot better and felt relaxed. She needed to go to the toilet and get a drink of water and wondered if the water in the bathroom was safe to drink. She pulled the covers back and was about to get out of bed when she noticed that there was a man sitting on the sofa. It was Seth's Dad. She gasped with surprise. He smiled at her.

"Sorry, I didn't mean to scare you."

"Do you want Seth?" she asked, flipping the covers back, pulling them a little further up her body.

"No, I wanted to come and say that I am sorry. I was out of order last night. Margaret says I made a fool of myself. I couldn't go to the market without seeing you first."

She didn't know what to say. She still hadn't got over the shock of seeing him sat there.

"It's ok, I…"

"Margaret and I are quite upset about Ivy and Ann. Such a terrible shame. Seth should have never taken you to the silent pool - it is cursed. I don't know what he was thinking of."

She stopped breathing for a moment as his words sunk in. He had just declared that he had witnessed her and Seth walking down to the pond on the day that they had discovered Ivy's body. She needed to change the subject.

"Thanks for milking the cows with Seth yesterday with such short notice. I don't think we could have coped without you both."

"It was no trouble. I'm sorry to hear about your Dad. There is another crying shame. Farmers all over the country are hanging themselves. It is a hard job eking a living out of the land and for some, it is a cross too hard to bear. I better get going," he said as he stood up. He collected the cups from the coffee table and headed towards the door. He stopped for a moment and turned towards her.

"Be careful, Jules, Sebastian has a temper and is a bit of a loose cannon. He breaks hearts. Don't get too close."

She was glad to see him go and stared at the closed door in disbelief. *He's a dreadful man!*

She picked up her phone from the side table; it needed charging. It was just after seven and she hoped that Seth would be back soon. After visiting the bathroom, she dressed, made the bed and sat on the sofa to wait for him. Jules didn't want to go downstairs alone. She knew that Margaret would be waiting for her and eager to chat. She wasn't in the mood for company. Feeling restless, she started to walk around the studio looking at all the pictures on the wall. There were many framed photos of insects in close up and the rest were of farm scenes and scenic landscapes. Some of the views she recognised and some she guessed had been taken abroad. Jules admired the composition of the photos and wondered who had taken such amazing shots. They put her photographic skills to shame.

A photo over the sofa caught her eye. It was of a field with a black barn on the horizon. She recognised that barn and turning away, shuddered. The door opened and Seth appeared holding two cups of tea and a plate with a pile of toast on it. His smile faded when he saw her sad face.

"What's the matter?"

"Somebody has taken a picture of our barn. Look?" she said, pointing to the photo on the wall. "Who took all these photos? They're incredible."

"It's a hobby. I've even sold some. Did you sleep ok?"

"Not too bad," she lied. "Thank you for being there for me. I dreamt a lot. Seth, something weird just happened. I woke up and found your Dad sitting on the sofa. I nearly died of fright. He came to apologise about last night. There's something else."

Seth looked worried and set the cups and plate down on the coffee table.

"He warned me about you."

"Did he? I thought he would. He still has a thing about me leaving the farm and going travelling. I am also the first Hearn that has ever gone to prison. He said I had let the Hearn family down. He tells everyone that I am a disappointment. I've got used to it."

"Yes, he said something like that. I took no notice."

"Really, I don't give a toss. As soon as I am a free man, then I will be out of this madhouse."

She didn't have the heart to tell him that his Dad had seen them walking to the silent pool together.

Chapter Thirteen

After breakfast, Seth had gone off to work in the top fields where they were going to harvest potatoes. He wasn't looking forward to it as it was going to be hard, messy work. The potatoes were going to be collected by hand to avoid bruising them. They had promised to text each other when they could and had planned to meet up after work at her house. She didn't really want to stay another night at Crow Farm. Jules had managed to get home without bumping into Seth's mother. She wasn't up to having a heart to heart talk with Margaret. *One day I will have to make an effort and get to know her.* She was, however, going to give Seth's Dad a wide berth.

Jules looked up at the sky and she could see dark storm clouds forming - it looked like rain again. As she walked through the courtyard, she noticed that the car was missing. She guessed that Peter must have driven down to the bank to pay in a cheque. She had seen one from the abattoir pinned on the noticeboard in the kitchen. The dogs greeted her as she walked into the kitchen and then ran to their food bowls, wagging their tails. It was strange that Peter hadn't fed them yet and she fetched the dog's food from the dresser cupboard. She half-filled each bowl and then put them down on the floor so the dogs could eat. They were really hungry and wasted no time devouring the food.

Jules checked the time; it was just before nine, she had plenty of time to check on the horses and give them some attention. She felt guilty for not seeing them yesterday evening and was trying not to think too much about that day. The unopened birthday card was still on the table, and she felt sad. Putting the card in a drawer, she took a deep breath and was determined to remain strong and support her Dad in any way she could.

As Jules went upstairs to change her clothes, she noticed her reflection in a picture on the wall. Her hair was looking really frizzy, she would have to tame her Ann Bridgewater-like hair before she left the house. She had seen photos of Ann but couldn't remember exactly what she looked like. When they moved into the farmhouse, they had replaced most of her uncle's photos with their own. She remembered seeing some old photos in a box in the study.

Jules quickly showered, used lots of conditioner on her hair and carefully dried her hair using a blow dryer with a diffuser head. She was fighting a losing battle and her hair fluffed up, so she tied it back in a ponytail. She dressed in jeans, a grey t-shirt and pulled on a green zip-up hoodie as she was feeling chilled. She would have a cup of tea and go and look for the photos. She really needed to see what her aunt looked like.

It took her a while to find the plastic box full of photos, and she sat on the floor of the study with her tea and started looking through them. Most of the photos were of her Mum and of her and Peter when they were babies. *I was such a fat baby!* These photos were worn around the edges, which didn't surprise her as she had seen her Dad looking through those photos many times. After going through most of them, she found one of Ann and her uncle and inspected it closely. She really was the spitting image of Ann at her age. Her Mum never spoke about her sister. *I wonder why?*

Jules walked with the dogs across to the stables and brought with her some chopped up apple to give to Connor and Barney. They must have smelt the apple straight away as they both trotted over to her to receive their treat. The dogs ran up and down their field, chasing imaginary rabbits, happy to be out of the house. She patted each horse in turn and ran her hand over their coats. Their fur was looking dull and a bit dusty. Connor had rolled in some mud, so she decided to brush their coats as they both enjoyed being groomed; it hadn't been done for a few days. It was a way of saying sorry to them too and would stop her thinking about Ivy. As she brushed Barney down, she noticed that he had small patches of itchy dry skin on his back and he quivered as she brushed these patches. She hoped it wasn't sweet itch; if it was, then he was being bothered by midges.

By the time Jules had finished grooming them and had filled up their water buckets, it was nearly time to go to the hospital. She decided that she would make sandwiches and bring a flask of tea for them both, to save some money.

Jules stood in the courtyard, with a cool bag over her shoulder and waited for Peter. She kept looking at her phone and wondered if she should text Seth to pass the time. She decided to wait until lunchtime as he would be really busy.

She had waited for half an hour for Peter, and she was beginning to get cross when another twenty minutes passed. She was starting to worry that he might have broken down somewhere or had an accident. Just as she was about to text Seth to see if Peter had been ok when they were milking, he drove into the courtyard and beckoned to her. He was looking hot and flustered. She put her phone away and climbed into the Land Rover and dropped the cool bag by her feet.

"You're late. Are you ok?"

"I'm sorry. I didn't sleep last night and after we did the milking, I went to bed and forgot to set an alarm. When I woke up it was nearly nine. I had to go to the bank and put that cheque in, or we are going to go overdrawn."

"Poor you, I must have just missed you."

"Did you sleep? Or should I ask that?" he inquired, turning the car around.

"Seriously? You're not suggesting anything went on, are you? The walls at Crow Farm are thin, and the house is brimming with Hearns. All I wanted to do was sleep. No, I didn't sleep well. I had weird dreams all night and woke up with Seth's Dad sitting in my room! So not the best of nights!"

"God, that's creepy. Why was he there?"

"He wanted to apologise for mistaking me for Ann Bridgewater. He's a complete nutter. Anyway, today is another day. Let's hope Dad is getting better. I fed the dogs, by the way, and they've had a little exercise. We will have to take them out later otherwise they are going to go stir crazy locked up in the kitchen all day. How did the milking go with Seth?"

"He did ok. We didn't talk much. It was a bit awkward, I think that he had something on his mind."

"Oh dear, I'll help you from now on. I'm feeling stronger now."

She knew exactly what Seth was upset about - he couldn't handle knowing that Peter had been seeing Ivy behind Jake's back. Even though Seth found Jake annoying and an idiot he would do anything for him - even go to prison for him.

She was relieved to see that their Dad had improved, and they were going to remove the ventilator as soon as the muscle relaxant and sedative had worn off. She took her place by his bedside and held his hand again, pleased that he was making progress. She hoped that when he woke up that he wouldn't be brain damaged, and most importantly of all, she hoped that he wanted to live. *What would we all do if he didn't?*

Peter was stood by the window of the intensive care unit and watched the seagulls circling in the sky outside. He seemed agitated. She could tell that there was something on his mind.

"You didn't tell Seth about me and Ivy, did you?"

She hadn't expected him to ask her this and went quiet for a moment, not sure what to say. She didn't want the chasm between him and Seth to grow wider.

"Jules?"

"Sorry. I was miles away. What did you say?"

"Did you tell Seth about me and Ivy?"

"No, did you want me to?" she lied.

"God no! Please don't. Are you sure you know what you are doing with Seth?"

"You're sounding like Dad now! He's good and kind to me and not like the other Hearns at all. His Mum is ok but his Dad is really crazy. I now understand why our uncle fell out with him."

Jules looked down at her Dad's hand in hers; she had felt it move. "Peter! Dad's hand just twitched, I think that he is coming 'round. We should tell someone."

Peter went to find a nurse and then returned. "The nurse said that it is just a muscle spasm. His muscles are starting to work again. They say that it will be a few hours yet before the drugs have worn off completely. Jules, do you have any change on you? I'm starving, and I haven't got any money on me for a snack. I didn't have breakfast."

Jules remembered the cool bag and flask she had left in the car. "There are some sandwiches and a flask of tea in the car if you're hungry."

"Great, you're the best." Peter went off to the car and she felt a little guilty for lying to him. It was strange that such a horrible few days had brought them so much closer together. She hoped that he would be honest and tell the police everything. Things were getting really complicated, and she still wasn't sure what she was going to say when she got to the police station. Seth had told her that it would be just a matter of saying when she had last seen Ivy and to just say what had actually happened and not what she had heard. She had to keep her statement simple. *This isn't going to be easy to do. I don't like lying.* There was nothing simple about Ivy's death.

***

The one good thing about today was that their Dad had started breathing for himself and the doctors seemed to be pleased with his progress. When they had left him, he had not woken up and she really wanted to be there when he did. She and Peter had agreed to go back to the hospital after making their statements. They left the hospital at quarter to two and walked across to the police station, leaving the car in the car park across the road from the hospital. It was only a three-minute walk so they got to their destination, following Google maps, in good time.

Jules was really feeling nervous, and she had pains in her stomach. Peter was looking anxious too, and she wanted to ask if he was going to tell them everything that had happened that night. She didn't want to lecture him again and hoped he had the sense to be truthful. Instinctively, she knew that this was not an accident and that someone had murdered both Ann and Ivy. It was no coincidence that they had both ended up in the pond and it was chilling to think that there was a cold-blooded killer in their midst.

They didn't have to wait long and were called to give their statements at the same time. Jules was starting to feel sick, and she watched as Peter, who was looking ashen-faced, was taken into an interview room further down the corridor. A female officer opened the door to her room and asked her to sit down at a small table. She closed the door and sat on the opposite side of the table to her. She watched the solemn tall woman, with dark hair tied in a neat bun, pull out a pen and an A4 booklet from a drawer. The booklet consisted of several pages and she wondered how she could possibly fill it. *I've only got a couple of things to say!* Her stomach ached again and she was thinking of asking for a glass of water but thought this might make her look guilty about something.

"Hello Julia, I am just going to ask you a few questions regarding Ivy Brown. Please try and remember everything you can about the evening of Saturday, 4 August, as this will help us with our investigation. I am going to write down what you say. After the statement has been completed, I will read it back to you and I will then ask you to sign and date it. Do you understand?"

She nodded, she was really feeling sick now.

"I am going to confirm your personal details first. Are you Julia Bridgewater, of Farm End, Long Furlong, Findon, Worthing?"

"Yes, that's correct."

"Is your date of birth 30 September 1997?"

"Yes, it is." She was starting to feel like she was on trial.

"Ok, Julia, please can you tell me the last time you saw Ivy Brown alive."

"It was at her engagement party on Saturday, 4 August."

"Was Ivy a close friend of yours?"

"No, but we went to college together. We rarely spoke to each other. She wasn't in my circle of friends."

"Did you speak to her at the party?"

"Yes."

"What was her mood like at the party?"

"Her mood?"

"Was she happy or was she upset about anything?"

"She seemed happy enough but she was really drunk. Ivy said that she was looking forward to being my sister. That's surprised me because I didn't think she liked me that much. She passed out while she was talking to me."

"Did Ivy say anything to you that would lead you to believe that she would harm herself?"

"No, as I said, she was happy enough but she said that she wasn't enjoying her party. She didn't say why."

"Did you notice anything unusual going on at the party or anyone acting in an abnormal manner?"

Suddenly all she could remember was Jake and Seth fighting. "No, I wasn't there long. I must have been there for less than half an hour."

"Why did you leave the party so soon?"

"My Dad didn't want me to go to the party, so I sneaked out and he came over to Crow Farm and dragged me home. It

117

was really embarrassing. The Hearns and the Bridgewaters don't really get along." She wished she hadn't said that and could feel her palms sweating with anxiety. She hoped that the officer wouldn't ask her why.

"At what time did you arrive at the party and then leave?"

"It was just after nine and I must have left around nine-thirty."

"Before the party, when was the last time you saw Ivy Brown?"

"It was at a meal in the Gun Inn on Friday, Friday 3 August and then on my way back home, I caught her and Jake riding one of my horses. They were really drunk. My pony is too old to carry them, and I yelled at them to get down but they took no notice and just laughed. Seth was in the lane and helped me get them off of Barney."

"Who is Seth?"

Warning bells were ringing in her head; she hadn't meant to bring him into it and was starting to panic.

"Just a friend," she said quietly.

"Are you talking about Sebastian Hearn?"

"Yes," she replied, wondering what the next question might be and she held her breath as she waited. This was turning out to be more of an interview than a statement. The officer turned a page of the booklet and continued writing. "From our records, on Monday, 6 August, it was you that reported finding the body of Ivy Brown. Is that correct?"

Relieved not to be asked any more questions about Seth, she exhaled silently. "Yes, she was floating in our pond."

"Can you remember what you saw?"

"Um...yes. When I got to the pond, I could see a bump in the middle of the water and wasn't sure what it was at first. The pond is covered in a green pond plant. When I stepped closer to the edge, I realised that I was looking at a body. I could see Ivy's face and her red dress."

"Can you explain why she was wearing your dressing gown?"

Her eyes widened, she felt like she had been given a kick in the guts. "No... I don't know. How do you know that it was mine? Ivy might have had the same one?"

"The forensic team have found long hair on the dressing gown that is probably a match to your own. They have also found collie dog hairs on it too. And this." The officer pulled out of the drawer, a small bag containing a bank card. She pushed it across the table, so she could see it.

"We found your bank card in one of the pockets of the dressing gown. Can you confirm that this is your bank card?"

"Yes, it is. Oh my, I really don't know why she was wearing it. I gave the dressing gown to charity a while back and I've been looking for my bank card. I was going to order another." She hoped that her quick thinking had produced an answer that would convince the officer and make her believe that she was telling the truth. She was shaking now and felt faint.

The officer asked her a few more questions about Ivy's relationship with Jake. She couldn't tell them much and after the officer had read through the statement, she signed it and was allowed to leave.

As Jules made her way to the door, the police officer had asked if they had the correct number for her father as they wanted to ask him a few questions about Ann Bridgewater. She had explained what had happened and that her Dad was in hospital after attempting suicide. The police officer had said she was sorry to hear that, but didn't sound sincere.

When Jules walked into the reception area, she realised that Peter was still giving his statement and she wondered if he was finding it as difficult as she had. Needing some fresh air and a moment to digest what had happened, Jules went outside. It was starting to rain, but she didn't care and sat on the steps in front of the police station to recover. She was still shaking and was sure that people passing by would think that she was a shady character. She felt dirty. *I'll message Seth.* She knew that she had to be careful about what she said.

'Hi, it's me. Dad is making progress and is breathing for himself. He's not awake yet so we are going back to the hospital when Peter comes out of the police station. I've made my statement and will tell you about it later. They made me feel like a criminal. Hope that you are ok.'

She waited for a message to appear, and it took a few minutes.

'I can't text now, I am up to my elbows in mud. See you at 5 xxx'

Jules stood up and looked up at the sky. Large drops of water were hitting the screen. She would have to go back into the police station and wait for Peter. She was feeling much calmer but was still quite disturbed by her ordeal.

Peter appeared twenty minutes later and he looked to be in a state of shock. He waited until they were in the street before he said anything.

"I might have to come back to answer more questions. They took my fingerprints and a swab from my mouth too. Jules, they think I killed Ivy! I know they do."

Chapter Fourteen

Jules and Peter hadn't stayed long at the hospital. It had taken them a while to find their Dad as he had been moved to a new ward. They followed the signs along the soulless corridors until they finally found him at the end of a ward, sat up in bed just staring into the distance. He didn't even acknowledge them being there. Disturbed by his condition, they had asked to see a doctor to find out why he was unresponsive. A nurse that had been caring for him had told them that physically, he should make a full recovery but they needed to assess his mental condition. It was likely that he was traumatised, and the lack of oxygen to his brain may have caused amnesia. He hadn't spoken to anyone yet and had cried when he realised that he was in a hospital. He was due to have a psychiatric assessment at four. They had gone back to their Dad and both had hugged him and he had cried but had said nothing.

The drive home had been a quiet one as they both contemplated what the future might hold for him, and for them also. She had sent a text to Seth to tell him about her Dad and she had cried when she sent the message. Seeing it in black and white had made it all too real.

That evening, after each cow had been milked, she painted iodine onto the cows' teats and without being prompted each cow wandered back to the fields. Peter sighed with relief as the last cow trotted out of the milking shed to join her friends.

"I'm glad that's over. The vat is full. We're due a milk collection tomorrow morning. All that rain has improved the pasture, the cows have exceeded themselves today. Dad would have been pleased."

She followed him out as he closed the gate to stop the cows returning. "Poor Dad." She was starting to well up again. "He looked so sad."

"I know, don't cry. They will know how to help him. It's going to take some time."

"Seth's coming over tonight. I want him to stay. I know it's hard for you to have him around but I am lost without him."

"I'll manage, I guess."

"Thanks, Peter. I'll get us some dinner. Is egg, chips and beans ok?"

When they walked into the courtyard, Seth was sat outside the house. He was dressed in his overalls and was covered from head to foot in mud. She smiled, he looked like he had been swimming in it. His brown eyes shone brightly in the evening sun, and he smiled when he saw her. It felt like they had been apart for an eternity.

"Hello, beautiful," he said, ignoring Peter.

"God! What's happened to you? I take it that the potato harvest went well."

"It's just a little mud. I'm used to getting dirty."

"I'm going to cook some dinner. Have you eaten? You could shower here if you want." She looked at Peter to make sure it was ok. He didn't object.

"No, that's ok, Mam's made something already. I'd better go back and wash at home and eat there. I need clean clothes. I'll come straight back. I just wanted to make sure you were alright first. You've had a bit of a hard day, haven't you? Are you up for a walk?"

"Yes, I'd like that. I'm just going to eat and then I'll be ready."

"Ok then, I'll see you in about forty-five minutes. Bring a coat; it can get windy where we are going."

Seth got up and walked towards her and kissed her gently on the forehead. She watched him disappear from view. Peter shook his head.

"God! You've both got it bad. It's like watching Titanic!"

***

She waited in the lane as she had just been to check on the horses. They had been munching on grass at the top of the field in a strip of sunshine and were enjoying feeling the warmth on their backs. They hadn't bothered to come down and see her. She didn't mind, it made her feel less guilty for not taking them out on a hack.

It was too warm to wear her coat and so she tied it 'round her waist, in case the weather turned. She didn't have to wait too long and spotted Seth walking up the lane wearing dark jeans and a black t-shirt. She could see his tattoo on each arm. He hadn't brought a coat with him, and she wondered if he even had one. She started to walk towards him and couldn't help grinning. It was true, she had got it bad as her brother had put it and couldn't wait to be with him.

As soon as they reached each other, Seth swept her up into his arms and kissed her passionately and held her for a moment. "I've been waiting to do that all day." He released her and then pointed to two hills in the distance. "We can watch the sun go down at the top of the first hill. It's about half an hour's walk. We should just make it. If you're too tired, then I'll understand."

"I'm fine. I need some fresh air and some good company. Lead the way."

The walk up Seth's hill was tough going, but she didn't mind. It was just wonderful to be outside. The fields were full of wildflowers, lazily bobbing their heads in a light breeze and red, yellow and blue petals shone in the evening sunshine.

They made it to the summit and sat side by side in the cool grass. The sun was not ready to set. She could see the sea shimmering in the distance. "I think we've got another hour before the sun sets. It's beautiful up here. Have you taken any photos of this landscape?"

"I've taken a few. I had to sell my camera. I needed some cash. You do realise that my Dad only pays us minimum wage and I am just a poor peasant boy? Everything you see below you will belong to Patrick one day. This is where I come to think. I haven't been up here for a while. A few years, in fact."

"So you haven't done much thinking lately?"

"No, I have done more than my fair share of thinking. You really can't do much else when you are locked up."

"It must have been hard for you. Don't think about it. We have to make the most of each day and always look forward to tomorrow. Although that is easier said than done."

"I'm sorry about your Dad; he doesn't sound good."

"No, he's not great."

"So what happened at the police station then?"

"Oh, that! The police lady that took my statement reminded me of a strict teacher, and she scared me. It was all going well and you were right, they just asked me questions about Ivy and then came a curveball. They have worked out that the dressing gown Ivy was wearing was mine. They found my hair on it and my bank card in the pocket. I don't know how I managed it, but I said that I'd given the dressing gown to charity and had lost my bank card so I didn't know how or why she was wearing it. I must order another bank card later. Anyway, I felt sick for lying."

"It was just a little lie, the dressing gown is not significant. It is not going to change anything. You did that for me, didn't you? I'm sorry that you had to go through that. Ivy could have fallen into the pond or committed suicide. It will be hard to prove that it was murder."

"It's ok, you would have done that for me. Something tells me that it was murder. Just a cold, dark vibe I'm feeling. I think that Peter thinks the same. He is convinced that they are going to arrest him soon. He didn't tell me what he said, but the police obviously had some difficult questions to ask him."

"Do you think that he killed Ivy? He might have."

"No, Seth! That's an awful thing to say. Peter is annoying but he is not a killer."

"I'm not saying he did it on purpose. It could have been a crime of passion."

She sighed and dropped her head down in despair, trying not to let her tears out. "I really don't know anymore. All I know is that there is a maniac on the loose and he could come for any one of us."

"I'm sorry, Jules. It will be ok. I didn't mean to upset you. I'll protect you. They'll find him," he said, putting his arm 'round her.

"Will you stay at mine tonight? I've cleared it with Peter."

"Of course I will. I was going to ask you anyway."

They had walked back to Farm End hand in hand, the sunset had been obliterated by clouds but the streaks of pink and red sky had promised them a sunny morning. It was dark when they reached the farmhouse, and she was relieved to find that Peter had gone to bed. She really didn't want to have to keep the peace between Seth and her brother. The dogs were pleased to see them and after she had made some tea, she allowed the dogs to follow them into the lounge.

Jules looked 'round the untidy room, and horrified, she started to straighten cushions and move junk mail from the chairs. She collected a couple of cups and plates and tucked a pile of bills under her arm. "Your Mum would have a fit if she saw this room. Peter is not very good at tidying up after himself, or Dad for that matter." She picked up a cup with the words 'Best Dad' on the side and looked sadly at it. She had given it to him on Father's Day. She hoped that he was having a better night and had been given some medication to calm him.

When she came back from the kitchen, Seth was sat on the sofa with the TV remote in his hand. She sat down next to him.

"Shall we watch something on Netflix?" she asked. "That's our one luxury in this household. We all love a good film. Do you like films?"

"Yes, there's nothing better. I'm a bit out of touch with current films. What do you want to watch?"

"Something cheerful and perhaps funny. It would be good to laugh again. Let me think. I know you boys like films like 'Aeroplane' and 'Weird Science.' There must be a film that we would both like."

"Guilty as charged. I'm easy, though. You choose."

"How about Paul? With the space alien. I like that one."

"Ok, not what I was expecting but it's better than Bridesmaids. Girls like that one, don't they?"

"No, not all of them. That one is a bit sickly - literally."

"See if you can find Paul, I'll get us some biscuits. Do you remember how to use a remote?"

"Cheeky, I haven't been away for that long!"

When she returned, both dogs were sprawled out on the sofa with Seth at one end, stroking the head of a happy dog.

"George! Pip! Get down. That's my place. Seth doesn't want to be covered in hair."

Obediently, the dogs jumped off the sofa and lay on the floor. George lay on Seth's feet.

"I think they like you." She brushed off the seat and removed a cloud of black and white fur and then dropped down next to Seth who was still trying to find the Netflix channel.

"Your remote has got me beat."

"Oh, I forgot! It's a different remote for films."

She looked around her and then saw the second remote was stuck between the cushions. "Here, let me do it. Custard cream?" she asked, handing him the packet. She found Paul and pressed play.

"I'd rather have you," he said, putting the biscuit packet and the remote she was holding onto the side table.

She stared at him in shock, and he realised what he had insinuated.

"Just a few kisses, I promise," he said, leaning towards her and then he drew her into his arms. She kissed him back and as the minutes passed, she could feel his kisses becoming more urgent. She ran her hands through his hair and kissed him harder too. He allowed her tongue into his mouth, and she traced the line of his lips and gently bit his lower lip. He gasped with surprise and then pulled away from her, smiling.

"You're getting the hang of this."

He kissed her neck, working his way up to her ear, he tugged at her earlobe with his teeth and then breathed hot air into her ear. It was her turn to exhale as a wave of pleasure washed over her. She hadn't expected that.

He was watching her intently, and she could see the love in his eyes. She let him slip his hand under her t-shirt and allowed him to run his fingertips down her back, unclipping her bra as he went. She quivered with pleasure as her skin formed goose bumps.

Kissing her, he lay her down, and his fingertips gently worked their way down her side and then up to her breast. He cupped one and trapped her nipple between his fingers. She moaned, her body yearning his. She wasn't sure how much more of this pleasant torture she could handle – her senses were on fire. His tongue found hers and danced with hers for a moment. She was ready to explode and wanted him more than anything. She felt him move away and when she opened her eyes, he was gazing at her with a playful twinkle in his eyes.

"We're missing the film."

"Don't you want me?"

"You must know I do, but I need to make you my wife first. I like to see you wild with desire. I also don't want Peter to walk in on us. I'll stop playing with you, if you want me to?"

"No, please don't stop."

***

It was late when she woke up with Seth's arms 'round her. She smiled as she thought about how crazy he had driven her. She must have fallen asleep before him and didn't remember seeing much of the film. They were both lying on the sofa and the television was still on although the sound had been muted. She reached for the remote and checked the time on the TV. It was five minutes past two; she had a couple more hours of sleep before she had to get up to do the milking. She turned off the TV and noticed that the moon was high in the inky black sky. It shone brightly, lighting up the lounge.

Jules stroked Seth's strong arm, marvelling at the feel of his skin. There wasn't much room for them both on the sofa and she wondered if she should wake him and find a bed for them to both sleep in. She sighed as she thought about the size of her tiny bed upstairs; it was not much better than the sofa. She hadn't thought about where they were going to sleep. Her Dad had a double bed, but it would be too weird to sleep there – she was sure that Peter would have a fit.

Seth was sound asleep and she thought it best if he stayed where he was. She slipped out of his arms, tried her best not to disturb the dogs, and then looked around for the throw to put over him. It was hung over the back of the armchair. She pulled it off the chair and gently covered him up. He looked so peaceful when he slept. She would have to sleep upstairs alone for a few hours, she hoped he wouldn't mind being left by himself.

The sound of breaking glass made her jump. Jules froze to the spot and listened. She could hear shards of glass hitting the kitchen floor. She held her breath when she heard the kitchen door open. The dogs looked up at her and growled. *Someone is breaking in!*

Chapter Fifteen

Instinctively, Jules dropped down low on the floor with the dogs, hoping that whoever had broken into the kitchen wouldn't come her way and see her. With her heart pounding, she watched the hall intently, hoping that the intruder wouldn't find her. She could hear footsteps getting closer and again she held her breath so nobody could hear her breathing. Somebody stopped by the lounge doorway for a moment and she could see the silhouette of a man – he was holding a shotgun. She couldn't move and dared not call out.

The man fell against the doorway, and her heart nearly leapt out of her chest. He righted himself and continued on his way into the hall. The stairs creaked as he climbed them and then she heard a picture fall off the wall. *Why did this man have a gun?*

"Seth," she whispered urgently. "Seth, wake up!"

"What time is it?"

"Seth, someone's broken in. I heard him go upstairs."

"Are you sure you're not dreaming? It's probably Peter," he replied, pulling the cover up higher.

"Seth, wake up. He's got a gun."

Seth's eyes opened as he realised the gravity of the situation. "Where did you say he went?"

"Upstairs. I couldn't see who it was."

132

Seth sat up and pulled the cover off him and looked worried. "Wait here, I'll go and see."

"But he's got a gun. It could be an armed robber. Shouldn't we call the police?"

"Jules, I've got an idea, I know who it is. Mam said he was upset. I'm going up after him."

"Who is it, Seth?"

"It's Jake. The little shite is after Peter. He must have got Dad's shotgun out. He doesn't know how to use it. I can stop him."

Jules didn't have time to argue with him as Seth had run out of the lounge. She followed him to the doorway and saw him run up the staircase. Her heart was beating hard in her chest. Seth was being rash. It could cost him his life, and she wasn't prepared to let that happen. An ear-splitting sound of a gunshot echoed through the house, making it shudder. She screamed and covered her mouth with her hand. As her heart recovered and her ears cleared she could hear Peter yelling and screaming. *Fuck! Has someone been shot?* She could bear it no longer and ran up the stairs to find out what had happened.

When Jules reached the landing, Seth and Jake were wrestling on the floor outside Peter's room. They were both holding the gun as Seth tried to get Jake to loosen his grip. Seth, being much stronger than Jake, finally pulled it off him and as he got up he kicked him hard in the side and he groaned and cursed him.

Jake lay on the floor crying, his hands up in defeat. Jules ran into Peter's room and flicked on the light; her brother was stood on the bed with his back against the wall. There was a gunshot in the wall above his head, and his eyes were wide with fear.

"Peter, are you hurt?" Seth asked, pulling Jake up onto his feet. Jake swayed on his feet and was having trouble standing up.

"That bastard nearly took my head off!"

"He deserved to… to die," yelled Jake. "The police told me everything. He was trying to take my Ivy off me. He was the one that threw her in the pond. Now she is dead. I can't live without her. I…" Jake started to cry. He was really drunk and stunk of alcohol.

"Seth, you're bleeding!" She saw blood trickling down the side of his forehead.

"I'm ok, I caught my head on the door catch when we went down."

Peter was looking shocked and slid down the wall onto the bed. He was shaking his head. "He was going to kill me."

"He's a drunk shite. He didn't know what he was doing," Seth said, wiping the blood away with the back of his hand.

"You can fuck off! You bastard! You owe me a car." Jake moved towards Seth in a threatening manner.
Seth, holding the gun in both hands, hammered Jake to the wall. Jake looked frightened. "For fuck's sake!" Seth released him and stepped back, shaking his head. He looked anxiously over at her. She could bear it no longer and was about to tell Jake that Seth had gone to prison for him but he gave her a desperate look to not say anything.

"He won't hear it. It's not worth saying anything. It will only make him angry."

She sighed. "So what are we going to do? Call the police? I would. Jake needs to take responsibility for his actions." She looked at Seth first and then at Peter. "Peter?"

"No, I don't want that. I don't want anything more to do with the police. If he thinks I killed her then I am sure that others will think that too. I... I need to get away from here."

"Please don't. If you run, then the police will think you are guilty," she pleaded. Her brother was in shock and wasn't thinking straight.

"Jules, listen to me. I'm going to walk Jake home and wake up Dad. He'll sort this out, the Hearn way."

"I don't know, Seth. It seems wrong."

"Look, nobody was hurt, thank God, and believe me if you upset my Dad then you will pay for the rest of your life."

"Peter, is it ok to take him home?" Seth asked.

"Whatever!" He didn't seem too interested.

Jules watched Seth open the gun up and take out a bullet. He put the bullet in his pocket and with the gun still open put the stock under his arm with the barrel pointing down. She could tell that he had handled a gun before. He grabbed Jake's arm and dragged him along. Jake resisted and seemed hesitant to go.

"Where we going? You don't have to pull me."

"We're going home to bed."

"I can walk," Jake added. Jake was so drunk that it was almost as if he had forgotten what he had done and seemed totally unaware of the ordeal that awaited him when they returned home. She wondered what Jethro Hearn would do to him. *What is the Hearn way?*

Silently, not wanting to hinder them, she kept a healthy distance as she followed Jake and Seth through the house. She watched Jake slide down the stairs and then pull himself up using the bannister. Seth looked furiously at Jake but said nothing and waited for him to catch up. As they walked through the broken glass by the kitchen door, Jake mumbled something about it being dangerous and that someone should clear it up. He had no memory of breaking the window. Without a word, Seth and Jake disappeared into the night.

She walked to the kitchen window and tried to see them pass by in the lane but it was too dark. She hoped that Seth would get Jake home safely. Seth hadn't even looked at her when he left and for a moment she felt hurt, and then cross with herself for being so needy. Seth would catch up with her tomorrow. *I hope.* She had to be patient and let him sort things out. *I can't believe that Jake has got away with it again.*

Peter came down to the kitchen looking pale and upset. He turned on the kitchen light and then sat down heavily on a chair. "They've gone, then? Back to see the Godfather!"

"I guess so. The Hearns like to sort out their own troubles. Peter, you're looking shocked, I'll make you a cup of tea."

She didn't wait for him to answer and put on the kettle and waited for it to boil.

"Jules, I'm in the shit. Tomorrow, once the DNA results come through, I will be carted off to jail for sure. How are you going to manage on your own and with Dad in hospital too? You don't even drive."

"You're jumping the gun! Oh God, I didn't mean to say that! Why would they arrest you? They have no evidence and most of all you are innocent."

"There were messages on her phone from me. The police asked me to confirm that it was me that sent them. I didn't deny it but some of them might have sounded a bit threatening."

"Why, what did you say?"

"I might have messaged her and said that she would be sorry if she went ahead with the engagement party."

"You didn't say that you would kill her."

"No, that's right. But there's one other thing that will count against me."

"What?"

"Christ! I can't believe I am going to tell my own sister this."

She waited for his reply and knew that it wouldn't be good news.

"I nearly suffocated her with your dressing gown belt when we were at it in the tack room. That's how we like doing it. Choking enlightens the senses. They call it breath play."

"You are joking?"

"No, I'm not. Even if the baby isn't mine then they will find my DNA inside her and maybe bruising 'round her neck."

"Oh my God! You're not making this up. Did you tell the police this?"

He shook his head and put his head in his hands. "Now do you see why I need to leave this place? I am going to get arrested for a crime I didn't commit."

Chapter Sixteen

With the milking done, Jules set off with the dogs for a much-needed walk. She climbed over a style and George and Pip ran through into the field. The sun was up and the dew on the grass was rising up in a hazy mist. She breathed in the fresh air, trying to wake herself up, and continued to walk upwards towards the hill that Seth had taken her to. The dogs bounded through the long grass, enjoying their walk. She needed to walk and think - the events of the night giving her plenty to dwell on. *My head is aching!*

Jules and Peter had not gone back to bed after the shooting incident. She had cleaned up the glass, not wanting the dogs to cut their paws, and had put her overalls on ready for milking. They had both drank hot sweet tea together as they recovered. Her Mum had always given her sugar in her tea if she was upset.

Peter was really lucky not to have been killed, and she was almost sure that she had managed to convince him not to run off. His revelation about his love life had been a bit of a shocker. *That could have gone so badly wrong. If consensual choking had resulted in someone dying, then would that be murder?* She just didn't know the answer, but she thought that it was likely. She would have to Google it. Her brother had talked about breath play as if it was the norm and everyone did it. Despite him nearly killing Ivy, she was sure that he was innocent. However, he could have so easily suffocated Ivy and dumped her body in the pond. *No, that couldn't have happened!* Her mind was in turmoil.

She wondered if Seth had ever tried breath play with Ivy during their drunken one nightstand. She hoped not. She didn't like to think of Seth and Ivy being intimate and shut the disturbing image she had of them from her mind.

After she had walked the dogs and checked on the horses, she and Peter were going to go to the hospital and visit their Dad. Peter had to wait for the milk to be collected first and he was going to fit a bit of board over the broken window pane. She had packed a bag of things her Dad might need in hospital. She hoped that he was starting to cope better with being alive but feared he might not be. His recovery was going to take time.

Feeling warm, she reached the top of the hill and found a shady place to sit, near to where she and Seth sat the previous evening. She could hear the skylarks overhead but the sea was lost in a mist in the distance. This was a lovely spot and she could see for miles. Most of the land below was Jethro Hearn's kingdom; where everyone bowed down to him and obeyed his every command. She could see his minions in their blue overalls, working in the fields, and she wondered which one was Seth. Even Seth, it seemed, thought that his Dad was above or equal to the law. *It was not right, Jake should have been charged with attempted murder, not hidden away and wrapped in cotton wool!*

Despite being cross with Seth for letting his Dad rule him, she forgave him also. She knew that he was protecting his mother from suffering any more than she needed to. He was a loyal son.

A mosquito landed on her bare leg and she brushed it off. *I shouldn't have worn shorts.* Jules had forgotten how much the bugs liked her blood. She stretched her legs out from the shade so she could soak up some sun and watch out for any bloodsuckers. The dogs had stopped chasing each other and were standing still looking over into the next field. They barked, spooked by whatever they had seen or heard and then ran up to her with their tails wagging. They lay down either side of her as if they were protecting her. *Or am I protecting you two?* They were such fraidy-cats. She couldn't see anything in the field. It was probably a pheasant strutting through the grass that had scared them. Stroking the dogs, she smiled. *They will never make guard dogs.* A man had broken into their house with a shotgun, and they had hardly raised an eyebrow.

Jules looked up and then saw movement in the next field, a woman wearing a yellow sundress was walking towards her. She didn't recognise the grey-haired woman at first but as she got closer she realised that it was Margaret Hearn, looking quite different with her hair tied up. She was waving to her and signalling to her to come over. Jules stood up, and calling the dogs to follow, headed towards Margaret. Jules jumped a ditch and found a space between the shrubs to speak to her. Margaret looked hot, her cheeks were red. She was fanning herself with her hand.

"Oh Jules, it's going to be a hot one today; I've changed once already. You look lovely and cool in your shorts. I'd like to wear shorts, but I don't think the one's I've got would fit me now. Jules, you haven't seen Jake, have you? Mark said he didn't come home last night. I know that boy is a rascal, but he's my youngest and the dearest. I'd like to find him. He's not been himself since Ivy passed."

Jules wasn't sure what to say. It was obvious that Margaret had no idea what had happened that night. "No, I'm sorry, I haven't seen him," she lied. "I'm sure he will turn up. He's probably sleeping it off somewhere." She regretted saying that, as Margaret might think she was being rude.

"Yes, you're probably right. I've walked 'round the farm twice, looking for him in all the usual places. He'll come home when he is hungry. He always does. Would you like to come down to the house and have a cup of tea? We can catch up and have a chat about things. How is your Dad doing?"

"Yes, I'd love to. He's physically alright now but mentally, Dad's not that great. Peter and I are going to see him later."

"I'm sorry to hear that. My Claire has had a few issues too. We have to keep an eye on her. She's doing a lot better now."

"Do you mind if the dogs come too?"

"Not at all, the more the merrier. There's a gate at the bottom of this field. I'll meet you there."

As they walked down to the farmhouse, she hoped that she would bump into Seth and find out what happened. Jake going missing was not a good sign.

By the time they had got to the farmhouse, Margaret had spoken about so many things that she was feeling overwhelmed and thought that she was perhaps the most talkative woman that she had ever met. Jules did feel relaxed though, and was under no pressure to talk about herself as Margaret was enjoying telling her about her family and about her numerous grandchildren. She felt like she had known Margaret all her life.

They sat in Margaret's pretty garden, under an umbrella, as the sun was starting to burn them. The dogs lay in the shade too, panting a little as they tried to keep cool. Margaret had poured her tea from a teapot into pretty teacups with matching saucers. Her Mum would have liked the rosebud design.

As Margaret chatted, the topic returned to Jake's absence. She looked sad for a moment.

"He's your cousin, you know!"

"Yes, Seth told me. He told me how you came to adopt him."

"Yesterday, the police came here and asked us if we knew Ann Bridgewater. We told them what we could. It was such a long time ago. If only we kept that letter then that would have led them to the bastard that killed her. She didn't write that letter. Thank the Lord he had the decency to spare her newborn's life. I never believed that Ann had run off with another man. She would never have left her tiny baby behind. Ann was a sweet young thing and not like that at all. Such beautiful hair; so like yours."

"Didn't you think of calling the police? Weren't questions asked?"

"No, I always thought that Ann would come back one day to get him. It never entered my head that anything could have happened to her. Your uncle, God rest his soul, wouldn't have been able to look after him. He drank too much. He was happy enough to give Jake up. Some people aren't meant to have children."

"That was such a lovely thing to do."

"No, it was the only thing to do. Would you like another cup of tea?"

"I've got to get back. Peter will be waiting for me and I need to pack Dad a bag. Pyjamas and wash stuff and his book. He's not shaved in days. I don't think he wants to."

"He will, just give him time and when he sees your sweet face again, then that will heal a thousand pains. Life can be tough, Jules, but you can cope with any trial if you all work together. A loving family is all that it takes to..."

Jules' phone started to ring. She took it out of her back pocket and saw that it was Peter. "It's my brother, Margaret. He probably wants me to come back home. Hi, Peter. I'll be back in a minute."

"Jules, the hospital rang. Dad's been moved to a mental health hospital. They want us to take him some clothes and anything he might need. Don't panic but this is normal procedure; they asked us not to pack any sharp objects, aerosol cans or anything with cords. They are going to put him on suicide watch."

"Really? Shit! Suicide watch! That's not good. What hospital has he been moved to?"

"You're not going to believe this. There wasn't a bed available in the local area, so he has been taken by ambulance to the Priory in Southgate."

"Where's Southgate?"

"Jules, it's in North London! I've looked at the route. It will take us two hours, ten minutes to get there if the traffic is good. I'm dreading it. You know what my driving is like."

"North London! That's crazy."

"The thing is, I haven't got enough petrol to get us there and I can't get any money out of the bank until the cheque has cleared. Do you have any money?"

"Yes, but I haven't got a bank card, I... I lost it. I need to order another one. I'll go to the bank with ID and see if I can draw some out. What about the milking? I could go up by train and then you could do the milking with Seth. I'm sure he wouldn't mind helping again. I'll be over in a minute. I'm just with Margaret at Crow Farm. I won't be long." She ended the call and looked up at Margaret's concerned face. "Dad's really not well, he's been taken into a mental health hospital in North London. The Priory, I think Peter said. There's no beds left in Sussex."

"I know that hospital. Jethro's sister works there. Your Dad will be in good hands. It sounds like you are going to have a job to get there. Jethro will take you. It will be a good excuse for him to see his sister again. I would have suggested Seth drive, but he hasn't got his driving licence back yet."

"I couldn't possibly ask Jethro to drive all that way. It would take us over two hours to get there! I am sure he is busy. He has your farm to run." Although it was a kind offer, she was not sure if she would survive the journey with Seth's strange Dad.

"He likes to think he runs things around here but Patrick manages the farm now. Jethro won't mind, he has too much time on his hands these days and gets under my feet. He is probably trying to while away the hours watching morning TV again. It will do him good to go for a drive. You go back home and get what you need for your Dad and Jethro will be over in a minute. I insist."

Jules felt that she had no choice. "If you are sure, then it would really help. I can pay you for the petrol soon. I just need to…"

"Don't you worry about petrol money. Jethro wouldn't take it. His old car needs a bit of run, and I am sure that he will jump at the chance to go for a drive."

"We'll have to work something out. I will make you a cake then. Ok, thank you. I know it sounds crazy, but I haven't been to London or on a train on my own before. The thought of it is a little scary."

"So that's settled then."

Chapter Seventeen

A very shiny, vintage BMW drew up in the courtyard. It was a cream colour and had been lovingly maintained. Jules was feeling worried, she wasn't sure if Jethro was a willing volunteer. Her fears dissipated as he smiled at her and waved. He had a similar smile to Seth and in some ways looked very much like him. He stopped the car and then got out to help her with her bag. He was wearing beige trousers and a shiny beige bomber jacket. She wondered if this was his driving outfit as it did compliment the car. Jethro put the holdall into the boot and then opened the passenger door for her to get in.

"It is very kind of you to drive me to the hospital. I really am most grateful. It's such a long way, though, for you." She got into the car, and Jethro closed the door. The car was stifling hot inside, she could barely breathe. The interior of the car was as shiny and clean as the outside and smelled of polish and of aftershave.

"It's a pleasure, young lady. It's a beautiful day for a drive. I am happy to be your white knight for the day. Margaret would not forgive me if I didn't help a damsel in distress."

"Thank you."

Jethro got into the car and turned the key in the ignition. It took a little cajoling to start the car and finely after a couple of turns of the key, the engine sprang into life. "It's been in the garage far too long. I haven't been to Southgate for donkey's years. It will do this old girl a lot of good taking her out on the road. I'll take the scenic route if that is ok with you. It might take a little longer but it will be worth it."

As they drove out of the courtyard, she realised that the car had no air conditioning and she was already starting to cook. She was relieved to see Jethro wind his window down and she did too. He didn't seem to mind, and it was lovely to feel the wind on her face as the car picked up speed.

Jethro looked up at the sky. "Another hot day to enjoy but it won't last, there's rain on its way."

He fiddled with the radio and picked up Radio Sussex. They were playing a 50's song that she didn't recognise, but Jethro seemed to like it as he tapped one of his hands on the steering wheel.

She thought she would try and strike up a conversation. "Does your band play at gigs or just at home? I saw you playing an accordion at Jake and Ivy's party. I like Irish music. It makes you feel happy. I like playing the guitar and singing too."

Jethro laughed. "We're called 'Windmill,' although there's not much wind in our sails these days. We used to play at festivals but now we are all getting a bit old for that malarkey so we only play at home now. That is how I met Margaret, she used to dance to our tunes. Can you believe that we have been married for fifty-eight years in December? She's been a good wife, I can't deny her that."

"Wow, that's a long time!" *Fifty-eight again, how spooky!* She looked over at Jethro's face and worked out that he must be in his seventies. He really didn't look that old.

Jethro noticed her looking at him. "I have weathered well, haven't I? I put it down to good food, a little whisky and plenty of exercise. Margaret keeps me on my toes and is a passionate woman."

Her eyes widened, she wasn't sure where he was going with his last statement. She had to change the subject and quickly. She was eager to know what had happened when Seth had woken him up in the middle of the night to tell him about Jake's mishap. She was still cross with Jake. *It wasn't just a mishap, it was very nearly a catastrophe!*

"Margaret is lovely. She is really worried about Jake. She can't find him." It was as if she had dropped a blow. Jethro's light mood changed and she could see a muscle in his face twitch as he gripped the steering wheel a little tighter.

He sighed. "Are now, there's a thing! Those boys are always getting into trouble. I had to take action last night. Things cannot continue this way any longer. They have brought it on themselves. It is out of my hands now. There is nothing more I can do."

Jules was puzzled. "What boys?"

"Jake and your Seth. A pair of irresponsible eejits! There are consequences if you play with guns, fight and mess a woman around. It had to be done. I've had enough. I swear those two have made my hair turn white. As for my poor Margaret, she shouldn't have to suffer this way."

She was becoming alarmed. "Did Seth come and see you last night?"

"He did. There is nothing you need worry yourself about. By the time we get home, it will all be over and we can move on with our lives."

"Why… I don't understand?"

"You know full well what happened last night."

She wasn't sure how much she should say about the shooting. Jethro seemed to be aware that there was a gun involved but she wasn't sure if he knew the whole story.

"I didn't tell Margaret but last night Seth caught Jake with a gun and they had a fight. Jake was really drunk."

"He's always drunk, that boy. He's going to kill himself one of these days. I can't let that happen. It was poor Ann's dying wish that we bring him up to lead a happy and healthy life. I've locked the pair of them in the cellar, so they can sort out their differences. It had to be done. It was a bit tricky getting them down there but I managed and now they have all day to talk and sort it all out. I should have done it years ago."

"Oh God! That's crazy!" She was horrified and thought it sounded like a recipe for disaster. She wondered what Seth had told his Dad and was sure that it wasn't everything that happened. Now he was being punished, treated like a child and trapped in a dark cellar with a crazy boy for company. It was a brutal way of dealing with things - barbaric even. Her head was spinning.

"Crazy, no. Desperate times call for desperate measures. Margaret best not know about this. She won't like her Jake being upset. Not after him losing Ivy. It will do him good not to drink. He needs to clear his head and see things for what they are."

"I hope it works," she said coolly. She didn't want to let Jethro know how furious she was. She pulled a bottle of water out of her bag and sipped it as she stared out of the window, trying to calm herself down.

As they travelled up the dual carriageway, she tried to imagine what Seth was going through. She hoped that Seth hadn't killed Jake. She also worried that Seth might not like her being in a car with his Dad. Would he be cross with his Dad and cross with her? Or would he accept his Dad's punishment as being 'the Hearn way' and leave the cellar in peace, having made up with Jake. She didn't think that would be the case. No wonder Margaret couldn't find Jake; he was in the last place she would have expected - right under her nose.

Jules was willing the hours away and wanted to get home and see Seth as soon as she could. He wouldn't be in a good mood, but she wanted to see him all the same – curious to see him at his worst. She needed to know what she was getting herself into. She kept looking at her phone, to see if Seth had left her a message but none came. She was worried sick.

Jethro was nearly as talkative as Margaret and as they neared London, he told her about his life in Ireland and about the cars he had driven over the years. He was extremely proud of his BMW and occasionally patted the dashboard. She had listened to him and had tried her best to engage with him, but it was a difficult task. *Jethro Hearn is a bit of a nutter!*

They reached the Priory just after lunch and drove up a drive lined by evenly spaced trees. They parked and walked up to a large red-brick Georgian house with white pillars. It was set high on a hill overlooking landscaped gardens below. Some of the residents sat at picnic tables or lay on the grass reading. She hadn't expected the hospital to be so grand and was surprised that an NHS patient would be allowed in. She had imagined a hospital with bars on the windows and people walking around in white gowns holding cut-throat razor blades. *I shouldn't think of mental patients like that!*

Jethro's sister was due to finish her shift in half an hour, and he had arranged to meet her on the grounds. She dragged the holdall into the reception area and hoped that she had brought her Dad everything he needed. She had placed his phone in one of the pockets but had left the corded charger at home. She hoped that the hospital had a place to charge phones.

The friendly reception lady directed her to her Dad's private room. The door was open, and a member of staff was sat in the hallway watching her Dad's room, and another patient also. He saw her approaching and whispered to her that he would just check through the bag. He found nothing dangerous. He asked her to keep the door open when she went in and to bring the empty bag out with her. It was a bit like being security checked at an airport.

Tentatively, she knocked on the open door hoping that he would greet her. Being met with a predictable silence, she didn't wait for him to reply and walked into an elegant bedroom with an ensuite. It was as good as, if not better than, a five-star hotel. Her Dad was sat by a neatly made bed, in a chair by a large sash window. He was staring at something into a small shady courtyard garden outside.

She didn't know what to say. She was going to try and sound cheerful at least and hoped that Margaret's words of wisdom would work. She had nothing to lose.

"Hi Dad, I've brought you some clothes, your book and your electric razor." He really did need to shave as he was now growing a grey beard which made him look odd. She sat on the bed next to him and tried to see what he was looking at so intently. Birds were gathered on a small planter hunting for insects. Her Dad clapped his hands, and the birds flew away.

"Dad?"

Realising that she was sat next to him, he clutched her hand.

"Jules, I did something terrible. I shouldn't be here. Why am I here?"

Disturbed by his croaky voice, she looked over her shoulder and could see that the man outside was listening and had picked up a clipboard and pen and started to write.

"You're in hospital, Dad. You're not well. You've got to stay here, and they will help you." She could feel the tears starting to trickle. Her positive attitude had faded away and had been replaced by anguish.

"Dad, listen. You tried to end your life. Seth and I found you. You nearly hung yourself in the barn."

"I... I'm sorry, I don't remember. I wouldn't do that to you, kitten."

"You just said you did something terrible? It has to be that, doesn't it?"

Her Dad shook his head. "I know something terrible happened. It was my fault. I just can't remember. I shouldn't be here. You should have let me die. I don't want to be on this Earth anymore. I need to be with your mother."

"Please Dad, don't say that. I don't want you to die. Peter doesn't want you to die either. We want you in our lives, to see us marry and have children. We would be lost without you."

"I can't, Jules, not now. It's too late for that. I hear her voice calling out to me. She's telling me to follow her. I'm sorry…I'm so sorry."

She watched the tears rolling down his face and realised that he had gone back into his own world; his mind spent. There was nothing she could do to save him.

The man in the hallway came over to her and whispered that she should unpack his bag and then meet him in the hall and he would talk to her about her Dad's condition. She nodded and unpacked the bag, doing her best not to cry.

Holding the empty bag, she left the Priory in tears and looked for a place to sit and try and compose herself before she found Jethro. She walked around the house towards some glasshouses and then saw some people waving at her from a picnic bench. It was Jethro and his rotund sister. She had no way to escape them and reluctantly walked over to join them. She couldn't compose herself, and the tears flowed freely. She climbed over the bench and sat next to Jethro.

"You poor girl, don't cry, my angel. Your Dad is in the right place." Jethro put his arm around her and gave her a quick reassuring hug.

"It was just so hard to see him so distressed. He doesn't want to live. How on earth are they going to stop him taking his life? He kept saying he was sorry and that he didn't want to be here anymore. The attendant watching him told me that he may be suffering from chronic depression and after they have assessed him will offer him medication and therapy. I doubt that he will let them. I feel so bad for him. There is nothing I can do or say to help him."

Jethro's sister smiled and took her hand - it was hot and she felt the warmth radiate through her. "You listen here, to me, my darling." Her Irish accent was much softer than Jethro's. Your Dad is just sick, and like a broken leg, his mind needs time to mend. They will talk to him, get him to join therapy groups and if he wants to take medication to reduce his anxiety then they will offer it to him. I promise you that he will recover. You just have to have faith."

"I'll try but it is so hard," she replied, drying her tears with her hand. Jethro's sister dived into her bag and found a tissue for her. Gratefully, she wiped her eyes and nose as she was beginning to look a state. Jethro's sister was probably the kindest person she had ever met. *She could be an angel.*

"Mary has worked here for over thirty years, she knows what she is talking about. It will take a while and a lot of patience on your part and eventually he will get better, I promise you. Our Claire did."

She nodded and sighed. *I hope they are right.*

Jules got back into the BMW and she realised that she was really tired. She felt emotionally drained too. As they drove home, Jethro started to chat again about his sister and how she had brought up seven children by herself and talked about what each was doing with their lives. She tried to listen and then found that she was drifting off to sleep. To wake herself up, she got her phone out of her pocket to see if Seth had left a message, and seeing that he hadn't she wondered if there was a signal in the cellar. She sent him a text anyway and hoped that Jethro wouldn't mind. She started to type.

'Seth, I can't imagine what you are going through. Your Dad has taken me to the Priory Hospital in North London. Dad has been sent there. At the moment, he doesn't want to live, and he needs help. Your Mum insisted that your Dad take me. He told me that he locked you and Jake in the cellar to sort things out. He is one crazy man but means well, I guess. I hope you are ok. Please text me if you can. Your Jules xxx'

The car pulled up outside her house and she realised that she had been asleep for the entire journey home.

"Oh my, I'm sorry, Jethro. I haven't been much company. I think I fell asleep not long after leaving the Priory."

"That's alright, my little angel. I listened to my tunes and you are probably sick to death hearing my voice. Margaret says I talk too much. You looked like you were in a deep sleep and you will feel much better for it. You are too young to have such worries."

"I feel much better. No, it's good to hear about you all. Seth is lucky to have such a lovely family," she lied.

"I worry for you, child. Seth is not right for you. You are an angel, and he will let you down. My heart bleeds when I think about the pain he will cause you."

"It's ok, Jethro, I know he has been reckless and has a temper but so do I. He loves me and I love him back. We are meant for each other."

"There is something I should tell you. As you may have heard, I am very attached to my daughters and I adore them all. Ivy was like a daughter to me too. I thought the world of her. A couple of weeks ago, she came to me and she was sobbing. She told me that she was three months pregnant."

"I know, Jethro, she told Seth that too."

Jethro sighed. "Did she tell him that the baby was his?"

"No," Jules replied quietly. "He didn't mention that."

Chapter Eighteen

Jules' mind was racing, bombarded with words and flashes of memories from the past few weeks. She was trying to stay calm and think through things clearly. Despite the hot afternoon sun, she shivered as she walked over to the horses to give them hugs and sit in her happy place behind the stables.

She sat on the wall where Seth had first kissed her and started to cry. She had cried too much today. Taking in a deep breath, she tried to calm her troubled mind. The truth was, she wasn't sure what to think anymore. *Had Seth known about the baby?* He had told her that his relationship with Ivy had been over two years ago. *Had he lied about that? What other lies had he told?* She could feel a horrible pain in her chest and alarm bells were ringing in her head, making it ache. She needed to watch his reaction when she told him what his Dad had shared with her. Then she would know.

Jules checked her watch and saw that she had half an hour to spare before she had to go and help Peter with the milking. She really should find him to give him an update about their Dad, but she had to see Seth first. This couldn't wait.

She could hear a row going on even before she got to Crow Farm. She could hear several angry voices, Seth's included. Jules hesitated for a moment, not wanting to walk in on a Hearn domestic. Perhaps this wasn't a good time to see

Seth. She started to walk back home and then heard Seth calling her.

"Jules? Where are you going?"

She turned to face him, unsure of what she should say to him. He looked like he was really cross and very tired. She doubted if he had slept since she last saw him.

"Are you ok? I heard shouting." She walked towards him, electing not to ask him her question until he had calmed down. He left the house and met her midway up the garden path. He looked rough and there was dried blood on the side of his head. His eyes were still blazing with fury.

"I'm fucking furious. I hear he took you to the hospital. Such a do-gooder! To the outside world, he is charming but behind closed doors, he's an evil bastard! Who locks people in cellars for Christ's sake? He has gone too far this time, Jules. I can't stay here anymore. I've got to leave this hellhole. That man needs certifying."

"You can come and stay at mine."

"I wouldn't be far enough away. I'm going to go to Cork tonight, and I am taking you with me."

"That is crazy talk. I can't leave my Dad or the farm at the moment. Anyway, you would be breaking your parole, wouldn't you?"

"Fuck the parole, I'm out of here in the morning. Come with me if you want to."

"You're angry, Seth. You need to calm down and think rationally. If you run away, then you are giving him what he wants. You are a thorn in his side, and he doesn't think much of you. He's got it in for you…he…"

She couldn't help herself and was going to tell him the very thing that she knew she shouldn't.

"What has he been saying now?"

She took a deep breath preparing herself for an outburst. "He said that you weren't good enough for me. He said that Ivy had told him that the baby was yours!"

"What the fuck! You didn't believe him did you?"

"No… but why would he say something like that?"

"You do believe him. For fuck's sake, Jules!"

"Truthfully, I don't know what to think anymore. I've had the shittiest day ever and now you are being a complete space monkey!"

"Do the maths, Jules! I wasn't here, was I? I could hardly have made a baby in prison. Could I?"

Jules shook her head. He was enraged.

"I'm sorry."

"Just go home, Jules. Go home! I've got a bag to pack!"

"Fine! Sod off to Ireland. Peter's in trouble and I've got a farm to run and cows to milk!"

She stormed down the path, slamming the garden gate behind her. Her blood was boiling, and she had no time for his pathetic tantrums.

As she reached Farm End, she noticed a police car was turning into their drive.

"That's bloody marvellous!" she shouted out loud, throwing her hands in the air. "That's all I need."

Her rage turned into fear as she speculated why the police were paying them a visit. *Oh God, they've come to arrest Peter*!

As she reached the courtyard she saw two police officers and Peter at the front door. One of the officers was putting cuffs on his wrists. She could hear him being given his rights. He looked drawn and pale. She really couldn't believe her eyes and ran towards them. "Why have you arrested him?" she asked an officer as they led him to the car.

"I'm afraid I am not at liberty to say."

"I told you, Jules, they think I killed Ivy. I am being arrested on suspicion of murder. I'm sorry. I've left the bank card and pin number on the dresser."

A police officer helped him into the back seat of their car and then got into the front. Their doors were slammed shut, and they did a U-turn and were gone.

She stood there for a moment with her mouth open. *This really was the shittiest day ever*! She was alone in the world now, with nobody to turn to.

In the distance, she could hear the cows mooing as they waited by the gate to be milked. The milking had to be done, there was no chance to curl up into a ball and shut the world out. She would have to get on with it.

Quickly, she changed into her overalls and had a quick drink of water. It was a short walk to the milking shed, and she hoped that the cows would behave. She took the dogs with her as they were used to being out with them on the milking runs.

The herd missed Hermione and there was always a different cow leading the herd to the shed. Today Pearl was leading, but she was not that confident and stopped half-way down the track. She sighed. *This is going to take time*. She swished her hands behind Pearl but this made things worse and sent her back up to the field. The others followed. "Oh shit!" She looked at George and Pip. "Go and get them, then." It had no effect. Not that she expected the dogs to do anything. They wagged their tails and thought she was going to throw a ball for them. They were hopeless.

"We need to get behind them and herd them down the path. Do you want me to help?"

She turned around. Seth was stood in the lane by the gate. She turned away. She hadn't forgiven him yet. He didn't look angry anymore.

"Where's Peter?"

"He's been arrested. Not that you care!"

"No! Christ! I'm sorry, Jules. I do care."

"I thought that you had to pack?"

Seth jumped over the gate and joined her. "I'm sorry, I was angry. I shouldn't have snapped at you. As you said, I can't break the parole conditions. I would be mad to leave now. Anyway, I couldn't go to Ireland or anywhere without you. I'd be a fool if I did. I love you, Jules."

"So you're sticking around then?"

"It seems so. Not at Crow Farm, though. I can't work for Dad anymore – not that I want to. I will have to get another job."

She gave him a sideways glance. He seemed genuinely sorry.

Pearl started to walk back down the path to the milking shed, the need to be milked driving her on. The other cows followed.

"Jules? You called me a space monkey!"

"I know, I'm sorry?" She was starting to smile. "I was cross. I'm sorry too."

"So what exactly is a space monkey?" he asked, smiling at her.

"I'm not entirely sure. I think it's got to do with choking someone while you are having sex."

"Really? Are you into that then?"

"No, of course not! I know someone that is though."

"I wouldn't hurt you!" Seth looked offended.

"No, not you, silly. My pervert of a brother has confessed to being a space monkey and is probably at the police station trying to explain himself. When he found Ivy in the tack room, he nearly choked her trying to get his wicked way. There's a lot of warped people in Findon and that includes your Dad!"

"Holy cow!"

The last cow entered the milking shed, and she and Seth followed her in.

"I'll help you milk them if you want me to. I'll understand if you want me to go. It will be easier if two of us do it."

She looked at his sad face and couldn't bear to see him suffer any longer. *You don't know how much I need you.*

"Seth, you do my head in sometimes but I couldn't be without you. If you want to stay at Farm End until Dad comes home then I would like that."

Seth smiled. "I'd like that too. Am I allowed a hug now?"

"Only if you help me with the milking. You've got to earn your keep now you are in Bridgewater territory."

"I will obey your every request. Come here and let me hold you. You are driving me crazy in that overall. You put it on to tease me, didn't you?"

Seth drew her to him and put his arms around her, embracing her warmly. He smelt of mildew having been in the cellar so long, but she didn't mind as she could feel his warm body next to hers and his heart beating. Together, they were the earth, the sky and the sea.

Chapter Nineteen

The alarm went off at four-thirty and Jules groaned as she reached for the phone. All these early starts were beginning to take their toll. She really couldn't believe that the morning had come so quickly. She was tempted to go back to sleep but knew that she couldn't. Gradually, she opened her eyes and tried to focus. An unfamiliar oak wardrobe materialised in front of her. One of the doors hung at an angle as the hinge was loose – it bothered her. It was strange being in her Dad's bedroom. The room was sparsely furnished and there were old pictures hung on the walls that were ugly and needed to go to charity. Little effort had been made to make that room his own. If only she had noticed this before, then she might have seen this as a warning sign. She wondered if her Dad had been watched at the hospital all night as he slept. *I will ring the hospital after breakfast*. She would only be able to visit him once a week as it was going to be expensive to travel there.

"Jules, turn the alarm off, it can't be time to get up. It is still dark." Seth sounded sleepy.

Wide awake now, she swiped the alarm off and turned over to face him and smiled as she watched him trying to wake himself up.

They had gone to bed early as both had been exhausted by their turbulent day. When Seth had showered, she had sat on the bathroom floor talking to him about their days. She couldn't help but stare at his muscular back as he applied her shower gel to his body. He didn't seem to mind. Watching him had all become too much for her, and she had to retreat to the bedroom to compose herself. She needed to sleep. As they were drifting off, she had asked him what would happen to Peter. Seth had reassured her that he would be released after twenty-four hours unless there was a crucial piece of evidence that linked him to the murder. He thought that it was unlikely.

"I'm not sure what kind of ship the Hearns run but you are going to have to rise before dawn if you are going to shine at Farm End."

Seth opened his eyes and smiled. He pulled her to him and kissed her.

"Morning, beautiful. What does a new recruit have to do to get breakfast here?"

"I don't know, you could start by making me a cup of tea."

"Just tea? Done. Just two more minutes with you. I just want to feel your body next to mine and breathe you in."

She turned over and snuggled into him. She could feel his skin on hers and her heart beat a little harder – he really was enjoying being close to her! He held her a bit tighter, and kissing her neck, he sighed and pulled away.

"I will have to go and get your tea now or I might not be able to help myself."

Jules turned over to face him. "You don't have to stop, Seth. If we took precautions, then it's fine by me. Not that I really know what to do. You do know that you'd be my first?"

"Really, you'd never know!" He had a mischievous smile on his face.

"Seth! You know you are!"

"I do. I just want to do things the right way this time."

"Do you believe in God then?"

"Not really. But Mam does, and she has done her best to bring up the Hearn boys with her moral principles installed into them. I am going to try and make her happy but if you keep staring at me with those longing eyes then I may crumble. Tea then?"

"Yes, please."

Dawn was breaking as they finished the milking. Both yawning, they walked hand in hand back to the house. She looked up and saw a few clouds in the sky, which was a good thing. It didn't feel as hot today as it did yesterday. She was pleased, it would be a good day to take the horses out.

"Do you want to go for a ride?" she asked, looking towards the horses' field. "Peter's old hat and boots are in the tack room, they might fit you. I don't think mine would. He had a go at riding, but he kept falling off Connor when he trotted. You could ride and I could follow and lead Barney alongside you. It would do them both good. I've got to take the dogs out too. What do you think?"

"That sounds great. It's been too long. You are a very generous employer. First, Jules, I am going back home to get my things. I've got a riding kit somewhere and I also need to tell Mam that I am staying here with you."

"How do you think she will take the news?"

"I'm not sure if she will approve but that has never stopped me doing what I want to do before. She will moan a bit, insist we sleep in separate rooms until we are wed. Later on, she will see that I am happy, and she will forgive me. She always does."

"You can have my bed if you like," she teased.

164

"I don't think that would be necessary. Part of my duties is to keep you warm at night. I think we can just pretend if she asks."

"I'm glad about that, I can't sleep without you. I guess your Mum will have crazy Jake to deal with and that will keep her occupied." She could see that Seth was looking a little cold faced at the mention of his name. "I didn't like to ask before but how did it go with Jake? Did you sort out your differences?"

"Being locked up with him was a living nightmare. He was so drunk and kept crying and talking to himself. So, he passed out and slept for hours and then when he did come around he had no idea why he was in the cellar with me. He threw up all over the floor and was in no mood to talk, thank God! So he lay on one side of the cellar dying with a hangover and I sat against the wall on the other side. I don't think we said a word to each other. He hates me and always will."

"Did you see my message?"

"No, I'm sorry. I've lost my phone. I can't remember where I left it. It will turn up." Seth smiled. "Anyway, we don't have to message each other now and meet up secretly. We will always be together. I won't need a phone."

After breakfast, Seth went up to Crow Farm to get his clothes and belongings. He said he would be a couple of hours as he needed to take down all the pictures and clean the room out ready for the next brother or sister to move into it.

Seth moving in with her just seemed to be the most natural thing in the world to do. When her Dad got home then they would find somewhere else to live. Somewhere in the village, until they were ready to move to Ireland. She couldn't imagine them ever living apart again.

165

As she made herself a second cup of tea, she noticed the farm's bank account card on the dresser and tucked it in her phone case along with the pin number as she would never remember it. She doubted if there would be much money left in that account as there were piles of bills to pay. A milk credit would be due into the account soon, but she wasn't sure when and was eager for Peter to return to take care of the accounts. She decided to order herself a replacement bank card so that they could live off her eBay profit. She doubted if Seth had much money, but he had already earned his keep that day doing the milking. If their finances didn't improve, then she would have to get a local job.

The kitchen was feeling hot as the sun got higher in the sky, so she opened the kitchen door and was surprised to see Jethro standing on the doorstep.

"Oh Jethro, you surprised me!"

"I'm sorry, I had to come 'round."

She was feeling a bit awkward and a little cross. He had been the cause of a fight between her and Seth yesterday. *Are you trying to split us up?* "If you came to see Seth, then he has gone back to yours."

"I know, I heard him come in. He should be in the fields working with the others, it is a busy time on the farm. No, it was you I came to see."

"Really?" She was starting to get cross.

"I just wanted to check that you were ok. You were so upset yesterday."

"I am fine, thank you, Jethro. It was such a hard day. You and your lovely sister made me feel so much better," she lied.

"I just wanted you to know I am there for you and if you need anything then come and see me and I will help you. I've done my best to make you see Seth for what he is. He stayed here last night, didn't he?"

"Yes, he did," she didn't want to say more than that.

"I will be disappointed if you lead him astray. It is not God's way and it is not the Hearn way to live in sin."

She could feel the heat rising in her cheeks with anger. He was making her sound like she was cheap. "Jethro, we are not living in sin! Seth wouldn't dream of it. If you talked to him, then you would know that. I can't believe you would think that!"

"I'm sorry, I didn't mean to upset you. That is the last thing I want. I will go home and hope that you forgive a sad old man. Come over when you can, you brighten up Margaret and my days."

Jethro left and as he reached the end of the drive he turned and stared sadly back at her and then walked on home. *He really is the strangest man I have ever met...*

While she waited for Seth, she started to pooh pick again in the field. She was amazed how much dung Connor and Barney produced. When it had dried a little on the dung heap then she would bag it up and try and sell it. In the past, she had sold a few bags to people that liked growing roses. Apparently, they thrived on it.

She had put on jeans and a t-shirt and was feeling hot. When she had finished this dreary task, she would go back into the cool farmhouse and change into something cooler, and she would ring the Priory to see how her Dad was.

She had felt nervous ringing the hospital. Images of her Dad crying kept flooding her mind and by the time she had got through, she was dreading what they might say. The reality was that her Dad's life was hanging on a knife's edge. She could only imagine what pain his mind was in. *Torture.*

Much to her relief, her Dad had spent a better night, having given his consent to receive medication. *This is a positive step.* She guessed they must have given him a sleeping tablet or two. She had breathed a sigh of relief as she terminated the call. Things looked a bit more positive.

She checked the time; Seth had been gone over two hours. He was probably having trouble leaving. She thought that he had underestimated his mother's hold over her family, and she would be reluctant to let him go. It was a strange thing, having so many of her children to live at Crow Farm even after they were married. She felt restless and was eager to go out for a walk with the horses and felt the need to tidy up. Seth's room had been immaculate; nothing was out of place. She felt excited thinking about his imminent arrival and hoped that he would feel comfortable living with her. To keep herself occupied, she decided to clean the bathroom, something she didn't do regularly enough.

Jules stood back to admire her handy work and then went back to the shower screen to wipe off a blemish and sighed a happy sigh. "There, all done, that's perfect."

"Just like you."

She smiled, Seth was stood on the landing dressed in his black riding trousers, long black boots, a riding hat and a suit jacket. In his hands, he was carrying black bin bags full of clothes.

She laughed. "You're not going to a gymkhana!"

"Very funny! I like to look my best when I ride. No, not really. I wore my suit jacket as I couldn't carry it. Where shall I leave my things?"

"Oh, I hadn't thought. Maybe we should use my old room as our dressing room. Leave your bags on my bed and I will clear some drawers and a space in the wardrobe for you."

"Ok."

She followed him to her room and watched him neatly lay his clothes in piles on her bed. She looked at her tiny wardrobe with concern, it was going to take a small miracle to make space in there, and she hoped that he wouldn't open the door and see how untidy she was. Seth took off his jacket, he was wearing a black t-shirt which showed off his muscular arms. He then went to the wardrobe to hang up his jacket. He opened the door and looked inside and was astonished.

"Wow, that's quite a disaster zone! When did you last have a sort out?"

"Um…not since we moved here. It's on my list to do."

With difficulty, Seth extracted a hanger and then hung his jacket on the back of the door.

"Is it ok if we eat first and then go out? I have cheese," he said, holding up a small plastic bag.

"Yes, of course, there's bread in the freezer."

She followed Seth down to the kitchen and got some bread out for them both. "You're not going to wear your hat while we eat, are you?"

"I forgot I was wearing it." He released the clip on the chin strap and put the hat on the kitchen table and then stood by the sink as she made them some sandwiches.

"We are going to have to work out what you can eat. I've never had to cook for a vegetarian before. Your Mum probably has some recipes she could give me. Was she ok when you told her that you were staying here?"

"Mam was as good as gold. I'm a bit surprised, though. I thought she would put up more of a fight. She said that it was for the best, considering what has been going on."

"That's good. What about your Dad?" She suddenly remembered her encounter with Jethro earlier. She wasn't sure if she should mention anything about it.

"No, I didn't go and find him. Mam said he had gone out. She is going to tell him. I would have told him if he had been there, I wanted to see his face."

"You wouldn't have found him because he was over here," she said, deciding that honesty was the best policy.

"Was he now? What did he want?"

"He came to see if I was alright after yesterday. He also noticed that you had spent the night here and said that we shouldn't be living in sin. I think I might have been a bit rude. Seth, he is such an oddball!"

"Don't worry about it. I'm sorry you are having to deal with him so much. If he bothers you again, then I will sort it out."

"It's ok, I can handle him. I think he means well."

She noticed something moving in the courtyard. A black car drew up and a tall man with blond hair and a gaunt face got out of the car.

Seth saw her looking out of the window and turned to see what had caught her attention. "It's the police."

"How can you tell?"

"Because of the car he is driving. He's probably a detective."

"I wonder what he wants?"

Chapter Twenty

After checking his identity, Jules allowed Detective Inspector Simon Black into the kitchen and offered him a cup of tea. He declined. Seth remained standing, and she could sense that he was feeling uncomfortable being there. He didn't leave and she was grateful. She was feeling anxious herself.

"Are you here because of my brother, Peter Bridgewater?"

"No, it's not about Peter. I wanted to ask your Dad some questions about Ann Bridgewater. I understand that he is in hospital. Is he able to talk to us by phone?"

"He's really sick. I think that he had a breakdown, and he's not really in this world at the moment."

"Oh, I see. I'm sorry to hear that. I don't suppose you know anything about Ann, do you? We are trying to piece together what happened to her. She died around twenty years ago. There was no missing report filed and we have been unable to track down any of her relatives."

"My Mum was her sister. Mum died about five years ago from cancer. My grandparents on her side are both dead. I think there's a relative in Australia but I don't know anything about him. Ann used to live in this house with my uncle but unfortunately, he's dead too. I've got a photo of her if that is any help."

"Yes, that would be good. Unfortunately, we find ourselves with a murder case on our hands. Ann had been struck on the head prior to being dumped in the pond. There is a fracture on her skull. Finding the murderer will be made so much more difficult as so much time has passed. Our forensic research has revealed that Ann had given birth. The Hearns told me about them adopting Jake Bridgewater. Unfortunately, we have no records of that either. Do you, by any chance, have any files or paperwork belonging to Ann or Mark Bridgewater?"

"Yes, there's a load of paperwork in the study. There are boxes and boxes of it. I think that it is mostly farm-related, though."

"Do you mind if I take it with me? It might help."

"Yes, that would be fine. Can I ask you something? Are Ivy and Ann's death related?"

"I think that it is unlikely. Why do you ask?"

"It just seems strange that they should both end up in a deep pool hidden in a copse that very few people know about. Are you going to charge Peter?"

"Peter is currently being questioned. So I am not at liberty to discuss this with you."

"He didn't do it, you know. I would know if he had."

"Sometimes we can be too close to someone to see the truth. Especially if the truth is going to hurt. I know this is a difficult time for you. If someone is out there harming others then we will find them. There is no such thing as the perfect crime – there is always a trail.

"Oh yes, there was something else I was going to ask you. Ann Bridgewater's remains will be released for burial soon. Are you able to cover the burial costs? Unfortunately, it can be quite expensive and it is unlikely that Ann left any funds to cover these costs."

"Oh goodness, I don't think that we could manage that. Things... things are a bit tight at the moment. The farm isn't doing that well."

"I have a proposal. The Hearns have indicated that they would like to cover the costs of a funeral themselves if you are unable to. The state could also bury Ann. Have a think and let me know what you would like to do."

She found the boxes of paperwork and the photo of Ann and watched as Inspector Black filled his boot and then left.

"That was nice of your Mum and Dad. I hadn't thought about having to bury her. I couldn't ask them to pay. It doesn't seem right."

"I told you, Mam was really close to Ann and I know that she would be upset if you don't let them. They can afford it and you are living hand-to-mouth. It would be silly not to accept."

"I guess. I need to ask Peter what he thinks when or if he comes back. Do you think he has been charged?"

"No, I don't, they have nothing but circumstantial evidence. They won't charge him. You'll see, he will be back in a couple of hours."

"I hope you are right."

***

It turned out that Seth was quite the expert when it came to riding Connor. Jules was impressed, and she had never seen her lazy horse look so lively. At times, it was difficult to lead

Barney alongside them and she had to let Seth canter Connor off into the distance.

When they returned home, Connor was sweating so Seth dried him off with an old hand towel and threw his cooler blanket over him. Connor kept looking 'round at his new rider with curiosity.

"He really likes you, you have a way with horses."

"They give me a lot of pleasure. I like working with them. We will have to work out how to get them to Ireland next summer. I am sure May will have room for two more. I'm looking forward to you meeting Moss. He is a bit of a character. I miss him. It's been too long, I hope he remembers me."

"He will. Black Beauty remembered his original owner."

Seth smiled. "He is black, actually! You're a bit of a romantic, aren't you?"

"I like happy endings. Are you…"

"JULES!"

Peter was at the gate. He looked tired, he was unshaven, but he had a smile on his face.

"Oh great, Peter's back! We'd better tell him that you are staying. He might kick off. I doubt whether he will have the energy though."

"We'll see."

They walked down the field together holding hands.

"So they didn't charge you then?" Seth asked. Peter frowned. "Did you think they would?"

"No, he didn't," Jules said, trying to smooth things.

"They can't pin this on me as there is no real proof. I remained silent for most of their questions. I didn't kill her, so

174

there was no point answering endless questions. The baby she was carrying didn't match my DNA." He was glaring at Seth.

"It wasn't mine!" He was starting to get angry. She needed to defuse the situation quickly.

"Dad is doing a bit better. He is taking medication. He was really ill when I went to see him. It was horrible." Both were beginning to relax and turned their attention to her.

"I was going to ask. They wouldn't let me ring anyone, apart from a lawyer. When do you think he will come out of hospital?"

"I think he will be in there for a while. It will take time, everyone keeps telling me."

"How have you been getting on with the milking? Did you manage by yourself?"

"It was too much for me so Seth has been helping. Peter, Seth is going to stay with us for a bit. Until Dad gets back. Call it a working holiday."

"No, it's not going to work. All your crazy family keep walking in shooting people. I just want to have a peaceful life and get things back to normal. I'm wrecked. I need to sleep. We'll talk about it tomorrow."

"Actually, we are in Dad's room."

"For fuck's sake! I'm gone twenty-four hours and you two have taken the farmhouse over. I'm going to bed. It's been a heck of a day. I give up! I'll leave the milking to you two." He stormed off, shaking his head.

"That went well. Nothing like a warm welcome."

"Take no notice of him. He doesn't like change. He can be like an old man at times. Peter will come 'round. He should! You saved his life."

Seth drew her to him and hugged her, he smelt of saddle soap and horse sweat.

The milking went smoothly and Pearl had led the herd down to the milking shed with confidence. Peter hadn't appeared for dinner. She guessed he was probably sound asleep and hoped that he wasn't sulking. She found some frozen broccoli and cauliflower in the freezer and attempted to make Seth a cheese bake. He had looked at her vegetarian meal offering with amusement.

"It looks interesting and smells ok."

"It isn't very exciting, is it? Do you cook?"

"No, not really. I can boil an egg and make toast and that's about it. Jules, don't worry, I am grateful for anything and I will contribute – I have savings. I do need to learn to cook. You'll have to show me how. Mam only taught my sisters how to cook and the boys work the land.

"It has always been that way. Did you see all that food at the engagement party? There was enough there to feed an army. Oh yes, I was going to tell you, next Saturday is Patrick's fortieth birthday. There is going to be a big do at Crow Farm. We will have to go. I will get a chance to dance with you at last."

"That hurly-whirly dance I saw? I could easily make a fool of myself. I'll try my best."

"That's my girl! I will teach you before, if you like. It's easy. The 'Siege of Ennis' is always a popular one. If you pass me your phone then I'll show you a demo on YouTube. It's so annoying not being able to have access to the internet on my own phone. I wonder where I've left it. It wasn't in my room. I will have to tell my supervising officer that I have lost it and also that I have changed my address and my job."

She passed Seth her phone, and he searched for the relevant film clip and then as he ate his dinner she watched it, and she grinned. "That doesn't look too bad but I will probably fall over. Yes, you really need to teach me."

"Ok, after dinner we'll have a little go. That is if I don't keel over first!"

"Dinner's not that bad!" Her portion had ham in it and it made all the difference. She ate her meal, trying not to reveal her dark secret - she couldn't survive without meat.

They had gone to her favourite spot behind the stable yard as there was a flat space large enough for her to learn to dance. Seth had found on YouTube different dances for her to try. She had laughed as she attempted to Irish dance with Seth. It was a bit like country dancing. She had done country dancing at school but that was a long time ago. It took her a few tries to get it right, but she couldn't quite get the foot movement the same and mostly skipped. Seth, she decided, had probably had lessons as a child as he was really good and she found this to be a really attractive quality. It brought out a side of his personality that she had not seen before. Watching him dance was mesmerising – *hot even!*

After at least an hour of training, she needed to rest. She realised how unfit she was and sat on the wall where they had first kissed. She could feel moisture on her skin. The sun had slipped down behind the hill and it was starting to get dark.

"Are you tired? You did well. I think that you will be able to hold your own if you practice every day until the party."

"I'm ok, I'm unfit. I just need a little rest. Where do you get your energy from?"

"It was the cauliflower cheese you made. It obviously had a hidden element."

Alarmed, she thought back to her dishing out the dinner and had to reassure herself that she had given him the correct side of the bake. *Surely he would have said something?*

"I will need to exercise again. Milking isn't physically challenging enough for me. When you work the land, you use every muscle. I will have to set up a circuit around the farm. If that is ok. You can train with me if you like."

"Oh I don't know, that sounds tough. I don't think I would have the strength to do that."

"You need to eat better. You eat like a little bird. I will have to feed you up if you are going to bear my children."

"Christ, it sounds like you are going to turn me into a breeding machine. So do you want children then?"

"Oh, at least fifteen. I don't want to let the Hearns down! No, actually, two will do but not for a few years yet. I am sure there are things you would like to do first."

"Perhaps. I know what I would like to do now and it involves Ed Sheeran. You have heard of him?" She picked up her phone and searched for a song she liked.

"I'm not a complete dinosaur and I do listen to the radio and keep up with the music scene. Even inside, you can listen to music." Seth laughed. "I bet I know which song you are going to choose."

"Go on then."

"It's 'Perfect' isn't it. You want to dance in the dark with me, don't you?"

She smiled playfully. "I might do." She tapped on the YouTube trailer and 'Perfect' began to play.

"Ok then, how can I resist," he said, taking her hand, and then he pulled her to him and slipped the other hand into the small of her back. She placed her free hand on his shoulder. Her heart was already beating hard and she could feel the warmth of his body. Slowly they danced in a circle, swaying gently to the music.

"You're perfect," he whispered into her ear.

***

'So sweet and yet it sickens me to see you act this way. My breath quickens as I watch you dance. Too long I have waited. I will come for you soon, my angel.'

Chapter Twenty-one

Three days passed by seamlessly. Seth and Peter had been carrying out the milking without incident and all was peaceful at Farm End. Seth had even managed to convince him to accept his Mum and Dad's offer to pay for Ann's burial.

Jules started to load up the washing machine; this was her second load of washing going in. She was keeping an eye out for Neal the cow man. Today, he was going to help Peter artificially inseminate the cows, so they would have calves in the early summer. Peter was used to carrying out this task and had actually invited Seth along to help. He was curious to see how it was done but was not going to stick his arm up a cow's bottom for anybody. She smiled to herself. *I will make a dairy farmer of him yet!*

Jules had already hung the first load of washing out to dry and could see them fluttering on the line at the end of the garden. It was a good drying day. The weather was due to change to rain in the evening, and she wanted to get as many clothes as she could dry before Peter went off to visit their Dad. She had packed him some more clothes and had asked Peter to bring his dirty ones back. He had suggested that he go and see him alone as he wanted to concentrate on the long drive. She had rung the Priory, and they had told her that he was improving but had not been taken off suicide watch.

Seth came into the kitchen. His shorts and t-shirt were wet with sweat. He had been working out in the barn. That was a place that she wasn't willing to go to again.

"Seth, do you have any washing? I am going to put a dark wash on in a minute."

"I do but I've got a full load. I'll do it later so don't worry. You can have this if you don't mind?" He pulled off his wet t-shirt and passed it to her. His chest and arms were pumped up and his skin was glowing red. She blushed when she saw him and he noticed.

"I'm sorry, I should warn you if I am going to strip. I know what you're like!"

The truth was that they were limited to just a quick kiss or a cuddle as Peter was in the next room to them.

"It's a good job Peter is around, otherwise I might have lost control. Does it hurt your arms pumping iron? What do you use?"

"I've found spare bits of farm machinery. I just keep lifting them until my muscle fatigues. It doesn't hurt now but might a bit later. I'm just going to have a shower and then I will be down and dressed, I promise. Neal is due soon, isn't he? I won't be long."

Seth disappeared upstairs, and she sighed as she added his top to the washing load. Her body yearned for him all the time since he had come to live with her – and she was finding it difficult to concentrate on daily life. She needed to think of other things and take up a hobby to keep her mind off him twenty-four seven. As she turned on the washing machine, she could picture him in the shower. It was impossible not to.

Jules walked out into the courtyard and she saw Neal draw up in his truck. She wasn't sure where Peter was. She guessed that he was getting cows into stalls in the winter barn. The dogs ran up to Neal to greet him. He loved animals and got down to hug and stroke them both. George and Pip licked his face, glad to see him.

"How are you boys?" he asked, still hugging them. "I've got a treat for them. If it is ok."

"Yes, that's fine. They haven't had any treats since Dad's been away."

"I'm sorry to hear about your Dad. I heard about what happened in the pub. How's he doing?"

"A lot better, thanks. Peter's going to see him later. I think Peter is up at the top cow barn already. I'll open the gate for you. Seth Hearn is going to give you a hand. I say that, but I am not sure if he will be much help." As if on cue, Seth arrived, wearing his overalls and his hair still wet, combed back.

"I'll do my best."

"Morning, Seth. How's your Dad, he's not been in the Gun recently."

"He's fine. It's been busy on the farm. I'm sure you'll see more of him over the winter."

"Do you want a lift, Seth? You can open the gate and save Jules' legs."

"Ok, no problem."

Seth gave her a quick side hug and kiss on the top of her head and climbed into Neal's truck. The dogs looked like they wanted to go too.

"Don't you two worry, we'll go for a walk when the washing's done." They wagged their tails hearing the word walk and followed her back into the kitchen.

As soon as she opened the gate to the cow field, George and Pip shot through and raced like greyhounds to the top of the field towards the cowshed, eager to find Neal.

She looked up at the sky apprehensively, there were rain clouds forming already. The field was covered in cow-pats. *I'm glad I don't have to scoop it up.* The farm had a machine to collect the dung and it was used to fertilize the arable land. She could see Neal's truck in the distance, and she hoped that the dogs were not getting in his way.

When she reached the shed, Seth was holding on to the dogs' collars. "These two nearly got kicked by Pearl. I don't think that she is keen on being done. Neal explained how he does the insemination and it sounds straightforward, but I'm not confident enough to insert either my hand or the gun into them. I would be scared of hurting them. It's quite a delicate process. It's also a messy one. You have to empty their bowels first. I respect Neal and your brother for their courage. I'd rather be ploughing a field."

"Don't worry, I wouldn't want to do it either. Do you want to walk the dogs with me?"

"I think I better stay and give them both moral support. They've only got another forty cows each to go! I'll see you at lunchtime. I'll make lunch. Are cheese sandwiches ok?"

She smiled. "Yes, cheese is fine. I'm going to explore the farmland up there." She pointed to a hill ahead. "I've never been this far before, I hope I don't get lost."

"If you're not back by dark, I'll send out a rescue team."

"Don't! I've got a terrible sense of direction, you might well have to. I used to get lost at school and be sitting in the wrong classroom wondering why nobody else was there."

"You do have your phone with you, don't you?" Seth was starting to look worried.

"Yes, it's in my pocket. I'll ring Peter if I get lost."

"I would give you a farewell hug, only these overalls have been splattered in shite. I've smelt better."

She laughed and blew him a kiss as she made her way to the top gate. Seth released the dogs, and they decided to follow her, eager to visit a new corner of the farm. She followed a narrow track between fields and wasn't sure if she was still on her land or the Hearns. The track was quite steep and was leading up to a hilltop - not the one she knew. It was nearly as high as Seth's hill and had a good view of Farm End. She was getting used to the farming life and thought it was a shame that the house and business were on the market.

She was pleased that the dogs were getting some much-needed exercise. This was a good workout for her too, and she started to power walk up the hill to work her muscles. She was nearly at the top of the hill when she noticed angry black clouds in the sky. A raindrop hit her bare arm and she shivered. She hadn't brought a coat, and not wanting to get drenched decided to go back home. She called the dogs to come to her and started to walk back down the track, hoping it would lead her to more familiar territory.

A pheasant ran out in front of her, and she watched it run down the track and then seeing the dogs, it diverted through the hedgerow back into the field it had just left. *Pheasants are the most stupid birds around!*

Jules saw something move further down the track. She tried to focus on the blue shape and work out who or what it was. There was a large oak tree on the right-hand side, and she was sure that she could see someone stood by it, wearing blue overalls. *Is it Seth?* The tree was hiding most of his body, and she thought that she might be mistaking some plastic caught on the tree for a person. Whatever she was seeing, it was making her feel nervous. Raindrops were falling more rapidly now, and she shivered again and was starting to feel chilly. To warm herself up and to get past the tree as quickly as possible, she started to run. If it was a person, then it was probably one of the Hearn's seasonal workers, having a cigarette.

She ran steadily towards the tree, her heart was starting to beat hard in her chest. She couldn't see the blue plastic or person anymore. The dogs ran with her and were not upset by anything. *This is a good sign.* If the dogs were not worried then she needn't be worried either.

Jules ran by the oak tree and turned back to check that whoever it was had gone. There was nobody there. Pip stood by her. George suddenly seemed interested in the tree and walked over to it. She waited patiently for him to finish sniffing and called him as the rain was making her feel really cold.

"George, come on. We're getting wet. Home!"
The dog paid no attention and stayed by the tree, his sniffing 'round complete. She started to walk towards the dog and getting hold of his collar pulled him away. George ran towards Pip and waited for her to join him.

"I'm coming…" She heard someone or something move. A man's hand went over her mouth and with his other arm, he slammed her backwards into his body. In fright, she screamed but his hand only released a squeal. She couldn't see him, but she could smell his sweat and stale cigarettes on his breath. She scanned the lane and field for anyone that could help her. There was nobody around.

"I have waited a long time for you."

She could barely hear what he was saying and his words sounded like he was talking below water. Her heart was hurting as it beat. She was petrified and wriggled desperately, trying to free herself from his grasp. She kept kicking back at him with her heels. *I'm trapped!*

"Hold still, my angel." His lips kissed her neck, and she strained to pull away from his wet mouth. His teeth grazed her skin as he worked his way down her neck. She was really frightened. He pushed his groin into her. *Please don't rape me!* With great force, she rammed her elbows into his stomach, and she knew that she had hurt him. He yelled and then bit hard into her neck and took out a small chunk of flesh. She shrieked out in pain, and furious, kicked back again.

The dogs started barking and then George leapt up at the man, and he roared out as the dog's sharp teeth clamped onto his arm. Her attacker's hold on her loosened, and she broke free. She felt a hand try to grab hold of her again, but she dodged it and began to run, hoping and praying that he wouldn't give chase. George seeing her run had let go of him and ran with her and Pip down the track.

When she was far enough away, she looked back to see if the man was following. He had slid away and was nowhere to be seen. Fear had been replaced with anger. She was angry with herself for going near that tree and angry at the world for allowing predators to prey on women. She kept on running, determined not to stop until she reached the end of the track. Her neck was bleeding and blood was pouring down onto her white t-shirt. *I mustn't look at the blood.*

When she reached the end of the track, she realised that she was behind the Hearn's garden. She noticed a wooden gate within the hedge. She could also see the roof of Jake and Mark's caravan above the hedge line. The only way she could get to the lane that led home was to go through their garden. She didn't want to go back up the track. She would never go there again.

Jules opened the gate and walked into the garden with the dogs. They stayed by her side, sensing her unease. She could smell the scent of roses as the rain beat down on their petals. Yellow roses were growing up the trellis which was hiding the caravan from view. She hoped that she wouldn't be seen as it was going to be difficult to explain what had happened to her. *What had just happened?* She felt emotionless and detached from the incident. The garden was quiet, and she was so relieved that she had made it down the track in one piece. Her neck throbbed, but she tried not to think about it. The rain was helping to keep her cool; she was sweating from all the running she had done. *Or was it from fear?* She didn't know.

"Jules?"

Her heart jumped, her tranquil moment had been shattered. She looked around. Someone had called out her name. Jake appeared below the arch between the trellis. He was wearing a blue overall, and she shuddered when she saw him. *Why aren't you working in the fields? Was it you?* He smiled and walked over to her. She held her breath and was ready to fight him off or just run. She hadn't decided. He gave her a friendly smile – she had not expected that. It was strange to see him sober; it was like meeting an old friend again. He gasped when he saw her neck and her blood-drenched t-shirt. "Jesus! What's happened to you?"

"I..." She was feeling dizzy. "Someone jumped me up there," she replied, pointing towards the track. "I need to sit down." *I'm going to faint.*

"I'll get you a chair and I'll get Mum." He didn't say 'Mam' like Seth did. He ran off and came back with a wet garden chair. She sat down heavily in it and then put her head between her knees and tried to breathe properly.

It only seemed like seconds ago that she had spoken to Jake, and yet he and Margaret were standing there, talking to her. She couldn't think how they had got to her so quickly. Margaret was asking her if she was ok to walk to the kitchen. She nodded, she had recovered sufficiently. *I must have passed out for a few seconds.*

"Yes, I think I can walk."

Margaret held her arm and walked with her, she'd forgotten where they were taking her.

The kitchen smelt of bread and three loaves sat on the side to cool. *A day's bread perhaps?* Jules was helped to a kitchen chair and she sat down. She had made it, but only just.

After asking where Seth was, Margaret sent Jake off to get him. Jake didn't complain and did as he was told. She hoped that he and Seth wouldn't argue. She looked up and suddenly realised that one of Margaret's daughters was in the kitchen also, and she was looking in a cupboard for something. Jules hadn't noticed her before. Margaret had put the kettle on and was looking worried.

"I'm sorry, Margaret, I'm being such a nuisance. I should be ok to get home; I need to clean myself up."

"Nonsense. Jake told us that someone attacked you on the hill track. Charlene is going to clean up your wound. How did you get that?"

"The bastard bit me! I'm sorry, I didn't mean to use a bad word."

"It's ok. You poor girl. Do you know who did this to you?"

"I don't know, he came up behind me and pulled me back. I didn't see his face. He smelt bad. I think he was wearing blue overalls. He'll have teeth marks in his arm. The dog bit him. I think George saved my life."

Margaret looked frightened.

"I need to call the police. Don't I?"

"Charlene, where's Dad?"

"I think he's in the office, Mam, with Patrick. Shall I go and get him?"

"No, I'll go. You take care of Jules. She's still bleeding and she might need stitches. See what you think." Margaret left the kitchen and looked back at her with concern.

Charlene smiled at her. She was a pretty woman, perhaps in her late twenties and had an Irish accent like her mother's. Charlene had long dark hair and the same dark brown eyes as Seth. She brought a green medical box over to her and took from the box a tub. She pulled a chair beside her and pulled from the tub a length of wipes.

"Jules, sweetie, this is going to hurt. You've gone very white. Are you feeling ok?"

"Not that great. I can't deal with blood and I'm feeling a bit shocked. Should I call the police?"

Charlene's smile slipped away. "I expect Patrick will deal with this. It was probably one of our foreign workers that did this. We don't check to see if they have a record. If your dog bit him then Patrick will find him and send him packing."

Charlene started to clean the wound and Jules took a sharp intake of breath as the antiseptic stung her.

"Sorry, sweetie, it will stop hurting in a minute. I don't think he's hit an artery or the muscle. It looks like there's some skin missing and some flesh too. I can see his teeth marks. You poor love. It's starting to clot now. I don't think you need stitches. Have you had a tetanus injection recently?"

"About five years ago when I cut my hand on a rusty nail."

"I would go and get a booster, you might be able to get one at a pharmacy. It's better to be safe than sorry."

"Are you a doctor?"

"I used to be a nurse but now I have three children to care for. I look after all the medical emergencies here. You'd be surprised how many accidents happen on a farm. They all keep me very busy."

Jules smiled at Charlene, she liked her very much. She had a kind soul. "Thanks, Charlene, for helping me. I'm feeling a bit better. Is it ok if I get a glass of water?"

"Don't move for a while. I'll get you one. I am going to put some antiseptic on the wound and then a dressing. You'll need to change the dressing every day and not get it wet. If the skin around the wound starts to get red and angry, then you will need to go to the doctors for some antibiotics."

Charlene got up to get her a glass of water and Jules heard the kitchen door open. Seth came into the kitchen and sat on the chair next to her. His eyes were wide with concern, and she could see that he was distressed. He took her hand and inspected the wound with a look of horror on his face.

"I'm ok, Seth. Charlene thinks that I'll live." She tried to make light of the situation, not wanting to make him any more anxious.

"I shouldn't have let you go out there by yourself. Fuck!"

"Really, Seth, I am ok. I didn't see who attacked me. The dog bit him hard and he let go of me. Charlene thinks it might be one of your workers." She wished she hadn't said anything. Seth stood up and looked furious. She could see that he was about to go out there and find him.

"Seth, sit down!" commanded Charlene. "Patrick will sort this one out. You will only make things worse if you go after him."

"Please Seth, don't do anything stupid. George bit him, and he will have teeth marks in his arm. Patrick will find him. Where are the dogs?" She hadn't seen them since she entered the garden.

Seth sighed and shook his head and sat down. "I just don't like to see you like this. The dogs are under the garden table keeping out of the rain." He looked at her t-shirt. "You are in such a mess. My poor beautiful girl."

Charlene gave her a glass of water and then started to dress the wound. Margaret, Jethro and Patrick came into the kitchen. Jethro frowned when he saw Seth and Patrick's eyes narrowed. "Look who's here! It's dairy farm boy! You've given me a right headache this week. Thanks to you, we are forty man-hours short!"

Margaret tutted. "Patrick, give the boy a rest. You've got plenty of help this year."

Seth just scowled at him. Jules could see that Seth was ready to blow. She couldn't help but stare at Patrick, amazed by what she saw. He was so like Seth but just looked a few years older than him and grey hairs ran through his thick, almost black, hair. He was, however, she thought, a meaner version of him. Her gaze turned to Jethro. He was stood at the back of the kitchen watching her. He was looking stressed and ran his fingers through his white hair. She realised that Margaret and he had a full-time job on their hands stopping their children from fighting.

Charlene finished applying the dressing and then looked up at Patrick. "You're wasting time, Pat. You need to go up the track at the back of the house and see if that bastard is still there. If it's not one of the workers, then this attack will need reporting. There's a psycho on the loose and this needs sorting now." She turned to Seth. "You need to get Jules home. She could go into shock. You'll need to keep an eye on her. In fact, don't leave her side for twenty-four hours. Do you hear me, Sebastian?"

"Of course, Charlene. Jules, are you ok to walk back?" he asked, looking into her eyes and then held the side of her face.

She nodded and was starting to feel embarrassed that she was causing so much trouble.

"I'll carry you."

She smiled. "No, you're alright, I will be fine to walk." She got up slowly and made sure her head didn't spin. The bite on her neck was sore, but she felt much better now it was covered up and had stopped bleeding. She really didn't want to faint in front of everyone.

They walked back home holding hands and Seth kept looking at her to make sure she was ok. "You look so pale. You are light as a feather. I'd feel better if I carried you."

"I can make it. My mind is racing, it is all just starting to sink in. Seth, this wasn't just a random attack. This man has been following me for some time. I just know it. It was something he said. I can't remember what it was. I'm scared, Seth. You mustn't ever leave me alone or he will get me."

"I promise. I won't ever leave your side," he said, squeezing her hand.

***

'I didn't mean to hurt you. Your blood is sweet. It is proof enough that my angel lives and breathes. You have returned to me.'

Chapter Twenty-two

The kettle was boiling furiously and Jules watched the steam puffing out of the spout with fascination. She was feeling cold and shivered. *Is the kitchen door open? No, it's not.* She could hear the rain beating down and she could see the raindrops hitting the window. The rain bothered her. There was something she needed to do. Something was out in the rain and shouldn't have been, but she couldn't remember what it was.

"Jules?"

She wasn't alone in the kitchen. There were others sat with her around her kitchen table. She was sure that she had been sat at another table only minutes ago.

"Jules, look at me?"

She turned her head, following the sound of the voice and her eyes met with Seth's brown eyes. *Such lovely eyes.* Why was he looking so worried? She felt his hand on hers; his hand, warm against her cold hand.

"Are you ok?"

She knew she had to answer that, but she couldn't put her reply into words. *I haven't been ok for a long time. Why was that?* She could hear a clock ticking somewhere. *Or is it coming from inside me?*

"No," she replied, trying to focus on his face. She didn't want him to worry. *My poor Seth.* "I am so, so cold."

Strong arms lifted her up and carried her through to the lounge. She felt herself being placed on the sofa and covered with something warm. Her skin felt clammy and wet. *Have I been in the rain?* She would sleep now or just close her eyes for a few minutes until she warmed up. *I will dream now, if I can.*

Jules was feeling hot and thirsty, the bed covers were tucked in too tightly around her body. She didn't remember them being this tight and so constricting. She didn't remember coming to bed. The covers were wet, and yet they didn't cool her burning body. *It's summer, I shouldn't have so many covers on me.* She needed to pull them off of her, but she didn't have the strength. *I will have to tell someone.* She would wake Seth, he would help her.

Jules sat up and looked around the room. The furniture looked unfamiliar. *Am I in my own house?* It was no wonder that the covers were different. *Where am I?* She tried to roll over to wake Seth but all she could move was her head. There was a dark figure lying next to her. *Who are you?* She could smell him and hear his rasping voice, saying he was coming for her. "NO, LEAVE ME ALONE! DON'T TOUCH ME!" The figure rose from the bed, his arms wrapping around her. She screamed out in terror.

"It's Seth, Jules! You're ok. It's me. You're dreaming. You're ok. Lie down and rest. It really is just me."

Her heart was beating hard, and she was crying from fear. The figure had gone, and she could see Seth's face over hers, feel his arms around her and smell his sweet body. She started to cry happy tears. *It's just Seth, my lovely Seth. Just a nightmare.* He hugged her, kissing her forehead and wiped away her tears with his hand.

"You're ok, just sleep. Your body is in shock."

***

Jules opened her eyes, she was in a strange room. Closing and opening them again did not change anything; the room remained the same, clinical and white. A mask was over her face, and then she noticed that the back of her hand had a cannula inserted into it and a clear tube was attached to that. *I'm in a hospital. How did I get here?* Her head ached and so did her neck. She remembered having her wound dressed by Charlene but nothing after that. She did, however, remember seeing Peter, Charlene and Seth standing by her bed in the night, looking worried and whispering to each other. *Why were they so worried?*

She carefully sat up. Her head was really hurting but other than that she felt like she was back to normal. *Did I manage to fight off the flu?* Seth was asleep next to her. He was sat on a chair and was sleeping on folded arms on her bed. Relieved to see him there, she took off the mask and stroked his hair and face. His face was showing dark stubble but she liked it. She hadn't noticed it before, but he had long, dark eyelashes. There was no doubting it, Seth was adorable. She was lucky to have him in her life.

Feeling her hand on his face, Seth opened his eyes and smiled. He sat up and stretched. "You're looking a lot better. You really scared me, Jules. I thought I was going to lose you. They nearly put you on a ventilator at one point. You didn't get sepsis though, you were lucky."

Her mind flashed back to seeing a machine breathing for her Dad, and she flinched. "What happened to me? I thought I just fainted or had the flu."

"You went into shock. Your body wasn't getting enough oxygen. I got Charlene to come over last night, and she called an ambulance for you. Do you remember being in an ambulance?"

"No, not at all. All I remember is you, Charlene and Peter by my bed. I feel ok now. I've just got a bit of a headache. I think I dreamed a lot."

"You had a fever. You were delirious, Jules. I did my best to calm you."

"Thank you for looking after me."

"How could I not? Are you hungry? You need to eat. I can't remember the last time you had something to eat. You need to stay strong."

"I'm ok, just thirsty. I promise I will eat something later."

Seth, still looking concerned, stood up, poured her a glass of water and passed it to her. She drank it, enjoying the cool liquid slipping down her dry throat. "How are we going to get home? I really am ok now."

"We'll see how you are and if the hospital thinks it's ok to go home, then Charlene said she will pick us up if it is not too late. We'll get a taxi if she's not free."

"Seth?"

"Yes."

"I love you."

"I love you too."

At lunchtime, Charlene met them in the car park. She was driving a brand new Range Rover. Seth opened the rear passenger door for her. Jules got in and he pulled the seat belt across her and clicked it in. Even though she knew he had been up for most of the night, he smelt so fresh and not like that awful man. She blocked that memory and instead thought of her happy place behind the stables.

"How are you feeling, sweetie?" Charlene asked.
Jules smiled, she loved hearing her voice. Her Irish accent was like a gentle breeze. "I'm ok, just a bit wobbly. Seth told me you came over last night to see me and called an ambulance. Thank you."

Seth climbed into the front passenger seat and closed the door. He looked back at Jules and smiled at her. "Thanks, Charlene, for picking us up. She's on the mend, but she's not eaten since the day before yesterday. I need to feed the little bird. Can we stop at a supermarket, please? I need to get some supplies."

She and Charlene waited in the Waitrose car park while Seth went in to get her a sandwich. She guessed it would be a cheese one. "He worries about me too much. I really am ok."

"Seth has a kind heart. He would do anything for you. You know he is smitten with you, don't you?"

"Your Dad doesn't seem too keen on us being together. He has warned me off him a couple of times."

"He is just a bit old-fashioned. He just likes things done his way."

"I don't think he likes Seth very much."

"Seth isn't like the other Hearn boys. That's why Dad gives him such a hard time. You should have heard the uproar when Seth went travelling. You'd think he had deserted the army."

"Do you like living at Crow Farm? Wouldn't you prefer to live elsewhere with your family?"

"I guess it is convenient for my husband Joe to live where he works, and we're not charged rent. Joe keeps himself to himself but he's had a few run-ins with Mam. Mam likes us all to be near her. It is what the Hearns do. When we moved over from Ireland in the nineties, Mam and Dad bought enough land to house us all. We had all lived in the same village near Dingle and so living on the farm together was not much different. Seth and I are only a year apart. A lot of people thought we were twins. We grew up thinking we were. Out of all my siblings, he is my favourite."

"Your accent is stronger than Seth's."

"He didn't really speak much to anybody until he went to school. He was the only Irish boy in the class here, so I guess he lost his accent trying to fit in with the others."

"I didn't think you would go to school. I thought you all would have been home taught."

Charlene laughed. "Most of the time we are just normal people, living normal lives." Charlene paused for a moment as she thought of something. "I guess I spent more time in Ireland than Seth. When I was thirteen, Mam and Dad sent me back to Dingle to stay with my grandparents for a while. I was a bit of a rebel back then and liked the boys a bit too much." She laughed again. "I had lots of boyfriends in Ireland too. I met Joe there."

"Seth wants to live near Cork. Do you have family there?"

"No, I don't think so. He has a good friend in Waterfall and she looks after his horse. He'll take you there, to be sure."

"Yes, I'd like that."

"Seth dotes on you. He'll be good to you, Jules. You are meant for each other."

Seth returned, carrying their lunch in his arms. He passed Jules a ham sandwich and some crisps and winked. "I know you like ham. Is it ok if we eat in your car, Charlene? Did Dad give you and Joe this car?"

"That's fine. The car, yes, he did. I told him we didn't need anything so big, but he insisted. You know what Dad is like."

Seth gave Charlene a chocolate bar. "I know you like this too! Thanks for picking us up."

"You didn't have to buy me chocolate, Seth Hearn! You know I would do anything for you."

"I know."

When Charlene dropped them off at Farm End, Seth's Dad walked into the courtyard.

"Oh God," whispered Seth. "What does he want now?"

"I was out for a walk and thought I'd stop by and see if you were back from the hospital. It was a shock for us all, you poor girl. Such a terrible thing to happen. How are you doing?"

"I'm doing ok, thank you."

"Dad, did you find out who attacked her?"

Jethro shook his head. "We went up the track to hunt the bugger down but there was no sign of him. Patrick checked every worker for bite marks but all were clean. The trouble maker, Josef, wasn't around yesterday. I'd place a bet on him as being our man. Patrick is looking for him."

"I don't think Josef is the one. He can be a bit mouthy, but he is no maniac. He just doesn't like being told what to do."

"We'll see. I just want to do everything we can to sort out this dreadful matter." He looked at her with concern. "You have no colour in your face. Take the child into the house, Seth, before she falls down again."

"I'm not going to let that happen."

"There is one thing, Jules, if it is ok with you. I'd like your aunt Ann to be buried here on your farm. It only seems right that she should remain here on the land that she loved."

"I don't know if you can do that. Won't she need to go to a cemetery?"

"Jules, the farm is the right place for her. I've run the idea past Peter earlier, and he agrees. You don't have to worry about a thing, Margaret and I will take care of everything. Even the wake. It's best to have it at ours, we have the space. It will give Margaret a good excuse to cook and will make her happy."

"If you're sure. That's very kind of you both. I will let the police know. Is it ok if I give DI Simon Black your number?"

"Of course, my angel."

"Dad, we're going to rest now."

"You do that, boy, and make sure that is all you do!"

As they walked into the kitchen, Peter appeared from the study, holding a pile of bills, and he set them down on the table and peered out of the kitchen window. "Has he gone?"

Seth's eyes narrowed. "He's gone, thank God! He has to throw a punch just as he is leaving. He does my head in!"

"I don't think he knows he does it." She was feeling weak.

"He does, believe me, he does." Seth pulled out a chair for her to sit down, and then checking to see if there was any water in the kettle flicked on the switch.

Peter sat down too, next to her. He held her hand. Jules was surprised, she couldn't remember him doing that, ever. Peter seeing her disbelief withdrew it. "You gave us all a bit of a scare. I was so relieved when Seth rang me this morning to say you had made it through the night."

"I used your phone, Jules. I'm still looking for mine."

"That's ok. I really didn't think I was that bad."

"Take it from me, you were not good."

"I'm fine now. Just a little bit tired."

"Do you want tea, Peter?" Seth asked.

"Yes, please, two sugars."

"So Seth, your Dad said that they hadn't found this freak. Isn't it time to call the police?"

She knew that he was talking sense. *But it doesn't work like that at Crow Farm.* "I'll give Jethro and Patrick a chance to find him and then I will call the police tomorrow."

"Mm… that seems a bit odd. I guess you have to do what you think is right. Did your Dad tell you and Jules about the home funeral? I said yes in the end; I didn't have much choice. If you look at the bills," he said, pressing his hand down on the pile, "then there is no way we could afford to bury her ourselves. I don't think our Dad will mind. Do you want to know where they want to bury her?"

"No, where?"

"Next to the pool, where they found her. It's a bit weird, don't you think?"

Seth sighed. "You haven't heard about the family tradition then?"

"Don't tell me that you own a home cemetery?" she asked.

"Kind of. There are several members of our family buried around the farm. There's no law against it. If you want to bury a family member on your land, then you can."

"Seriously?"

"I think Mam and Dad believe that you should become part of the land you were raised on. It's to offer nature something in return for providing you with food and water. Dust to dust and all that."

Seth handed her and Peter their tea and sat down next to her. "I lost a brother when I was small. He had a weak heart. David is buried up on the hill I took you to. I think you will find the planting ceremony interesting. I've never forgotten it."

"It would give me the creeps having bodies decaying nearby," Peter said, starting to arrange the bills in order.

"So why did you agree to Ann being buried by the pool?" she asked.

"I don't know, I just didn't want to upset Jethro or Margaret. Ann will be just bones, it won't be the same… Seth, are you all pagans, then?"

Seth laughed. "I wouldn't say that. Most of my family believe in God. I think back in history, the Hearns were God-fearing Catholics. Over time their beliefs have evolved and now Mother Nature rules their lives. Me, I'm just a free spirit trying to make his way in life and doing my best to be kind to others when I can."

She took a sip of tea. "That's sweet."

"Is it? I sound like a freak now!"

"No, you don't. The tea is really sweet. How many spoonfuls did you put in?"

Seth smiled. "Maybe one more than usual. I'm trying to put some colour back in your cheeks."

"Jules, I was going to tell you, Dad's got a bed at Worthing Mental Health Hospital. He was moved there yesterday. It's a good job I didn't go up to London as it would have been a wasted journey."

"Didn't they ring you first?"

"No, the bed was only being held for a couple of hours, so they just rushed Dad down there in a taxi. They did ring me when they got to Worthing but I missed the call. I rang them back this morning."

"How is he? I want to see him."

"They are still watching him, but he is improving."

"Can we go and see him tomorrow? He probably needs some more clothes. Oh, the washing! It's still on the line."

"Yes, of course, if you are up to seeing him."

"I should be. Seth, I am really tired. You must be too. I'm going upstairs to sleep for a bit."

"I'll get the washing. Seth, would you be ok to help with the milking later - it's hard work on your own," asked Peter.

"Yes, no problem. Jules, you will have to come too. I don't want to leave you on your own. Not at the moment."

"I just need a couple of hours. You need to sleep too, Seth. You're looking tired."

"I'll be along in a minute. I just need to shower."

Chapter Twenty-three

Meadowfield Hospital was only a ten-minute drive from Farm End, and as Jules and Peter drove into the car park she sent a text message to Seth to say that they had managed to get to the hospital without incident. Grey rain clouds had gathered over the hospital complex, daring them to enter into the buildings. She stared at the screen for a moment, hoping that he would reply to her message and then remembered that he had lost his phone. *How stupid to send him a message.*

Jules had seen the pain in Seth's eyes when she had said that it was better if he stayed at home. He had protested as he really didn't want to be parted from her. He didn't say, but she knew that he was worried that she might be attacked again. She tried to believe that it had been a one-off incident and whoever it was that had grabbed her had been caught. A small voice in her head told her to be cautious. *Bastards like that did not get caught easily.* She had promised faithfully that she would stay with Peter and not go anywhere on her own. She had asked Seth if he would exercise Connor, and he had smiled weakly at her, realising that she was trying to occupy him while she was out.

"You're looking a lot better today, Jules. Does the wound on your neck still hurt? asked Peter. "I can't believe that anyone could do such a thing."

"It throbs occasionally. I'm trying not to think about it. They changed the dressing at the hospital and gave me a tetanus boost, so I should be ok. Do you know what ward Dad is on? This doesn't really look like a hospital; it reminds me of a primary school."

"Do you think so? They told me but I can't remember. We will ask at reception. Are you ready?"

"Yes, ready as I'll ever be. I think you will be shocked when you see him. He's probably got a full beard by now. I hope he's stopped crying. I think we are going to find this hard. Peter, please don't tell him what happened to me yesterday."

"No, silly. That would just send him over the edge again."

"If he asks about the dressing, then I am going to tell him that it is an infected mosquito bite."

They found their Dad sat in a communal room with others, all looking equally depressed. When they had walked into the hospital wing, they had been welcomed by a jubilant woman that told them that she was going home soon. She was hoping that she would be allowed to visit her baby. Her baby had been taken into care. The woman's name turned out to be Julia too. A member of staff asked her to leave them alone and come and get her medication.

There was a vast difference between the Priory and Meadowfield. She found it quite difficult to be in such close proximity to so many patients that were clearly very ill. She felt guilty for feeling like that.

Their Dad was sat in an armchair in the middle of the room. He had his book on his lap but was just staring into space in deep thought. She was pleased to see that he had shaved and changed his clothes. He looked a little better. She touched him on the shoulder.

"Dad, it's me and Peter. How are you doing?"

He smiled. "I'm glad you're here. I want to go home. They're all a bit mad in this hospital."

She looked around her, hoping nobody had heard him and had taken offence.

Peter sat down next to him. "Do you know why you are here?"

"Depression isn't a crime! I shouldn't be locked up in here."

"Dad, you did something really bad to yourself. Do you remember?" Peter asked.

I wouldn't have asked him that!

"No, not really. I remember bits when I try to sleep. I think the tablets they give me affect my mind. I feel so tired all the time. Shall I pack?"

Peter looked at Jules with concern. "Dad, you are still being assessed. When they have finished all their tests and if they think you are well enough, then I'm sure they will let you come home. Jules and I have been running the farm ok. I've been looking at the accounts and think I have found a way to make the farm run better and make money. There is really nothing for you to worry about."

She was pleased that Peter was talking to him. He was doing much better than she had.

"How's my little kitten?" he asked, taking her hand. She pulled up a chair and sat next to him. He held onto her hand.

"She's fine. I've been taking Connor out a bit more and have done a bit more milking too. Pearl has become the matriarch now and leads the others."

"There is something I was going to ask you both but I can't remember what it was. It's got something to do with the barn. I can't think what it was. It will come to me, I suppose."

She looked at Peter with alarm. Any minute he would remember hanging himself. She needed to change the subject. "Dad, where's your room. I need to take your washing back. I have some clean clothes in this bag for you."

"See that door there," he said, pointing. "That's my room. I always have to keep the door open, in case I harm myself. I don't know why they think that."

"Do you want to harm yourself?" Peter asked.

Their Dad looked really sad for a moment and a tear rolled down his cheek. "Sometimes?"

She took a deep breath, hoping she wasn't going to ask something he didn't know how to answer.

"Why, Dad?"

"There are a few reasons. I miss your Mum, the fear of turning fifty-eight. I know that sounds crazy and I despise myself for sinking so low and not wanting to see the sunrise. And of course, there was Ivy. Beautiful, dead Ivy. I feel such a terrible sorrow. The guilt eats into your soul." He sighed and the tears were starting to run down his cheeks.

"Dad, how do you know Ivy?" Peter asked. She could see that he looked traumatised, and they were about to hear something awful.

"You might as well know. I can't keep this inside me anymore. I came across Ivy in our hay barn a few months ago. I didn't expect to see her there. She was crying and said that she had been dumped by Jake. I told her that she would find someone else and that she was young and beautiful and had her life in front of her. We talked for ages and then... I am ashamed of myself for allowing it to happen but it did. Maybe that is why I was trying to remember the barn. It meant nothing and for a moment I forgot your mother and was young again. I guess I was flattered that a girl so young would find me attractive and want me... I could have helped her."

She was shocked and saw that Peter was about to cry or fly into a rage. She'd never seen him so emotional before. He was about to lose the plot. She tried to stay calm but she felt appalled. "Dad, Ivy was three months pregnant. Do you think it was yours?"

Her Dad shook his head. "No, it can't be mine. I had the snip years ago."

She could see Peter was about to yell. "Peter, go and get Dad's washing. I think you need some fresh air, don't you?"

Peter shook his head and picked up her bag and stormed off.

"He's cross with me. I am a monster!"

"No, Dad, he is just upset. He has been seeing Ivy for a while now, and he thought the baby was his. God knows who the father is! He is upset that she is dead. You know that she drowned in the pond, don't you?"

"I remember now. I remember seeing her on the night she died. She came to our house before dawn. I was up early as usual – I don't sleep much. She was quite drunk and wanted to come into the house. She wanted to see Peter and not me. I was jealous, I think. I told her to go home. She staggered out of the courtyard and I really should have helped her home. If I had helped her back then maybe..." He was crying again.

"Dad, it's ok. We don't know why she chose to go to the silent pool. She drank too much and if it didn't happen on that night then it could have happened on another. You can't blame yourself. It is not your fault."

"I tell myself that over and over but I can't let it go. Voices in my head taunt me. Maybe I should stay at the hospital a bit longer. The voices are driving me mad. You will come back and see me, won't you, kitten? You don't think I am a monster, do you?"

"No, Dad, of course not!" She was on the verge of tears herself. "They will help you here. You have to promise you will let them."

Peter returned with a few clothes in his bag. "We'd better go, Jules. I've got a few things to do around the farm."

"Peter, I'm sorry. I'm just a stupid old man. Why didn't you tell me about you and Ivy? I didn't know."

"It's ok, Dad. Just get better."

"I'll try. I'm just a stupid old man."

The car ride back to Farm End had been a quiet one. Peter was really upset, and she wanted to tell him that everything would be ok, but she couldn't think of the right words to say. All their lives had been altered dramatically and sometimes she hardly recognised herself.

He stopped the car and looked at her. She realised by the look on his face that he had something bad to tell her. "Jules, I've reported your attack to the police. I did it online yesterday. It is only right. The attack or those Hearns have addled your mind. They act like they are the mafia and are above the law. If there is a maniac out there then he needs to be caught. Others could suffer at his hands or worse. You know this had to be done. I know you wouldn't go to the police yourself. I gave them your number, so I guess they will be in touch. Are you mad with me?"

She shook her head. "No, you were right to do that. I should have reported it. God, Jethro and Patrick are going to be really mad with me!"

"What about Seth? Will he be cross with you? I'll tell him where to go if he is."

"No, he's had enough of his family." *I hope he won't be cross.*

When Jules got to the kitchen door she noticed that a large bunch of red roses had been let on the doorstep. She liked surprises. "Oh, they're for me," she exclaimed, smiling as she read the label. "Seth must have got..." Then she saw the words. '*I have waited a long time for you.*' She screamed out loud, dropping them on the floor. "They are not from Seth. Oh Peter, they are from the man that attacked me. I remember him saying this." She passed the card to him. He took the card, just holding the card on its edge and reading the words. He looked worried. "Jules, this could be evidence. It could have fingerprints on it."

Icy chills ran up and down her spine, and she scanned the area to check nobody was lurking nearby and fled into the kitchen. Peter followed. "Can you find a box or something to keep these in? I don't want to see them again. I will call the police, I don't want to go down to that police station again. They will come here, won't they?"

"I am sure they will."

The kitchen was quiet and there was no sign of Seth. "SETH," she called out, hoping he would appear. "He must still be out with Connor. Peter, will you stay with me until Seth gets back. I don't want to be by myself. Peter, I'm scared."

"I won't leave you, I promise."

She found her phone and decided to call the police straight away. She pulled out Inspector Simon Black's card from her phone cover and hoped he wouldn't make her go through a different channel to report the incident. She had to speak to him anyway about releasing Ann's body to the Hearns.

Is this a bad idea? Simon was out of the office, so she left him a message to call her back.

Peter couldn't find a box, so he put the roses and the card in a dustbin sack and shut them in a cupboard. She couldn't bear to watch him doing this. The roses sickened her and the thought of her attacker knowing where she lived and what door they all used to enter the farmhouse was creeping her out. *Had he ever been into the house? Was he there now?* She trembled. Seth needed to come back soon. She needed him to calm her. She was starting to lose her mind with worry.

Seth walked in the kitchen and looked hot, he was wearing his riding gear and had on a black rain jacket which he took off and hung on the back of a chair. *So you do have a coat!* He had a big smile on his face and had obviously enjoyed his time with Connor.

"You know your horse is quite a charger, he took off in the top field." He then saw her face and realised something was wrong. "Jules, are you ok?"

She shook her head. "Seth, the psycho that attacked me has left me flowers – blood red roses! His calling card said 'I have waited a long time for you,' the very words he said when he grabbed me. I've had to contact the police. I've left a message with Simon Black to call me. Seth, your Dad is going to be livid with me."

"Sod him, you were right to make the call."

She sighed silently, it was such a relief to hear Seth say those words, and she started to cry. He put his arm around her.

"Don't cry, I'm here now."

Her phone started to ring. The display showed that it was Simon. She picked up the phone. "Hi Simon, something bad has happened and it may be related to Ivy Brown's case."

'Red roses for my angel. I saw you embrace them and then discard them. Your obstinacy upsets me. In time, you will learn to love me again.'

Chapter Twenty-four

Feeling tired, Jules rested against the door frame of the spare room with her arms folded and looked at the untidy room in despair. It was another beautiful day and sunlight streamed in through the small window onto dusty piles of boxes and furniture covered with dust sheets. This room had become the dumping ground for all their unwanted things. It would take weeks to sort it all out and it was a daunting task. Most of the boxes were filled with shoes, crockery and trinkets that her Mum had bought from local charity shops. The boxes all needed to be gone through and a small selection be retained for sentimental reasons. She would save that chore for another day. Her energy levels were at an all-time low since she had been assaulted.

A few days ago, the police officer that had come to Farm End on the day she had found Ivy's body had taken a statement from her. Jules had given her as much information about the attack as she could but felt bad that she couldn't give a description of him. The police officer had recommended that she keep herself safe and to ring the emergency services if the man showed up at the house. *How will I know if it is him*? Jules had also been given a link to a website, advising her how to protect herself from a stalker. *Is that what he is, a stalker? Or is he more than that?*

Jules felt safe in the house with Seth. Feeling anxious and really vulnerable, she had gone with him to Worthing so he could go to a parole meeting. She had sat in the reception room, glad that there were others waiting there too. The receptionist had smiled kindly at her which was unsettling. She had found it difficult to concentrate on the magazine she was reading. 'How to give your nails a professional nail polish' seemed to be too much for her to digest. She had sighed with relief when Seth had appeared.

After the meeting, they had visited the bank, and she had drawn out two hundred and fifty pounds out with her new bank card. She didn't know why she had drawn so much. There was something reassuring about having cash in her purse. They had also visited the Worthing Registration Office and had obtained a death certificate for Ann and this now meant that the Hearns could collect her from the morgue. She really couldn't imagine how they would transport the body back to Crow Farm. Seth thought that one of his brothers would make Ann a woven coffin out of willow. A home funeral really was an alien concept to her. *Did many people have home burials?*

Her attention turned to the large mahogany wardrobe filled with her Mum's clothes. Later that evening, Ann's burial was going to take place at the silent pool, and she had nothing suitable to wear. She hoped that she would be lucky and find something, otherwise she would have to wear dark blue jeans and a black t-shirt. Jules opened the doors and stood back, surveying the rail of brightly coloured dresses. She couldn't remember seeing her Mum wearing black, but there was a chance that there might be something tucked away, suitable for a formal occasion.

Jules worked her way through each item of clothing and some of the dresses brought back pleasant memories for her. She could now understand why her Dad had kept her clothes. She could smell her Mum's perfume on them and it felt like she was in the room with her.

It had been a long time since she had seen her Dad, and she was feeling guilt-ridden for not going to see him sooner. She had tried to broach the subject with Peter, and she realised that he needed some time to get his head around him sleeping with Ivy. She decided that she would ask him if they could go on Sunday. *The next couple of days are going to be busy*. It was good to keep busy; keep her mind from dwelling on the past. The funeral was today and then Patrick's fortieth birthday was going to be held on the next day, Saturday. She was dreading both occasions. Amongst other worries, it was proving to be very difficult for her to leave the house - her safe haven.

She finally found a black skirt and pulled it off the hanger. It would need an iron but it would be ok. She had some navy pumps at the bottom of her wardrobe and the skirt would go with the black t-shirt she had left on the floor of her bedroom to wash. *I really should have looked for something to wear sooner.*

She walked into the kitchen, the radio was playing Bon Jovi's 'It's My Life', which always lifted her spirits. Seth was stood at the stove cooking and was singing along. *Wow, he's got a really good voice!* He stopped singing and smiled when he saw her. "Seth, you've got a great voice. You didn't tell me you could sing!"

"Thanks, but I'm not as good as Patrick. Are you hungry?"

She looked at the clock and realised that it was nearly lunchtime. She hadn't eaten anything yet and her head felt light, so she knew that she should eat.

"A little. What are you cooking?"

"Do you like vegetable curry?"

"Yes, but I didn't think we had any ingredients to make one."

"I have gathered together all of your wilting vegetables in the fridge, searched your cupboard for spices and found a jar of curry sauce and some lentils. I have fried the vegetables and added the lentils and sauce. What can go wrong?"

She smiled. "It smells lovely." She was sure that the jar of sauce had been in the cupboard for over a year and was probably out of date. She had no idea where the lentils had come from.

"We'll have to have it with toast. I was going to make naan bread but you don't have any plain flour." The toast popped up from the toaster. "There, it is done. Can you get some plates out, please?"

She put her ironing on a chair and got out a couple of plates and a knife and fork. Seth served up lunch and they sat and ate. It was surprisingly good; she hadn't realised how hungry she was.

Seth smiled. "I bet you didn't realise that I had so much talent in the kitchen, did you?"

"No, you did very well for your first attempt. It could be just a fluke, though."

"A fluke! I'll have you know that us Hearns excel in everything we do."

"Do you need me to iron you a shirt for later?" she asked, knowing that this was one area he did not excel in.

"Yes please, learning how to iron is one bridge too far. Did you find yourself something to wear?"

"I think so. I found a black skirt in Mum's cupboard and I plucked out a t-shirt from the wash. I think it will be suitable. What about you? What are you going to wear?"

"Just a black shirt and black jeans. You don't want me to wear a suit and black tie, do you?"

"No, that's ok. It's strange, it doesn't feel like I am attending a funeral of a relative. Will your Mum and Dad be wearing black?"

"No, I don't think so. They might if they were going to a relative's funeral in a cemetery. For home funerals, they usually wear quite bright clothes and have a party to celebrate the life of the deceased after."

"Is that why your Dad called it a wake? Is that what wakes are? A party? They won't have Ann's remains on show in an open coffin, will they?"

"No, that would be rank! They are not barbarians, you know!"

"They are not like other people though, are they? Nothing would surprise me. Have you seen Peter? He's feeling nervous about this evening. I don't think he wants to go down to the silent pool either. He doesn't show it, but he is having a hard time dealing with Ivy's death."

"I think he is coping ok. He seems more positive about running the farm and has gone to the bank with a business plan to try and turn the farm's finances around."

"I didn't know that. He didn't say anything about it to me."

"He wants to make dairy products, cheese and ice cream on-site, to sell locally. I read his plan and it could work.

More people these days like to buy local produce. He's done his research. He just needs to get a loan to buy some equipment."

"I'm so glad that he is starting to get over losing Ivy. I'm just not sure if he will ever forgive Dad, though."

"He will in time."

***

After milking, Jules, Seth and Peter, walked up to Crow Farm, all dressed in black. She held Seth's reassuring hand. Seth had suggested that she collect some flowers from the garden to take with them to the burial, and these she carried in her other hand. She had gathered together what she could and was sure that some of the blooms were just pretty weeds. She hadn't thought about ordering a wreath. Seth said that his parents would prefer the garden flowers. She hoped that he was right.

Jules could feel herself trembling, she wasn't sure if it was from nerves or because of the cool breeze. She was glad that she had brought her dark green zip-up hoodie with her as the evening was cooling down rapidly.

Feeling her shiver, Seth looked down at her and then squeezed her hand. "It's going to be ok, I'll be with you all the time."

As they approached the style that led down to the woods, she noticed fairy lights nearby and as she got closer, she realized that little white lights ran down the side of the field and into the woods. She wondered if the coffin was going to have to be lifted over the style, but then she saw that some of the fencing next to the style had been rolled back to give access.

There were more fairy lights along the path leading up to the Hearn's front door. The door had been left open. It then occurred to her that she was about to see Seth's entire family.

She was beginning to feel really shy and took a deep breath. She looked at Peter and realised that he looked frightened too. *I wonder how he will react when he sees Jake?*

They walked into the lounge and it was filled with family. Gentle Irish music was playing in the background, and she could see a small child-size willow coffin, placed on a table, covered with a white cloth. *There can't be that much of Ann left, to have a coffin so small.* On top of it, were wildflowers interspersed with roses cut from the garden. Hundreds of tea light candles had been placed around the coffin and burned brightly. There were several conversations going on, and she scanned the room for Charlene, trying to find a familiar face. She was going to do her best to avoid talking to Margaret and Jethro, feeling that they may be angry with her about her calling the police and not letting them find her foe.

Children who were dressed in their best clothes were running around the coffin, playing. Some of the more boisterous boys were scolded and told to be careful of the candles.

She bit her lip, she could see Margaret who was wearing a long white, lacy dress, walking over to them. Her hair was tied in a huge bun on the top of her head, and she wore dangling earrings. Margaret forced out a smile and hugged her; she ignored Peter and Seth.

"I hope you like what you see, Jules. Ann would have loved all this. She appreciated our ways."

"It's beautiful, Margaret. Fairy-like even! Thank you for doing all this for us."

Margaret smiled. "I'm glad you're pleased."

Jules looked around the room. She couldn't see Jethro; she felt thankful. "Where is Jethro? I wanted to thank him too."

"He'll be along in a minute. He had something to attend to. He's going to bear the 'end of life basket' with Patrick, James and Jake - if he turns up! Jake should be here to help carry his birth mother to her resting place. We'll start walking down to the woods in a minute."

A small girl with dark hair and big brown eyes tugged at Margaret's skirt. "This is little Bryony, Charlene's smallest. She's a little darling, aren't you a poppet?" Bryony smiled sweetly at them and then hid her face in Margaret's dress. Margaret swept her up and hugged her. Bryony whispered something into Margaret's ear. "Come on then, let's find your potty. What a good girl you are." Margaret took Bryony off to the bathroom.

"She is really cute, she looks like a mini Charlene," she said. *I wonder where Charlene is?*

Peter was looking nervously around. She decided that he must be looking for Jake.

"Jake's not here," Seth said. "I doubt if he will appear. He's probably in his caravan. He has been keeping himself to himself lately."

She could feel Peter's tension ebb away.

"There's some wine on the side, do you two need a drink? I know I do!"

She shook her head. "I don't think we should, until after."

Jethro walked into the room wearing a long white tunic; his feet were bare. There was a garland of flowers around his neck, and he had others hanging over his arm. He saw the three of them and walked over to them.

"You're going to wear the garland this time, I hope, Seth?"

"No, thank you. I'm good, Dad. Jules will wear one. Give them to the girls this time, they will appreciate them more."

Smiling, he placed a garland over her head and stared into her eyes, making her feel uncomfortable. "He is such a heathen," he said scowling. "Peter, you'll wear one won't you?"

"I'd rather not, Mr Hearn, it will give me hay fever."

Jules watched Jethro as he circulated around the room with his garlands of flowers. It was such an odd sight to see the family complying and allowing him to place the flowers over their heads. When this task was completed, he stood by the top of the coffin and James and Patrick joined him. He looked around the room for Jake, and seeing him not to be there asked another of his sons to join them. All held a small handle on the side of the coffin and picked it up. She had thought that they would put it on their shoulders but it was carried out of the room at hip height. Each of the bearers had a serious expression on their face, which made her smile - she didn't know why. The coffin seemed to be really heavy, which surprised her.

Seth whispered in her ear. "The basket is full of moss, earth and flowers. Ann has been planted in there."

"Wow!"

They followed the coffin down the side of the field towards the woods; the fairy lights sparkled in the evening light. Everyone seemed to be in high spirits and not sad at all. The children ran alongside them through the long grass, laughing and chasing each other. She felt like she was going to a party, rather than a sombre burial. It seemed so natural to celebrate someone's life like this, rather than grieve for their loss.

As they approached the edge of the woods, something caught her eye. It was a long piece of fabric fluttering from a tree. She recognised the blue and orange pattern immediately and her heart stopped for a moment as she realised that it was the belt from her dressing gown. *How did it get there?* The last time she had seen it, it had been in Peter's hand in the tack room. She thought that Peter had taken it. Perhaps he had dumped it in the lane somewhere and it had blown through the fields and got caught in the tree. It was a bad omen, and she started to feel anxiety sweep over her. *Has someone hung it there purposely to freak me out or is it just a coincidence?* Either way, it was sending chills up and down her spine. She held Seth's hand more tightly. She hoped that Peter wouldn't see it. He had enough to deal with today. She had seen the way Margaret had looked at him and knew that she was aware of his involvement with Ivy.

They reached the water's edge, and she saw that a deep hole had been dug where she and Seth had stood when she had first seen the pool. The family gathered around the pool and the children were asked to hold hands with their parents. The coffin basket was placed on the edge of the pond ready to go into the grave, and Jethro and Margaret stood at either end of it, ready to give a speech.

"Please hold hands and shut your eyes."

Everyone held hands forming a semi-circle around the coffin. She held Seth and Peter's hand and looked at everyone's face. Seth's siblings were so alike it would be hard to remember who was who. Not wanting to annoy Jethro, she closed her eyes. She could hear the birds chirping in the surrounding trees as they found a roosting place.

"We are gathered here today, to celebrate Ann's life. We remember with fondness her angelic spirit. She was born from the earth and will be returned to the earth but in our hearts, she will always be with us.

"Ann was a dear friend to us all and a mother to Jake. We will never forget her. She brought light into our lives. We have brought her home to her resting place. Her spirit will always be here at Silent Pool. We will think of her with every rising sun, when we are far away and when we are near. Ann, you are loved more than you will ever know."

A loud splash made her open her eyes. There was a gasp from everyone's lips as they saw Ann's coffin floating on the pond amongst the lilies.

"That wasn't meant to happen!" whispered Seth.
Silently, everyone watched the coffin, laden with earth, sink down into the pond. Accepting and unfazed by what all had witnessed, those holding bunches of flowers threw them onto the pond. She watched everyone incredulously. This was the most bizarre funeral she had ever been to.

As she walked back to Crow Farm, still holding her bunch of flowers, she threw them into the hedgerow along with the garland. She was feeling cross and very much confused. When she got back to Crow Farm, Seth, seeing that she was enraged, took her out into the garden to calm her down.

"I know that was weird and probably not what you are used to. Is there any point in burying anyone? In the end, all we have of someone is memories."

"Your parents need locking up! They are not normal. Is that really what Ann would have wanted? Or is it what they wanted?"

"Probably not. They should have asked you and Peter if they could do that. I don't think it was planned, otherwise, my brothers wouldn't have dug a grave. Let it go, Jules, they will only kick off and cause you and Peter grief."

She huffed and folded her arms. The Hearns were doing her head in. Seth was doing his best to calm her, and she felt sorry for him for having such crazy parents. She looked around for Peter and doubted if he was in the house.

"I'm ok, I'm not going to murder anyone now. You can relax. They are just so crazy and manipulative. It is a wonder that you turned out so normal. I think that Peter is cross and has gone home. They didn't make him feel welcome."

Seth smiled, and hugging her, rested his head on hers. "Yes, I saw him walking up the lane to Farm End. We will sit in the garden for a little bit and then go home. Twenty minutes tops, I promise."

She sat under the big umbrella in the garden and pulled her cardigan around her; she was really cold now. Seth returned with some food and a glass of wine. Charlene was with him and she was carrying Bryony. Jules smiled; Charlene was another normal Hearn family member. Seth sat next to her and Charlene sat opposite with Bryony on her lap.

"How are you doing, sweetie?"

"I've had better days. It was a good job it wasn't my Mum they launched."

"Seth said you are annoyed. I'm sorry that you are upset. Mam and Dad are a law unto themselves. They mean well most of the time."

"I'll get over it. Your Bryony is so beautiful."

"She's going to be a heartbreaker."

"How old is she?"

"Nearly three."

"Splash, Mam!"

"Oh dear, she said that when the basket went in the pond. That's the third time she's said 'splash', this evening."

"Charlene, where's Joe?" Seth asked.

"He's at home looking after Michael and Rowan. Michael is our oldest."

"Are they sick?" she asked.

"Just a bit of a cough, they should be alright for Patrick's party tomorrow. I was a bit worried about them falling in that pond. They can be a bit lively at times and it wouldn't have gone down well if they had fallen in. You'll enjoy the party tomorrow. You'll find us Hearns can party like the best of them with no hidden surprises. Are you both coming still?"

"Splash Mam!" Bryony hit the table with both hands to emphasise the coffin hitting the water.

"Yes, Bryony, sweetie. Splash! You like water, don't you?"

"She is so sweet. Yes, we are looking forward to it. Aren't we, Seth?"

Seth looked surprised by her sudden enthusiasm; she didn't want him to think that she was a complete misery.

"With this stunning girl by my side, it will be a night to remember."

Chapter Twenty-five

As the cows came into the shed for milking, Jules stripped each teat, checking that the cow's milk was the right colour and consistency. This told the cows to relax and to let the milk down. She then applied iodine and then wiped the teats clean with a cloth. Seth and Peter followed behind her and connected the milking cups to each cow. She was starting to like having to get up each morning to milk them. There was something very reassuring about working with animals and it was quite rewarding too. Each cow would leave their station less burdened, and she could almost sense their euphoria as they returned to the fields.

This morning, Peter seemed happy with the milk production and announced that most were producing five percent more than yesterday. Seth was having a harder day and had got soaked twice as the cows urinated on him when he removed the cups and applied the iodine. He didn't complain too much and got on with the job.

She thought back to the funeral and hoped Ann would be happy at the bottom of the pond. She still couldn't get over how everyone had just accepted Margaret and Jethro's actions as being normal. Perhaps that was normal to them. Seth hadn't been too upset, either. She was starting to question her own sanity.

It was the party this evening, and she was still looking forward to it, and her breath quickened as she imagined herself dancing with Seth again. She hadn't practised any of the steps he had taught her, and she hoped that she would remember what to do.

Seth had taken her around his farm exercise course, and she had found watching him workout almost too much to endure. Her body longed for his. It had been difficult to find time alone with him. Peter had the habit of just walking in on them, to ask her something.

Seth was showering and as she waited her turn, she had a look inside her wardrobe to see if there was anything she could wear to the party. Her wardrobe was a mass of clothes that were only suitable to wear around the farm and for riding. She couldn't face wearing her Mum's clothes again.

In a box on the top of her wardrobe was her prom dress. The blue beaded material flowed over a net petticoat to the floor. It was too formal for her to wear to a party but if she cut the skirt down to above her knee then it would be the perfect party dress to wear on a hot summer's evening. Jules tried the dress on and looked at herself in the mirror. *I look like Cinderella*! She wasn't going for that look and needed to make the dress look less grand. The plaster on her neck made her feel ugly. She needed to change it and so pulled it off, to see if she could go without wearing one. The wound looked like a hideous love bite. *I still need a dressing, otherwise, people might stare.*

"Why are you wearing your prom dress?"

She turned around. "Oh Peter, I didn't hear you come up the stairs." He had startled her. Her nerves were ragged.

"Sorry. Are you going to go to the Hearn's party wearing that? You shouldn't go back there. They are a bunch of nutters. Except Seth, though, he's not like them."

She smiled, Peter was beginning to take to Seth. "It's Patrick's fortieth and Seth wants us to go. I don't really have any party clothes. I was going to cut this down. I am not likely to wear it ever again and I like up-cycling things."

"You could just wear what you wore yesterday. You were wearing a black dress, weren't you?"

"Peter, you are a complete moron! It's a known fact that girls have to wear a decent dress to a party, otherwise, they will be laughed at. Anyway, I have nothing else; this will have to do."

"Ok, keep your hair on! Your neck looks a bit rough. You look like you've been bitten by a vampire. I think you need to cover it up."

"Thanks, Peter! You're making me feel a whole lot better about myself."

"Are you two coming back tonight?"

"You are sounding really like Dad now! Yes, but it will probably be after twelve. You could come to the party too if you want."

"No thanks, I'd rather eat my own hand off! Just be careful Jules, they're an odd bunch."

"Peter?"

"Yes."

"Do you want to go and see Dad tomorrow? He will need some more clean clothes."

He looked troubled for a moment. "I'll drive you over and see how I feel when I get there. Is that ok?"

"I understand. Thanks."

***

Jules thought that the morning was going quickly, she had managed to cut down her dress with kitchen scissors. She was sitting in the lounge watching 'Escape to the Country' as she tried her best to sew a hem into the fine fabric. Seth had taken it upon himself to dust and hoover the house and occasionally came over to sit with her and to talk. She could see that he was having difficulty being cooped up in the house with her.

"Seth, you can go out for a walk if you want. I will be ok. I've got to learn to be independent again. There's been no sign of the stalker for days. The police might have arrested someone by now. I don't like to see you so... so penned in."

Seth smiled. "I am happy, Jules. I am happy when I am with you. That is all I want from life. To be with you. I have been thinking though, that we should venture outside more together. Do you want to go for a ride? You could ride Connor and I will walk by you, ready to fend off any unwanted company. What do you think? Your horse is missing you. It huffed at me the other day; a sure sign of a breaking heart."

"I know what you are saying is right, but I have this knot inside my stomach. I don't mind walking up to Crow Farm or visiting the horses but anything more feels scary. Do you think Connor's heart is breaking, then?"

"For sure."

"I do miss riding him." She smiled, realising that Seth was using Connor's breaking heart to entice her outside. She would be safe up high on her oversized horse and with Seth walking beside them. There was very little that could go wrong.

"Seth Hearn, you crafty thing! Ok, but not too far and not up that track behind Crow Farm."

Seth grinned. "You'll feel so much better. You'll see."

Chapter Twenty-six

Jules breathed in the fresh air, savouring each breath. It was a beautiful day. She sat on Connor's strong back and could see for miles. The landscape unfolded around them as they walked. Seth seemed happy to be out too and patted Connor's neck as they walked along. Connor seemed to be more careful where he trod, and she was sure that he had a bit of a spring in his step. Seth had obviously worked his magic on him. She suspected that Seth was a horse whisperer. The three of them had wound their way along tracks and through fields until they reached the view point where she had met Seth weeks ago. She slipped off Connor's back, and they sat on the style-like table and bench and looked across the countryside, both absorbing the amazing views.

"Do you remember me asking you to kiss you up here? I think I scared you."

She laughed. "You didn't scare me. I wanted to kiss you, but I was a bit shy. I didn't really know you well enough then."

"I know. I couldn't help myself. I'm glad you didn't run off. I think it was when I saw you riding towards me; it was then that I knew."

"Knew what?"

"That I loved you. What about you? When did you know I was the one?"

She thought back. It was strange but she couldn't exactly say when. She felt like she'd known him forever, and yet they had only been together for a few weeks. "I think it was the night you came to my rescue. The first night I saw you. There was something about you." She put her arms around his neck and kissed him. "Yes, it was love at first sight and when you kissed me for the first time, it was then that I really knew."

He kissed her back, taking her breath away.

***

Feeling a little nervous, Jules pulled on her dress and hoped that she hadn't cut it too short. If her Dad had seen it, then she was sure that he would have made her take it off. She smoothed down the skirt, did up the zip at the back and then inspected herself in front of the mirror. Jules was pleased with her handy work. She was showing a little cleavage as the dress had much needed push-up pads in the bust area. *Not too bad!*

The next task was to put on the right amount of makeup, to make herself look natural and not overdone. She applied a little mascara, blusher and some lip gloss to her lips, not sure if she had done enough or too much. Jules put her phone into a small silver bag and then put the strap over her head. She didn't want to be carrying it around with her but had to bring her phone, in case she had to ring 999.

Her next dilemma was what she should wear on her feet. She only had trainers, her navy pumps or sandals. She hadn't thought about shoes before. Her Mum had some old shoes at the bottom of her wardrobe, in boxes, but most were really ugly and too big. She needed something to dance in. She decided to wear her pumps, as these were comfortable and wouldn't hurt her feet. The next problem was what to do with her hair. She decided to keep it down and just clipped her curls back, out of the way. This exposed her dressing more, but she knew that her hair would get on her nerves if it kept falling in her face when she danced. Nerves were really starting to kick in; she didn't want to mess up.

Seth came up to find her as it was nearly time to go. He was wearing his black jeans and a short-sleeved pink shirt. His tattoos were showing, and she liked seeing his muscular arms. He was holding a tissue on his chin. He saw her and his face lit up. "You look amazing! Is that what you were sewing earlier? I'm going to have a hard time keeping my hands off you! Jules, you don't have a chap stick or something similar, do you? I've cut myself shaving."

She handed him her pot of lip gloss. He took it and looked at the label suspiciously and opened the lid.

"Take some up on your finger and rub it in. I thought you were meant to tear a piece of tissue and stick it on to the cut."

"That was in the dark ages. I don't know who told me to use a chap stick, but it works." He rubbed the gloss into his cut and smiled. "There, good as new."

"Do you think this dress is too much? I could find something else?"

"No, it's perfect. The Hearn girls like to dress up. You'll see. Although, some will be wearing kilts!"

"Really? I don't think they are going to be very impressed with my dancing skills."

"Just relax, they will help you and so will I. You're a natural. Come on beautiful, let's get going. I'm dying to show you off."

Patrick's party was in full swing when they arrived. The kitchen was crowded with family, laughing and drinking. The table was covered with party food and there was a large fortieth birthday cake at one end in the shape of an American car. *Another car enthusiast!* She could hear music coming from the front room and imagined Jethro and Margaret playing in the band. She could hear a man singing an upbeat Irish folk song. The song was about whiskey blowing someone's head off and it made her laugh. She was curious to see who was singing.

The next song started to play, she couldn't remember the name of the song, but she knew she had danced to it with Seth.

Seth whispered in her ear. "I love you. Come and dance with me." She didn't have a chance to feel nervous or object. He took her by the hand and led her into the lounge to join the merry throng of jubilant dancers. They passed the band, at the top of the room as before. She noticed that there were more band members this time. Margaret and Jethro were playing and, lost in the music, both had their eyes closed. They had not seen her come into the room, and she was glad to slip past them.

She surveyed the dancers' clothes to make sure that she was wearing the right dress. Most of the girls were wearing party dresses so she felt at ease. No one was wearing a kilt but some of the dancers were wearing black shoes that tapped as they danced. She hesitated for a moment, wondering what she had let herself in for and then saw Charlene calling her over. Seth smiled at her and led her around the dancers, and they slipped in, forming the next dance pair in the line. Seth held her hand in the air and started to dance. She took a deep breath and joined in. She copied Charlene when she could. Seth guided her through the dance too until the sequence of swaps and turns became embedded in her mind. Her fears of looking foolish faded as she gained in confidence. Jules was finding dancing easier than she had imagined. *This is fun.* Seth beamed at her and was brimming with pride as he twirled her around.

After a few more set dances, she was feeling hot and needed a drink. Seth was still grinning at her, and she could see that he really loved dancing with her. Jules signalled to him that she needed to stop and she was glad that he understood. He gently swung her out of the dance and led her to the kitchen.

"You were grand! Like I said, a natural. You look hot. What would you like to drink? Mam and Dad probably have everything in."

"I don't know, what are you going to have?"

"Just a beer. I don't really drink spirits."

"A beer would be fine, or a coke. Just as long as it is cold. You can work up quite a thirst dancing."

Seth opened the fridge and found two cold beers. He found her a glass and tipped hers into it. "I can't have you drinking out of a can in that dress. Here's a plate, we'll have something to eat now. You're going to need your strength. I have been known to dance until the morning!"

Jules took the plate and helped herself to a little food, but she wasn't that hungry. The beer was lovely and cool, and she felt much better sipping it. Seth got himself something, and then he led her through to the garden. Every shrub and tree was covered in fairy lights; it looked magical. The garden was full with children playing together. They sat down, side by side, on the grass and stretched out their legs. It was then that she noticed that he was wearing shoes like the others. "Seth, you're wearing tap shoes. I didn't notice you had those on."

He smiled. "They're not exactly tap shoes. They are similar, though. They're called reel shoes, they have harder heels, I think."

"Can you river dance?"

"No, but you'd be surprised to know that Jake can and most of my sisters do."

"I haven't seen Jake. He wasn't dancing, was he?"

"No, I didn't see him. He's probably fluthered, somewhere."

She laughed. "You're so funny. Do you mean drunk?"

"Yes, or high. Both, probably."

"Oh dear." She looked around the garden, trying to remember where she and Ivy had sat. The engagement party just seemed to be a distant memory now.

Seth led her back to the party and this time the music was a lot slower, and she realised that Patrick was singing a ballad. She was surprised how good his voice was. Jules hadn't heard 'The Fields of Athenry' before and decided that she would find the words for the song and learn to play it on her guitar. Some of the guests stood around him, watching him but most people were dancing in pairs and were circulating around the room in a slow stepping waltz. *I don't know if I can do this.*

Seth smiled. "Just let me lead you and relax, you'll be fine." He put her hand on his shoulder, held her other hand out to the side and then placed his other hand in the small of her back. He showed her a simple side step, one way and then the other. This she found easy to do. He started to move 'round the room with her. She clipped his toes a couple of times, but he didn't seem to notice. Jules tried her best to relax but it would take a few more dances before she mastered it. She smiled and looked into his eyes. When the song finished, he held her chin and kissed her on the lips. He drew her to him and held her for a moment. People clapped and cheered for Patrick, and he raised his glass to thank them all for coming to his party. She thought that the Hearn's love of music was an endearing quality. *How can they be so bonkers one day and then so normal the next?*

The hours passed by quickly, and after the last traditional slow dance Seth had kissed her, and she had seen a look of desire in his eyes. "Come with me," he whispered.

They walked through the garden and he took her to the fence that she had climbed through when her Dad had dragged her away from the last party. Instead of walking her down the lane, he led her up the side of the field to a small barn. The path along the side of the field was, well, worn. *How many people have been up here? Is this where the lovers go?*

He pulled the barn door open, switched on a light and closed the door. This was where the Hearns stored hay for the sheep. The hay smelled lovely but there was another sweet smell in the air too.

"Are you ok, my little dote? I just wanted to be alone with you. You know I want you so much, don't you? You make me the happiest man that ever was. I live and breathe only for you. I love you so much."

"I love you too. Hold me, Seth, and don't let me go." He held her and his lips found hers. She kissed him back passionately; tasting him. He ran his hands down her body and finding her bottom cheeks, pulled her into him. She could feel him harden and knew that he wanted her there and then. He stopped kissing her and looked longingly into her eyes. "I will if you want me to. I have brought something with me. Do you want to?"

She looked at him and wanted so much to say 'yes.' Her heart and body were screaming at her to give herself to him. *I can't. Not here in a barn. Not on Crow Farm. I have to stop. Can I stop myself? I don't think I can.* "Seth… I want you so much. You know I do, but not here. Not like this." She hoped that he would understand. *His eyes are burning with desire, but he is not angry. My lovely Seth. If you ask me again, then I will lose control. I need to feel you inside me.*

"Thank fuck for that!" Jake appeared from the back of the barn. He was holding a can of beer and was smoking a cigarette.

"Shit, that was close!" *Is he smoking weed?*

"You two need to get a room!"

Seth spun 'round as Jake walked over to them. Her heart was beating hard from the shock of seeing him.

"What are you doing here, Jake?" Seth demanded.

"Just minding my own business. Can't a man have a drink and a smoke in peace? Did you bring Ivy here too? I wouldn't bother with him, Jules. I've heard that he can't get it up. As for you; you are just a prick tease!"

She gasped, she could see the rage in Seth's face. Furious, he threw back his fist and gave Jake a right hook on the chin, which sent him flying.

"Seth, what on earth are you doing? Leave him be and get some air." Seth's eyes were burning with fury. "Just go for a walk, please."

Still angry, Seth headed out of the barn. "Just give me a minute."

Chapter Twenty-seven

Jules glared at Jake, who was still lying on the floor nursing his chin. "You are such a dickhead! You hate Seth because he screwed Ivy, but then so has every man in Findon! Do you have any idea what he's done for you in the past? For God's sake, Jake, he went to prison for you! I think you know that, don't you? You just choose not to hear. You are such a piss head these days. You used to be alright when we were at school together."

"You don't know what you are talking about, he's playing you."

She was getting angry. "You bastard, he's a better man than you will ever be. He went to prison for you and you let him. He didn't want your Mum to know, because you are her favourite. Seth has had your back all this time and you just like to press his buttons and stir up trouble. For fuck's sake, Jake, grow up!"

"He still owes me a car!"

"Just piss off, Jake!" Still fuming, she started to walk away. Her phone pinged telling her that she had a message. She took her phone out of her bag. It was from Seth. "He must have found his phone," she said out loud.

'I'm sorry if I upset you. I'm down by Silent Pool. Come and find me there. Seth xxx'

"Is that from your boyfriend then? Messaging you to say he's sorry?" he asked in a sarcastic voice.

"You'll be glad to know that he isn't coming back to finish you off. He's at the silent pool. I wonder why he's there?"

"Shit, no, Jules! Don't go there on your own. That place is evil."

"I'll be fine. It's just a short walk from the lane and the fairy lights are still up from the funeral." She left Jake in the barn and hoped that he would think about what she had said. *He's such an idiot.* She headed towards the lane along the side of the field. As she passed the Hearn's garden, she noticed that most had left the party and there were only a handful of people left talking in the garden.

Soon, she was in the lane and could see the fairy lights lighting up the side of the field and the entrance to the woods. She shivered, the night air was turning cold. She climbed over the style and could feel her head swim a little. *I'm such a lightweight, I only had one can of beer!*

As she walked along the track to the woods, she thought back to Seth's wild passionate moment and how she had so nearly let him take her. She was right to have stopped him, she didn't regret it and it would have been even more humiliating if Jake had found them at it. It wouldn't have been special and would have just been a wild moment and soon forgotten. *I'm not like Ivy.*

She could see Seth waiting for her at the entrance of the woods, and she smiled. It would be good to be in his arms again. As she reached him, she realised that it wasn't him. It was Jethro. He grinned at her. "Jethro? What are you doing here?"

"Seth didn't want you to walk down through the woods to see him alone. He's not doing great. I think he has had a little too much to drink. It was a good job I saw him walking down here. Come with me."

She frowned, she hoped Seth hadn't had anything more. She followed Jethro down the path. The fairy lights twinkled as she passed them by. They reached the pond and they stood by the edge. The moon lit up the water and thousands of lily pads shone in the moonlight. She looked around her. She couldn't see Seth. "Where is he?"

"He's not coming."

She looked at Jethro suspiciously. "I don't understand. You said that he was here."

"It was me that sent you the message. I found Seth's phone."

"What! Why did you do that?"

"Because, Ann, I knew you wouldn't come to see me. This used to be our favourite place to be together. Do you not like roses anymore?"

"Jethro, you are scaring me." She started to move away from him.

"Don't be afraid, Ann, I would never hurt you."

"Jethro, please. I'm not Ann." She went to run, but he grabbed hold of her wrist and she tried to pull it away from his grasp.

"You are my angel. You have come back to me. Don't fight me."

She was panicking. "For God's sake, Jethro, I am not Ann. Do you hear me? Let me go. I won't say anything. Please!" *Was he the one that attacked me by the oak tree? Is it him?* She yanked her arm away from him. "Get away from me, you bastard!"

Jethro was getting angry. "Don't you leave me again! I didn't mean to hurt you before. I want my last moment with you to be special. Don't you see? I have to have you one more time! I want you to lie with me like we used to and then I will watch you die as my soul floods into yours. I will let you go forever then. Just one last time, Ann. Then you can go back to your watery grave."

He dragged her into his arms, almost crushing her. Jules felt like she was going to suffocate. She could smell his body, a horrible smell of body odour doused in aftershave. *It's him*! He planted his lips on her mouth trying to get his tongue inside hers. She clenched her teeth together and turned her head away. She could feel his teeth on her cheek as he struggled to find her mouth again.

Desperately, she tried to wriggle out of his cruel embrace. The more she moved, the more she could feel him becoming aroused. She had to wait and pick her moment to get away. He threw her down onto the damp earth next to the pool and straddled her, trapping her beneath him. She screamed out, and he punched her hard in the face. Her head spun.

Urgently, he undid his trousers and pulled them down past his hips. He was erect. She could smell fish coming from him. She felt sickened by it. "HELP! PLEASE HELP ME!" She yelled and started to cry, knowing that she wasn't strong enough to stop him. She could feel his hands on her breasts and then ripping at her clothes as he tried to pull her dress up. There was no doubt, he was going to rape her. All she could do was yell and beat him with her fists.

"Hush now, Ann, you know it makes me angry if you scream. Ivy used to scream when we made love. She would be alive today if she hadn't got herself pregnant – stupid bitch! Just one more time. It's your fault you died, you shouldn't have had that child. You gave me a son that is cursed."

Jules was becoming hysterical, he was clawing at her underwear. His nails gouged into her skin as he got his fingers under the elastic. *Just a few more seconds and it will be too late.* "NO, PLEASE NO! Don't do this, Jethro. Please..." she screamed out in defiance, as she prepared her body to resist the assault.

"NO!" Then an ear-piercing shriek in the night stopped Jethro from entering her. A heavy body slammed into Jethro's, sending him flying. She heard the splash as two bodies hit the water. She screamed in terror. *I'm ok. Thank God! Someone has found me. Saved me. He has gone. I am free.*

Still crying, she sat up and watched as two men wrestled in the water. *My lovely Seth, thank God! How did you know I was here?* He had come to her aid, and just in the nick of time. The two men fought, both trying to drown each other. Someone was going to die that night. She could barely watch this tragedy unfold. "STOP, FOR THE LOVE OF GOD! Stop this madness!" She yelled out into the night. She could see the rage on both men's faces as each tried to force each other down into the water. As they wrestled, she could see bite marks in Jethro's arm. *It was definitely him, the bastard. He was the one that bit me. This is going to end badly.* "Please, just stop," she sobbed.

Hands locked around each other's throats and Jethro and Seth disappeared beneath the waterline. Her eyes widened with fear as she waited for both men to reappear. The water rippled between the water lilies; the moonlight on each tiny wave sparkled. Time seemed to stand still as the trees around the pool mocked her for believing in the living. *No, please!* She held her breath and waited. Each second tore at her heart.

They had been gone too long. She imagined them descending to the bottom of the murky, black pond in a death roll. Were they both going to die in that watery grave? It was a living nightmare. She was sobbing again. *Nobody can be underwater that long and survive.* The water was still and the lily pads had settled into an unbroken jigsaw. It was done, she was alone. *I've lost him! I can't continue without him.* If she was meant to die, then she would do it of her own hand. Like Ophelia, she would slip into the water and let the water lilies engulf her and take her to find her star crossed lover on the other side. She moved closer to the edge of the pool. *I can't be without you!*

Seth broke through the surface of the water, gasping for air and choking on pond water. She screamed out hysterically. *He has returned to me.* Jethro had not made it. "OH MY GOD, SETH! I thought you were dead." She was ecstatic and tears of joy and shock rolled down her face.

Seth swam over to her. He was crying too, bawling painful sobs. "I couldn't let him do that to you. Why would he do such a ghastly thing to you? Jules, are you hurt? Did he hurt you?"

"No, Seth, don't cry, please don't cry, he didn't touch me. You came just in time. He thought I was Ann. He was going to rape Ann and throw me in the pond to join her. Seth, he pushed Ivy and Ann in here. He killed them both, I'm sure. He murdered them because he got them pregnant. He is… He was a monster!" She lay on her front and reached down the steep mud bank to touch his hand. She could only just reach. "I can't pull you out of here. Can you get yourself out? The banks are so steep."

Seth tried to hold onto a tree root to pull himself up but his weight was too much and it broke away in his hand. "I told you that this pond is a death-trap. You'll have to go up to the house and get some of my brothers to help me out. I will be ok. I can tread water for a while."

"Ok, I won't be long." She got up and looked around for her bag. It had her phone inside. She couldn't see it. It must have dropped into the pool.

"Jules, what have I done? I've killed my Dad. Fuck! What am I going to do?"

"He would have killed us both had you not stopped him. It was the only way, Seth. Don't cry.

"I'll go and get help." Her dress was all torn, and she wasn't sure how she would wake up Seth's brothers and explain why she looked so awful. "I'll go and get Peter and bring some rope."

She started to walk away from the pond and looked back at him. She didn't want to leave him. He smiled weakly at her. He was lucky to be alive. When she turned to go, Margaret was next to her.

"Jules, what are you doing here?"

She inhaled sharply and was horrified to see her there. She wasn't sure what to tell her. "Seth has fallen in the pond. I can't get him out. I need to get him some help."

"Your dress is all torn."

"I fell over," she lied.

"Seth?" Margaret walked over to the edge of the pool. She followed her. "Seth, you poor boy. Why are you in here?"

"Mam, Dad...Dad is gone. He's at the bottom. He tried to rape Jules. I'm sorry, Mam, I knocked him into the pond. He wanted to drown me!"

246

"Seth, don't upset yourself. I knew he was up to something. It is all over. He is at peace now."

"What do you mean? What's over?"

"For over twenty years, I've had to put up with his shenanigans. Jethro liked the ladies too much and it is something I have had to live with for far too long. He was obsessed with Ann Bridgewater, and now he is with her. God rest his soul."

"Mam?"

Jules watched Margaret curiously. *She's not upset that Jethro is dead.* "So you knew that he was seeing Ann and then killed her?"

"No, Jules. I killed Ann! My dear friend was playing with fire. I tried to warn her as any good friend would do, but she wouldn't listen. I was angry and hit her over the head with a vase. She wouldn't listen to me. I never meant to kill her; I loved her. Jethro was devastated, of course, but he did what he was told and helped me bring her body down here. And like yesterday, we threw her into the silent pool; where she belongs."

"Mam, I think that he killed Ivy too. The baby was probably his. Did you know that?"

Jules could see the pain in Margaret's eyes, and she cried out. "Not poor sweet Ivy. How could he do that to Jake? This is all too much to bear. My poor Jake. It all has to end tonight." She turned towards her, and almost spat out the words. "You came here to torment us, Jules, you are a ghost from the past. You cannot fool me. Our little Ann, who we both loved, came back to haunt us." Her eyes narrowed, and catching Jules off guard, she shoved her over the edge of the pond, causing her to slip down the steep muddy bank and into the pool. Jules screamed out and hit the icy water hard. She felt herself sinking

247

down towards the hands of the dead. Fearing they would grab hold of her, she held her breath and swam back to the surface to join Seth.

"WHY DID YOU DO THAT? Seth called out angrily.

"It's time to bury the past and to keep my family from knowing the truth, so they can live full and happy lives on the farm. Your Dad cannot live without Ann. He will have her back soon. You will be dead by morning. It will just be a tragic end to you both. Seth, you were never mine. Just another one of his mistakes." She started to walk away.

"MAM, COME BACK! Jesus, she's not coming back, is she?"

Jules' teeth were chattering together, the water was so cold. "No, I don't think she is." She was finding it difficult to stay afloat.

"FOR THE LOVE OF GOD!" he yelled out into the night, punching the water. "We're fucked!"

Jules swam over to him. "Seth, we'll find a way to get out of here. I don't like to see you in pain." Treading water, she held his face in her hands. "We'll be ok. Concentrate, Seth, it's going to be ok." He was starting to calm down, and he was focusing on her. "Maybe. I hope so. Jules you're going to have to tread water with less energy. We might be here a while. You just need to fill your lungs with air and move your arms like this. Move your legs slowly. Like this."

She watched Seth's demonstration and tried to imitate him. She was starting to sink.

"You need to relax."

She tried to unwind but it was difficult for her. To help, she thought of her happy place behind the stable block. She did her best and inhaled and exhaled slowly; treading water was getting easier.

Happy with her progress, Seth looked around the pool for another way out. "Stay here, I'm going to swim around the edge of the pond to see if I can find any tree root or rock we can use to climb out."

"Ok, there has to be something."

Seth began to swim and circle the pond, feeling his way along the banks. Finally, he returned and he looked downcast. "Nothing!"

"I'm so cold, Seth." Her teeth were still chattering. "Come here, let me hold you. Lie on your back and put your head on my shoulder. I'll put my arm under your neck and I will hold your head. Just relax and float. I'll keep my legs and arm moving and try to keep you warm with my body."

She lay in the water looking up at the moon and the stars. She had never seen so many stars. "Someone will find us, Seth. I know they will. It is not our time yet. How did you know I was here?"

"Jake came and found me. He told me where you had gone. I shouldn't have hit him. He just makes me so angry."

"No Seth, you shouldn't have. Seth, your Mum is willing to let you die to hide her dirty family secrets. How could she do such a thing?"

"I don't think she ever liked me. I wasn't hers, was I? Don't think about dying, Jules."

The hours past and at times she found herself drifting off to sleep. Each time Seth woke her, worried that she was fading away. She was so tired and so, so cold, but she could feel Seth's warm face against hers, and she thought only of surviving this nightmare.

***

Beautiful birdsong echoing around them and Seth shaking her awake made her realise that it was dawn. For a moment she thought they were in bed; the lily pads their covers. She put a cold hand up to feel his face. His cheek felt warm: it was obviously hard work to keep them both afloat. "Seth, you must be tired. I will try and swim so you can rest for a bit."

He hugged her tighter. "No, don't. I like to feel your face next to mine. It is keeping me going, knowing that I can keep you alive."

"Do you hear the birds? It's going to be light soon. Somebody will miss us or him on the bottom." She couldn't say his name anymore. Warm rays of sunshine were seeping through the branches and onto their faces, telling them that there was hope.

"Seth, I love you and I always will. No matter what happens. You know…" A dog barking in the distance stopped the birds from singing and made her heart leap in her chest. "Seth, did you hear that?"

"Yes, I did."

"I know that bark, like a ewe knows the sound of her lambs bleating." Another dog barked in reply.

"It's George and Pip! I know it is." She called out their names and listened. The dogs barked again and they sounded as if they were getting closer. "Seth, they're coming to find us."

George arrived at the waters' edge first, followed by Pip, and they crisscrossed as they ran along the edge of the pond, excited to see her. Their noses scuffed the edge of the bank as they weighed up whether they should jump into the pond to see her. Feeling alarmed that they might be tempted to dive in, she called out "Go and get Peter. Fetch". They barked again and ran off. Anxiously, they both waited, hoping that Peter would arrive. It couldn't have been more than a minute's wait but it felt like a lifetime. Peter and Jake suddenly appeared on the edge of the pond, making them jump with fright.

"Jules, Seth! Oh my God! Jules, your face! Are you hurt?" Peter squatted down on the side of the pond and held out his hand.

"We're ok, just really cold. Peter, we can't get out of here, the banks are too steep. We've been in here for hours."

"We'll get you out. The dogs were going crazy this morning and when you didn't turn up for milking, I knew something was wrong. The dogs brought me here, Jules. They knew you were in trouble. Maybe they heard you calling out. I met Jake in the lane. Mr Hearn didn't come back last night either. They have been looking for him since sunrise."

"I'm sorry, Seth. I was such an idiot last night," Jake said.

"It's ok, Jake, I'm sorry I hit you. Jake, something bad happened here last night. Mam left us here to die. Mam and Dad have done some terrible things. You haven't seen us, Jake. Our lives are depending on you. You must tell no one."

He frowned. "Some family we've got! Fuck them all!"

Peter got on his knees, so he could reach her hand. She grabbed onto Peter's warm hand and did her best to help him drag her up the bank. She lay on the ground, staring at the sky, shivering but glad that she had escaped death. It took both Peter and Jake a while to get Seth out of the pond and when he got onto the earth he kissed it. He crawled over to her and kissed her. "Morning beautiful. I love you." He was smiling.

"I love you too." He stood up and pulled her up onto her feet and kissed and hugged her. She smiled and breathed in the cool morning air. Today was a new day and despite the horrific night they had endured, she felt elated that they were both alive.

Jake went back to Crow Farm, promising that he would tell nobody that they had survived. Holding hands, they followed Peter and the dogs back to the farmhouse. As they walked they scanned the fields and hills for others, fearing that they would be seen.

"It's not over. Is it?"

"No, Jules, it's not."

Chapter Twenty-eight

The house was eerily quiet. George and Pip were by her side and looked up at her sadly. Unable to bear the silence, Jules turned on the radio, desperate to hear music and the reassuring sound of voices. *Did all this really happen?* Her torn dress dripped pond water onto the kitchen floor, telling her that this was not just a terrible dream.

"Don't worry, boys, I'm here now," she said, patting the dogs on their heads to reassure them.

Seth looked out of the window into the courtyard. He was watching the lane uneasily and sighed. "We are going to have to hide out in here and hope that we don't get seen. They think we are dead and it needs to stay that way."

Peter frowned. "What happened out there, Seth? Why has Jules got a black eye?"

"My Dad tricked her into going down to the silent pool, and he tried to rape her. I caught him before it happened. I think he did the same to Ivy. We fell into the pond and then we fought. I won." He looked lost for a moment. "My Dad drowned."

"My God!"

She could see that he was having difficulty telling him the next part of their sorry tale so she continued it. "Seth's Mum came down to the pool. I thought that she was going to help me get Seth out. She told me that she had killed Ann and they had dumped her body in the water. She said that Ann had an affair with Jethro and she was glad that she had killed her. Peter, they both thought I was Ann, risen from the grave. She pushed me in the pond so I could be reunited with Jethro. That woman needs locking up."

"Jules, you need to ring Simon Black now. This has gone too far!"

"I can't, Peter! Don't you see, it's our word against hers? She will say that Seth killed Jethro and with his record they will believe her." He shot her an injured glance. "Even if Margaret is taken into custody, then her family will stand by her and there will always be a Hearn waiting, ready to do her bidding. Margaret thinks that we are dead, and we need to flee this place and start our lives somewhere else. Peter, we're going to have to leave you, Dad and Farm End forever." She was shivering now.

"She's right, Peter. You don't know what my family is capable of."

He shook his head and his eyes were red with emotion. "She left you to die in that pool? One day, you have to let me see you again. One day, when you are both forgotten. You promise me both?"

"We promise you, Peter."

"Look, you have to hide away in here. Don't come into the kitchen or you might get seen. I… I've got to go and milk those cows, they can't wait. Please don't go until I get back. We can work out how to get you out of here."

He hugged her, and she could see tears on his cheeks. He went out of the kitchen door and locked it behind him, and she watched him walk towards the lane. "We can say goodbye to him, can't we?"

254

Seth nodded and then hugged her. "My poor wee dote, you are freezing."

"You are too. We need to warm up. I'm going to run a hot bath to try and revive myself. No, I can't wait, a hot shower will do. Let's go upstairs and out of the kitchen. We are like two sitting ducks in here."

She shut the bathroom door and turned on the shower and let it run to warm up the water. She looked over at Seth, and he looked distraught. "Seth, it will be ok. We have each other."

"I bet you wished you had never met me. Look at your face. You look like you've been fighting with a bear. Your dress is torn, and because of me you nearly died. Now we have to go on the run. I am no good for you."

She walked over to him. "You saved my life. I am still breathing and I breathe better when you are with me. Take off your clothes, Sebastian, and warm up in the shower with me?" She started to unbutton his shirt. 'Hole In My Soul Can You Fill It,' was playing on the radio. His tears were falling and dropping onto the back of her hands. She wiped away the tears on his cheeks and kissed him gently on the lips. "Don't cry. I'm ok. He's gone now and I just have a sore eye. He won't break us. Be strong, Seth. Help me out of these rags." She turned around so he could unzip her dress.

Together they stepped into the shower and let the hot water run over them, allowing it to warm their battered bodies. Lost in the torrent of hot water, they reached out for each other.

***

Jules woke in Seth's arms, she wasn't sure how long they had slept. He was still asleep, and she could feel his warm breath on her neck. *I live for every moment I have with you. The here and the now is all that matters.* Everything they had been through had faded into the verdant green hills around them. She inhaled deeply as she remembered him take her. Her body was still pulsing with pleasure. Seth had been tender and gentle, and they had made love, lost in each other's souls until they had become one. She didn't want this day to end, and yet she knew that there were hard decisions to be made and soon they would have to leave Farm End.

Needing the bathroom, she slipped out of his arms, and naked she walked to her room to find something to wear. Jules picked up a long t-shirt and as she put it over her head, she heard someone downstairs. She froze to the spot, as she listened for another sign of life. She checked the time on her alarm. It was eleven twenty. *It must be Peter.* She looked around her room and put on a pair of joggers. She visited the bathroom and then walked downstairs, avoiding the kitchen and breathed a sigh of relief when she saw Peter in the lounge. He was not alone, Charlene and Jake were with him. She was surprised and a little alarmed to see them all sat there.

"Charlene, Jake, what are you doing here? Jake?"

Peter looked surprised to see her. "It's ok, Jules, I was going to wake you. Jake has only told Charlene about you both still being alive. I told them the whole story, Jules, I had to. Charlene is going to help you both get out of here."

She had been crying and she blew her nose. "I'm sorry, sweetie, I'm so sorry. Your poor face."

Seth appeared behind her, still sleepy, and she was glad that he had thought to put on some pyjama shorts. He came up behind her and put his arms around her. It was then that he noticed everyone else in the room. "Jake? Charlene?"

"Don't have a go at Jake, Seth," Charlene pleaded. "I heard what happened. He came to me because there is a lot going down at home. Some of your brothers are out for blood. Dad…Dad is still missing and Mam is going crazy. You know what I mean by crazy, Seth? You know what she is like, when she has had a drink. I knew she was capable of dark things, but murder too?" Charlene started to sob.

"Please don't cry, Charlene," Seth said, going over to her and putting his arms around her. "Do you think anyone knows we are alive? Did anyone see you two come over here?"

"I don't know, Seth. Mam is acting very odd. I can see that she is working on some horrible plan. How do you know she didn't see you walking back to Farm End this morning? I think you need to find another place to go. Just in case. I have a friend in Worthing. You could stay with him. You can't stay here, it's not safe."

"Charlene, we are going to go to Ireland. We'll go today. Can I ask you to drive us to Southampton? We can make our way from there."

She nodded. "I'll do that for you. I'll have to tell Joe. He won't say anything. He doesn't care for Mam."

"We should get a taxi, Seth." Jules didn't want to take any chances and get Charlene in trouble.

"The thing is, taxis can be traced," Seth said. "I'll be skipping parole and I don't want the police to be able to trace me. I'll have to borrow someone's ID to get on the ferry."

Jake put his hand in his back pocket and pulled out his wallet, and then plucked out his driving licence card. "Here, Seth, borrow my licence. The photo isn't that great, and we could easily pass for brothers. They won't look too hard at the date of birth."

Seth took the licence and looked at the picture. "I'll have to shave well before we go. Thanks, Jake. That's perfect. I'll send it back to you."

Charlene got to her feet. "You two should go now. Pack what you can while I get the car. I'll empty the boot. I think you should stay in there, until we're well on our way. Jake, if anyone asks you, then tell them that I've gone to IKEA."

"Ok, Charlene. I'll message you if anything happens at home."

"Oh my, I didn't think we would be going so soon. Seth, the horses. What am I going to do about them?"

"I'll look after them," Jake volunteered. "I've worked at a livery yard before, so I know how to ride and look after them. It will be a way of saying sorry for being such a jerk."

"When we're settled in Ireland, we'll arrange for them to be brought over somehow. Thanks, Jake."

Peter looked at her sadly. "You're really going then?"

"Yes, Peter, we have to. Don't be sad. Hug Dad for me. Tell him that I have gone travelling." The tears were now streaming down her bruised face.

"I will."

***

Peter had gone into the loft and found two small suitcases and had handed them down to her. In a blind panic, they had thrown into them everything they could and then wheeled them through to the hall. She had to hunt for her passport and then, much to her relief, she had found it in the drawer of her Dad's desk. She was relieved to find that it was still in date. Her photo did look very childlike, but that is all she had as ID. She had found a small handbag and put a cap, sunglasses to hide her black eye, passport, bank card and money into it. She wasn't sure if she would be able to use her bank card again as the ATM would show the police where she was and would lead them to Seth.

Jules and Seth stood in the hall waiting for Charlene to arrive. They both wore jeans, dark t-shirts and a mac as it looked like rain. She had tied her hair back into a ponytail and wore a baseball hat. She just wanted to blend in with everyone else and not draw attention to themselves. Her guitar had to come too, she couldn't leave it. "I hope Charlene managed to get away without anyone stopping her."

"She's probably had to sort one of the kids out. They are a real handful. Be patient."

Peter came downstairs and found them in the hall. "She's on her way. I was watching from your bedroom, Jules. I'm going to miss you both. Will you message me when you get to wherever you are going? It is best you don't tell me where exactly. I just want to know you are both alright."

Jules looked sadly at her brother. "Peter, we have both lost our phones and if we had them with us then we could be tracked. I promise that I will find a way to contact you; even if it is by pigeon."

"Oh God, Jules, Give me a hug." He hugged her, and she could see that he was tearing up. "Take good care of her, Seth Hearn."

"I will, Peter. Don't worry. She will be fine."

Charlene reversed the car right up to the doorstep and then got out and opened the boot up. Cautiously, Seth opened the door, making sure nobody was around.

"I'm sorry I took so long. Bryony got a nose bleed because Rowan tripped her over. They'll be the death of me, those two. Are you ready? I've put some cushions in the boot. I'll stop near Buck Barn and then let you both out. I'm not being too dramatic, am I?"

"No, it makes sense, Charlene. Thank you." Seth was looking at the boot and Jules could see that he was going to have trouble fitting in it with her.

"Seth, I will lie in the footwell at the back of the car. I will cover myself over with a throw. We can't both fit in there. Buck Barn is not too far from here, so we won't be hidden for long." She ran back to the lounge, picked up the throw and ran back. When she returned Seth was in the boot and Peter was putting the suitcases and guitar on the back seats. She looked around and climbed into the car and curled herself into a ball on the floor of the car. Peter covered her over and patting her back, shut the door. She called out to Seth to make sure he was ok, and he said that he was missing her and that he was fine. She heard the car start, and she could feel the car moving away from the farm.

They turned right out of the courtyard and drove along the bumpy lane towards the main road. She realised that she had been holding her breath for ages and exhaled as the reality of it all hit her. This was probably the last time she would see Farm End again, and perhaps Peter and her Dad too. She felt sad to leave and tried not to cry.

"Are you ok, sweetie?" Charlene called. "It should take us just another ten minutes before we get to Buck Barn. My heart is beating like a drum. Is yours?"

"It's thumping like crazy. You don't have to take us all the way to Southampton, Charlene. We could get a train from

Horsham. We should be far enough away from here by then. I don't think we would be detected."

"Have you seen 'Hunted,' Jules?"

"No, is it a film?"

"It's just a TV series, where couples go on the run to win money and have to avoid being tracked down. You'd be surprised how easily these people are caught. There are cameras everywhere. You are going to have to be careful when you travel together. Don't look up at any cameras and don't use your phones."

"Oh dear. We will do our best." *Oh my God, we are on the run!*

"I want to do one last thing for my baby brother, and for you, of course. I'm going to miss you both. We will come and see you when we visit Ireland for a trip. In secret, of course."

"I'd like that, Charlene."

They turned off at Buck Barn and Charlene took a left down a quiet lane and pulled into a lay-by. Jules wriggled out from her blanket and peeped out. She slowly slid a suitcase along the seat and sat next to it. She kept low and looked around her to make sure nobody was watching. The lane was quiet, and she couldn't see anyone following them. She wondered if she would ever relax again.

Charlene let Seth out of the boot, and he stretched and held his back. He had obviously suffered from being cramped up in the boot. He opened the car door and took out their luggage and put it all in the boot. He too was looking over his shoulder to see if anyone was following them. Seth then got in the car and sat next to her. A red car went past them, and they both sunk down in the leather seats to avoid being seen. When he sat back up again, he sighed. "It won't be like this all the time. When we get to Ireland, we will be free as a bird."

She smiled at him and held his hand. "We just have to be really careful until we get there. I think we should buy our ferry tickets separately and sit apart. Cameras are everywhere. You will need to wear your cap and keep your eyes down all the time. You mustn't look up at the cameras."

"Oh goodness! You've really thought this through."

Charlene started the car, and they continued on their way to Southampton.

They had been driving for over an hour, and she found herself drifting off to sleep. She moved into the middle seat, strapped herself in and snuggled into Seth. He put his arm 'round her, and she laid her head on his chest to sleep. He smelled so nice and delightful memories of their morning together flooded her mind. Charlene was playing dreamy music to keep herself and everyone calm, and she chatted merrily to Seth. Jules wanted to talk too but was still so exhausted. She drifted off into a troubled sleep.

Jules was woken from her slumber when she heard Charlene exclaim that she thought that they were being followed. She opened her eyes and noticed that Seth had sunk lower into the seat. Seeing that she was awake, he whispered to her to keep low.

"Who do you think it is?" he asked Charlene.

"I don't know. I just recognise the car. It is following the car that is behind us. What car is Patrick driving now, Seth?"

"I think he's been borrowing one of Dad's. Is it an old black Honda Accord?"

"I don't know the make but it's definitely Dad's. It's black and I recognise the registration plate." She sighed. "Was Dad's! It might just be a coincidence."

"I don't think it is. Damn!"

"Charlene, we're coming up to a service station soon. Let's pull in there and see if the car follows."

"I'm going to be really annoyed if Patrick's following us. We were so careful. Anyway, what can he do? He can't stop you two going to Ireland. You will just have to change your identities."

Jules was starting to feel really anxious.

"Seth, I think the car has turned off with us. It has to be Patrick. He stopped me when I was leaving and asked me where I was going. I told him that I was going to IKEA. He was angry that I would want to go shopping when Dad was missing. I told him to stop being so dramatic. He knows I'm up to something. I just know it. I'm going to give him a piece of my mind."

"Charlene, don't, he will go mad. Look we're nearly at Southampton, we can make our own way from the service station. I don't want you to get in any trouble."

"I'm going to drive around the car park and then find a spot at the back so we can watch where he parks. I don't want to abandon you here."

"Don't worry about us. We will hitchhike and then get a coach or two to Fishguard."

"Seth is right, you have helped us enough."

"I can just see the car pulling in further up. I am furious. I have every right to go shopping if I want to. Patrick has no right telling me what I can and cannot do. It has to be done. I'm going to give him a piece of my mind. Keep low, I'll be back in a minute."

"Charlene, no, please don't."

"I have to, sweetie, I am tired of Patrick treating everyone like eejits." Charlene jumped out of the car and slammed the door behind her.

Seth smiled. "She's a lot like you. She has a fiery side too."

"You will have to watch out then and never cross me, Sebastian Hearn!"

"I dare not. We'll find someone to give us a lift to Southampton or further, if we can. That's how I got around in Thailand, by hitchhiking. Let me do the talking, and I'll soon get us a lift."

"We could get coaches to Wales, I don't think National Express costs too much. We will need to be wary of the cameras, though."

"Jules, did you bring any money with you?"

"Yes, that two hundred and fifty I drew out the other day and I have little change. How about you?"

Seth pulled out from his jean's pocket notes rolled into a bundle. "It's a good job Dad paid everyone weekly in cash, otherwise I would have had to go to the bank. We should be ok for a while. You do realise that we are going to have very little money and each other is all we have from now on. I'll try and be good to you and make you happy. I love you, Jules."

"I love you too, Seth."

Charlene returned to the car and looked annoyed. "He wasn't in the car. Perhaps he is travelling this way as well and has gone to get a coffee. Maybe I am being paranoid."

"No, you aren't. He must think something is up. There is no reason why he would come all this way after lecturing you about leaving the farm. He hardly ever leaves the farm. Look,

I've had an idea. Jules, we're going to borrow his car. He needs to be taught a lesson. It's a long way to Fishguard. You'll take him back to Crow Farm, won't you, Charlene? It's not as if we are leaving him here without a ride. I would love to see his face when he sees that the car is missing."

"Seth, that's crazy. He will know for sure that we were with Charlene!" She was a little shocked.

"I don't think so. If you leave your car unlocked then you are just asking for trouble. Anyone could steal it. The car has no key, so you have to hotwire it to make it start."

"Anyway, you don't have a license at the moment or insurance."

"Dad insured us all to drive the cars and farm machinery he owns. The license part is just a small technical detail. We need to be quick, Jules, before he comes back. Charlene, do you think I should do this. I'll leave the car near Fishguard. I don't know if Patrick's seen us, but if we stay here much longer, then he will see us for sure."

"I think you should. Seth, you have to be careful though, I don't want you to have another accident. Oh, but you didn't, did you? Jake told me that you went to prison for him. You're one crazy brother. I love you, Seth. I really am going to miss you. Seriously though, you haven't driven for a while."

"Oh, did he? Well, I never! I'll be fine, Charlene, I've been driving farm machines and haven't lost my touch. Jules, are you ok with this?"

"I suppose it's not stealing. I am scared though. Thank you for bringing us this far. I'm going to miss you."

"I'll miss you too, sweetie. We'll see you both again, soon enough. You must go."

They jumped out of the car and Seth opened the boot and pulled out their suitcases and guitar. They both ran towards the car, pulling them along. Seth opened the back doors, and they threw everything onto the back seat. She jumped into the passenger seat and Seth into the driver's seat.

"You keep watch and I'll start this thing up." He started to fiddle with some wires below the steering wheel. Panic-stricken, she scanned the car park for any signs of Patrick. Her heart was thumping really hard in her chest, and she thought it might burst.

"Anyone coming?"

"No, it's all clear... Hold on! I can see Charlene waving at us. It looks more urgent than just a goodbye wave. Seth, she's seen him!"

The car's engine sprang into life and Seth smiled. "We're out of here! Put your seatbelt on, Jules."

She clipped it in as fast as she could. He slammed his door shut, and putting his foot on the accelerator, shot out of the space. She could see someone approaching Charlene's car, but she couldn't see who it was. "I think it is Patrick? I'm not sure though."

Navigating the one-way system at speed, with tyres screeching, they hurtled out of the car park and joined the M27. She was frightened witless, but she could see that Seth was handling the car well. They had made it out of the service station in one piece and were speeding towards Wales at breakneck speed. When they had clocked up a few miles, Seth took his foot off the accelerator and began to relax. He grinned at her with a victorious look on his face. Jules settled back in her seat and began to breathe again. "We're free, Seth, free as a bird."

NATASHA MURRAY

***

'Forgive me, my love, for letting Jethro hurt you and for leaving you to die. Each time you were with him you broke my heart. He is gone now. I see the wind in your hair and your rosebud lips and I want you more than ever. The Irish Sea will never be wide enough. I will follow you, Ann, to the ends of the earth. I will come for you soon and then I will watch you dance again.'

58 FARM END

I hoped you enjoyed 58 Farm End. I wrote this during lockdown. If you could leave me a small review, then I would be most grateful. Authors are lost without reviews.

You may be interested in reading Julia's Baby – the next book in this intense romantic suspense crime series.

5.0 out of 5 stars <u>Gripping!</u>

Reviewed in the United Kingdom on 13 September 2021

58 FARM END

'Yes!!! A great sequel, was everything I hoped for and more. I was hooked from the first page and really feel invested in the characters. Roll on the 3rd book! A great read!!!'

After only a month of being together, Julia Bridgewater and her hot boyfriend Seth Hearn are on the run. Fearing for their lives, they escape from Sussex and flee to Ireland with the hope of starting a new life together.

To survive, Jules and Seth must earn a living without being discovered. Seth, having worked at a riding school in Waterfall on the edge of Cork, hopes that the owner May will give them work. Will Moss his black cob remember him? When they visit May's run down Manor House, Seth has the distinct feeling that something is terribly wrong.

The streets of Cork offer Jules and Seth a financial solution to all their money worries. Hidden talents are revealed, making their bond stronger. Seth never fails to surprise Jules.

Things are looking up until unwelcome visitors come to Waterfall West and cause major headaches for them both. Their lives spiral out of control with disastrous consequences.

The question is: Can you lead a normal life if you are always looking over your shoulder for those that mean you harm?

You can run but you cannot hide.

About the Author

Natasha Murray is an award winning West Sussex author. She is a diverse writer and produces books for all ages. She would be very grateful if you could leave her a review or star rating on Amazon or Goodreads.

During lockdown, Natasha has written a romantic crime thriller series 58 Farm End, Julia's Baby and Waterfall Way (The Waterfall Way Series). These books are set in Findon, West Sussex and Cork, Ireland. She says, "I love writing and it is both a pleasure and a compulsion. My dream of course is for my creations to be well known and to make people smile."

For more information about Natasha and her books, then please visit her website at https://cutt.ly/5fR483w

Or her Facebook
https://www.facebook.com/NatashaMurray3004

Twitter https://twitter.com/NatashaM_Author

Instagram @natashamurray1426

TikTok @natashamurray16

NATASHA MURRAY

58 FARM END

Printed in Great Britain
by Amazon

78496427R00159